THE FIFTH BLACK BOOK OF HORROR

Selected by Charles Black

Mortbury Press

Published by Mortbury Press

First Edition
2009

This anthology copyright © Mortbury Press

All stories copyright © of their respective authors
Cover art copyright © Paul Mudie

ISBN 978-0-9556061-4-4

This book is a work of fiction. Names, characters, businesses, organisations, places and events are either the product of the author's imagination or are used fictitiously. Any resemblance to actual persons, living or dead, events or locales is entirely coincidental.

All rights reserved. No part of this publication may be reproduced, stored in a retrieval system, or transmitted, in any form, or by any means (electronic, mechanical, photocopying, recording or otherwise) without the prior permission of the author and publisher.

This book is sold subject to the condition that it shall not, by way of trade or otherwise, be lent, re-sold, hired out, or otherwise circulated without the publisher's prior consent in any form of binding or cover other than that in which it is published and without a similar condition including this condition being imposed on the subsequent purchaser.

Mortbury Press
Shiloh
Nantglas
Llandrindod Wells
Powys
LD1 6PD

mortburypress@yahoo.com
http://www.freewebs.com/mortburypress/

Contents

MRS MIDNIGHT	Reggie Oliver	5
THE MAN WITH A HOLE IN HIS HEAD	Marcus Gold	31
STARLIGHT CASTS NO SHADOW	Ian C. Strachan	47
LEIBNIZ'S LAST PUZZLE	Craig Herbertson	54
HANGMAN WANTED: APPLY IN WRITING	Paul Finch	76
IN THE GARDEN	Rosalie Parker	92
THEIR OWN MAD DEMONS	David A. Riley	97
WINTER BREAK	Raymond Vaughn	131
DE VERMIS INFESTIS	John Llewellyn Probert	133
NO SUCH THING AS A FRIENDLY	Richard Staines	159
SCHRÖDINGER'S HUMAN	Anna Taborska	168
THE CHAMELEON MAN	David Williamson	182
TWO FOR DINNER	John Llewellyn Probert	194

*Dedicated to Clarence Paget
1909-1991*

*****

Acknowledgements

Mrs Midnight © by Reggie Oliver 2009
The Man With A Hole In His Head © by Marcus Gold 2009
Starlight Casts No Shadow © by Ian C. Strachan 2009
Leibniz's Last Puzzle © by Craig Herbertson 2009
Hangman Wanted: Apply In Writing © by Paul Finch 2009
In the Garden © by Rosalie Parker 2009
Their Own Mad Demons © by David A. Riley 2009
Winter Break © by Raymond Vaughn 2009
De Vermis Infestis © by John Llewellyn Probert 2009
No Such Thing As A Friendly © by Richard Staines 2009
Schrödinger's Human © by Anna Taborska 2009
The Chameleon Man © by David Williamson 2009
Two For Dinner © by John Llewellyn Probert 2009

Cover artwork © by Paul Mudie 2009

*****

Also in this series:
The Black Book of Horror
The Second Black Book of Horror
The Third Black Book of Horror
The Fourth Black Book of Horror

MRS MIDNIGHT

Reggie Oliver

What's the worst thing about being a celebrity? The intrusive press coverage? Forget it! I do. No. It's being roped into these charity projects, because nowadays you've got to be hands-on, or they mark you down as a complete toe-rag. Oh, look at Lenny Henry, they say, look at Julie Walters: they weren't prepared just to swan around like celebs, they got their hands dirty, their feet wet: they endangered some extremity or other. And if you present a program like *I Can Make You A Star*, you're generally assumed to be someone who got where they are by being lucky, or sleeping with the right people, so you have to prove yourself all the more. Well, I got to be the presenter of *I Can Make You A Star* by sheer hard graft, and it tops the ratings because I am bloody good at my job. My qualifications: a first class honours degree in the University of Life, having passed my entrance exam from the School of Hard Knocks with straight A's in all subjects. That's the sort of bloke I am, as if anyone gives a flying fuck. Pardon my French. Anyway, that was why I was recruited to head up the Save The Old Essex Music Hall project.

The Old Essex: what can I say about the Old Essex? It's a glorious relic of those magical bygone days of Music Hall? No, it isn't. It's a filthy, rat-infested, dry-rotten, draughty, crumbling, mildewed dump that hasn't had anything to do with show business for well over a hundred years. Most recently it has been a hangout for winos and junkies; before that it was a warehouse and a motorcycle repair shop. Before that, God knows. The only reason it's survived is that some nutter slapped a preservation order on it. A few of its original features have remained intact, not that they're much to write home about. But I can't say all this, can I? I have to say something like: 'It's an amazing piece of living history which must be revived to serve the needs of the modern community.'

Mrs Midnight

Call me a cynic, if you like. I prefer the word realist.

The Old Essex fronts onto Alie Street, Whitechapel, and it was in some godforsaken courtyard round the back of it that Jack the Ripper did for one of his victims. Which one? Look it up for yourself. I have never understood why people should take the remotest interest in that squalid old monster, whoever he or she was. Eh? Well, why shouldn't it have been a *she?* I'm no sexist; I'm an equal opportunities sort of guy, me. I merely mention the fact, just to give you an impression of the kind of glorious, heritage-packed part of London we're talking about. As a matter of fact it was shortly after the Ripper murder that there had been a fire at the Old Essex, after which it stopped being a theatre, and embarked on its chequered history as a hangout for bikers and junkies. God knows how or why it escaped the Blitz: the Devil told Hitler to give it a miss, I reckon.

It was a mad March day when I first saw the Old Essex and the rain was blowing in great icy gusts across the East End. Even though it was eleven in the morning the sky was nearly black, and street lights were reflected fitfully in the water-lashed pavements. There were three of us who got out of the minicab outside the Old Essex, all kitted-out with yellow hard hats, Day-Glo jackets and torches. There was Jill, a bloke with the stupid name of Crispin de Hartong, and me, Danny Sheen, as if you didn't know. There was also supposed to be a camera crew, to film the whole thing for posterity, but their van had got lost – a likely story! – and they didn't show up till a lot later.

Jill was the reason I was in on the project, as a matter of fact. Her name is Jill Warburton and she has some sort of cultural adviser job in the Mayor's Office and had adopted this project as her baby. I hadn't much taken to her when she first rang me up because she had a posh accent, but at least she wasn't pushy so I invited her to come round to see me at my house in Primrose Hill. After a few minutes in her company I felt easier about her. I'm not saying she's a raving beauty or

Mrs Midnight

anything, but she looks nice. She's tall and quiet. She laughed at the jokes I made, and she wasn't faking it. That counts a lot with me. I know it sounds weird of me to say this, but she seemed to me like a good person. So I agreed to help the project, before almost instantly regretting it, and that was why I was here, about to inspect a derelict building in the pouring rain.

The other bloke tagging along, Crispin de Hartong, was there because he was an architectural expert. He was also a minor celeb who pronounces on that TV property makeover show, *Premises, Premises...* You remember: he's the poncy type who goes in for shoulder length blonde hair, bow ties and plum-coloured velvet jackets. I got the impression that he had his eye on Jill, and maybe that didn't exactly endear him to me.

The frontage of the Old Essex is mostly boarded up now to stop the druggies getting in. Jill undid a number of padlocks and we entered. At least we're out of the rain, I thought.

We shine our torches around and immediately Crispin starts raving about pilasters and spandrels and architraves. I don't want to hear all this rubbish, especially as I know he is just showing off to Jill. I only want to look.

We are in what I suppose was once the foyer. It is quite a narrow space and everything has been covered at some stage with a thick mud-coloured paint. The floor is covered in rubble and bits of plasterwork that have fallen from the ceiling, some of them quite recently, so I am glad we are wearing our hard hats. Our feet crackle and crunch on the floor. The most powerful thing in this area is the smell: it's a mixture of damp, decay, dust and death. You know when your cat has brought a dead rat or something into the house and has left its remains somewhere. Then you get that awful sweetish smell that seems to stick in your nostrils and as you haven't the nose of a dog and your cat can't tell you, you drive yourself mad trying to find out where it is coming from.

The other thing that I don't like is that there's a draught that feels like it's come straight from the Arctic, but, like the smell,

Mrs Midnight

I can't locate its source. I wet my finger and put it up to gauge the direction, but it's no use. Now I have a numb finger.

"Let's go into the auditorium, shall we?" Says Jill. She opens another temporarily padlocked door and we enter the Hall proper.

This is something of a shock. After the reeking claustrophobia of the foyer, it seems vast. The roof looks as high as a cathedral's and we can see a little without our torches because grey shafts of light come down at crazy angles from holes in the roof and from broken windows on either side high up. Through these shafts of light little sprinkles of rain fall down from outside like silver dust. We have come in under a gallery which curves in a great horseshoe around the auditorium supported by thin wrought iron columns. Facing us is the desert of an auditorium stripped of its original seating, and strewn about with all sorts of debris from its motorcycle and junkie days.

"Watch out for the odd used needle," said Jill. "As you can see we haven't even begun the clearing up operation."

Beyond the auditorium is an oblong black hole which I assume to be the orchestra pit and then the remains of a raised stage, its floorboards cracked and rotten, with a dirty great hole in the middle. Part of the stage is thrust forward into the pit beyond a great rounded proscenium arch behind which hang a few tattered threadbare remnants of curtains and stage cloths. Close to the stage, at either side under the wings of the gallery I can just detect the remnants of two long bars where customers once drank as they watched the entertainment. I feel as if I am breathing an eternity of dust and decay. I don't think I would have liked the place even when it was alive. It would have been too much like a giant version of those Northern clubs where I once had a brief inglorious career as a comic.

'Get off! We want the bingo, not you, yer boring boogger!'

That voice from the past echoed in my head almost audibly. I look round at the others, half expecting them to have heard something, but they were just staring at it all. I was left to my own thoughts. The night I 'got the bird' in that club all those years ago was the night I quit the show business for tabloid journalism. It was the best move of my life. And now I'm presenting *I Can Make You A Star*, and the man behind the 'Get off... yer boring boogger'? Cancer, heart failure maybe: he had been a fat bloke with a face like a potato. I can see him now through a haze of booze fumes and cigarette smoke, and his voice still echoes. No, revenge is not sweet.

Meanwhile Crispin had said that thing that people always seem obliged to say when they enter some great cultural edifice: "What an incredible space!"

I was happy to be spared the necessity of saying that stupid, meaningless phrase myself. Anyway, Jill was paying no attention; she was on her mobile to the camera crew.

"Look, where the hell are you...? Hold on, you're breaking up... Look, just come now... The doors are unlocked... We'll be here for another... Fifteen minutes—"

I shivered and said: "Wouldn't it be better to cancel them and come back some other time when the weather's a bit better?"

"No, I'm sorry, Danny," said Jill. "I just can't afford to waste them. We're on this incredibly tight budget."

I thought of offering to pay for the camera crew to come back later, much later, but something prevented me. I thought it might lower me in Jill's estimation, but why should I care about that?

"You know," said Crispin, pausing after this introduction in that way people do when they feel they have something incredibly important to announce, "I have a theory that this could be a very early Frank Matcham." He looked at me. "Matcham, you know, was the great theatre architect of the late nineteenth, early twentieth centuries and—"

"I know who Frank Matcham was," I said. I caught Jill's eye and she smiled, but even this little victory didn't make me any happier. I was cold, I needed a drink; I was beginning to hate the Old Essex with a passion. The idea of waiting around here for another quarter of an hour for a poxy television crew made me livid. I strode away from the other two towards the bar on the left side of the auditorium.

"Careful how you go," said Jill. "The floor can be a bit treacherous."

As I crunched over to the bar, I heard her and Crispin having an earnest discussion about Matcham and architecture: "The Old Essex was thoroughly renovated in 1877 by the firm of Jethro T. Robinson who was Matcham's father-in-law, and so it could be..." I didn't want to leave those two together. After all, Crispin may have been a ponce but at least he was her age and her class; he wasn't a twice divorced forty-year-old father of three, as I was. But I felt so angry.

What was I doing here? I shone my torch. The bar was in surprisingly good condition with a fine marble top, cracked in two places and thickly overlaid with dust, but otherwise intact. I began to shift a lot of debris to get behind the bar. I had this vague idea, you see, that I might find some ancient bottle of Scotch or brandy, or something. A likely scenario! Even a bottle of Bass would have done.

I managed to squeeze behind the bar by shifting several wooden joists and a broken chair or two. It probably wasn't at all safe, but I didn't care. There were some shelves behind the bar into which I shone my torch. Their contents consisted mainly of rubble, the odd dead rat and, as Jill had predicted, a used needle or two, but at the back of one I thought I saw a wad of paper. I reached in a gloved hand and tentatively drew it out.

It was a sheaf of handbills from the Old Essex days. They were singed at the corners and buckled with damp but still legible. I was excited almost in spite of myself. The date on the top sheet was 1888, the year of the fire at the Old Essex, the year it closed down. The acts were listed and some of the names were familiar:

GUS ELEN
ALBERT CHEVALIER

MARIE LLOYD
DAN LENO
LITTLE TICH
Then there were others who were not known to me.
LITTLE Miss ELLEN TOZER
The Juvenile Prodigy
THE GREAT 'HERCULE'
Astonishing Feats of Strength
And then, this:
Mrs MIDNIGHT
And her Animal Comedians

I don't know why, but that name Mrs Midnight struck a chord somewhere. Was her name really Midnight? It sounded too good to be true. And what, for God's sake were 'animal comedians'?

I looked up from the bar where I had laid out the papers and across to the stage. I was not shining my torch in that direction, but I thought I caught sight of someone sitting just behind the proscenium arch in what legits call the 'prompt corner'. It looked like a great bulky old woman with a shawl over her head and shoulders, wearing a floor length dress, but I could barely see more than an outline in the gloom. The figure was leaning forward slightly and quite motionless. The face was completely obscured by the cowl of the shawl, but I had the impression that it was staring in my direction.

I flashed my torch towards the figure and saw at once that it had been an illusion. It was no more than a pile of furniture and junk covered by a tarpaulin. All the same it had been uncannily lifelike. I switched the torch off to recreate the effect, but the magic had gone. It just looked like a pile of junk covered with a tarpaulin.

"Are you okay, Danny?" said Jill.

As a matter of fact I was shaking all over, but I said: "Come over here! Look what I've found."

Jill was very excited by the old music hall bills; even Crispin was reluctantly impressed. I don't know why – to please Jill I suppose – but I said I would do some research into the playbills and the history of the theatre. Then Crispin started offering me advice about how and where to research. I let him go on a bit; then I quietly reminded him that I had been quite a successful journalist for over a dozen years, so I did know a little about the techniques of research. Crispin shut up, and again I thought I saw Jill smile.

Finally the camera crew arrived and we did some fake shots of us arriving at the Old Essex and being amazed. Crispin repeated his line about it being an incredible space and his Matcham theory. He wanted me to ask him who Matcham was on camera, but I wasn't playing ball. We were about to film my 'discovery' of the playbills when the crew started to get technical glitches: jams in the camera, gremlins in the sound system, erratic variations in the light levels. The sound technician was particularly jumpy. At one point he said he had got the noise of some animal crying out in pain, perhaps a cat, on his cans; but the rest of us had heard nothing.

I know camera crews: they can be very touchy and difficult when they want to be. Perhaps it's because they think they are doing all the work and us guys in front of the camera are taking all the credit. I could see they were getting into a state, so I tried to calm them down, but it was no good. The sound man said straight out that the place was giving him 'the willies'. At this Crispin started to be very sarcastic until I told him to shut the fuck up. It was all beginning to get a bit hairy so I made a cut-throat gesture at Jill to let her know that I thought we should wrap. She understood immediately, gave the word and we cleared out. I wasn't sorry to go.

For about a week or so I put the Old Essex out of my mind. I was heavily into meetings with some producers about hosting a new Reality TV show called *Celebrity Dog Kennel*. Apparently they were finding it hard to sign up even the B and C listers who were asking silly money anyway. In the end it was Jill who spurred me. She rang me up and asked me how the research was going. I was vague but invited her to have

Mrs Midnight

dinner with me in a couple of day's time when I would tell her all about it. The following morning I took myself off to newspaper library at Colindale.

I had already got the bare facts about the Old Essex from Mander and Mitchenson, that the theatre had suffered a very damaging fire on Saturday, December 1st, 1888 from which its fortunes had never recovered and it had been abandoned as a place of entertainment very soon after. So I began my researches by looking in the newspapers of that period for reports of the fire at the Old Essex.

Most of the national dailies contained little more than a few lines stating that the fire had been started shortly after the Saturday night performance and that there were no 'human fatalities', but that one man, a Mr Graham, had been severely injured. I did, however come across a passing reference to it in a letter to the *Times* on December 5th, stating that: '*the recent riot and conflagration at the Old Essex provides further evidence of the extreme unrest among the denizens of Whitechapel following the appalling murders recently perpetrated in that district.*' I presumed that the writer meant the Ripper murders, the last of which had been committed in November 1888. Rather fatuously the letter ended by urging the Metropolitan Police to '*redouble their efforts in hunting down the person responsible for these unspeakable atrocities.*'

Eventually I tracked down a more detailed account of the fire in a local paper called the *East London Gazette*. Monday, December 3rd, 1888. In it I read as follows:

'...*the evening's entertainment at the Old Essex was proceeding as normal when, towards the end of the bill, there was introduced an act known as* Mrs Midnight and her Animal Comedians. *In it a lady by the name of 'Mrs Midnight', dressed as a gypsy vagrant (but in reality personated by a Mr Simpson Graham) appears on stage with a number of animals, including a cat, a Learned Pig, a miniature bulldog, a cockerel and a Barbary ape. These creatures under instructions from Mrs Midnight performed a number of astonishing mental and physical feats. Especially notable we are told was the 'Learned Pig' Belphagor who was capable of solving elementary mathematical conundrums with the aid of numbered cards. On this particular evening, however, parts of the audience, especially those who had been drinking at the bars, were restive and took against Mrs Midnight. These vulgar objections reached their height while the Barbary ape, called Bertram, was performing the act of rescuing the miniature bulldog, Mary from the top of a miniature tower of wood and canvas, designed to look like a castle keep. Coins and other small hard objects were thrown onto the stage, one of which hit Bertram, the ape. The animal was so provoked by this act that he became visibly agitated and having reached the top of the tower, instead of rescuing the bulldog, Mary, he bit her head off.*

'That disgusting incident, needless to say, only incensed the troublemakers further and a full scale riot ensued. The local constabulary was summoned and the theatre was cleared. The artists appearing on the bill, which included Mr Dan Leno were led to safety, but Mr Graham remained behind because he was fearful of being set upon by the mob who were indeed calling for him. It was at this point that smoke was seen to be coming from one of the dressing room windows at the back of the theatre, though precisely when and how the fire was started has been disputed. Our reporter who arrived on the scene with the fire brigade was told by one member of the crowd that the reason for the animus surrounding 'Mrs Midnight' was that her impersonator Mr Graham (formerly, we understand, a medical practitioner) was suspected by many to have some connection with the Whitechapel Murders, though quite why he should have fallen under suspicion we have been unable to ascertain. The gallant members of the Fire Service, under their leader Captain Shaw, soon had the fire under control and were able to spirit Mr Graham away unseen by the crowd. However Mr Graham is understood to have sustained severe injuries from the blaze and his entire

menagerie of 'animal comedians' has perished in the conflagration.'

As I was coming out of Colindale with my photocopy of the article I had a brain wave. My last job before TV celebrity took me to its silicone-enhanced bosom was as Showbiz Editor of the *Daily Magnet*. There I got to know Bill Beasely, the head of crime news. We had worked together on the Spice Girl Shootings and rubbed along fairly well. He wasn't a bad bloke if you could put up with his smoker's cough, and the fact that he smelt of gin and peppermints at nine in the morning. One of his fads was his fascination with the Ripper Murders: he'd even come up with a theory of his own about it and done yet another Ripper book. I think his idea was that it was Gladstone and Queen Victoria in collaboration, which is loony of course, but not as loony as that daft American bint who thinks it was Sickert the painter. (I happen to own a Sickert. I'm not a complete muppet.) I thought Bill might know about this Graham bloke if he was a suspect.

I gave him a ring and he asks me over. I suggest meeting in a pub, but he insists I come to his flat. I don't want to go because Bill is a bachelor – well so am I at the moment, but you know what I mean – and a bit of a slob and lives at the wrong end of Islington.

My worst fears are confirmed. There is even some old gypsy tramp woman with a filthy plaid shawl over her head crouching on his doorstep. She holds out her hand, palm upwards for cash. Luckily Bill buzzes me up fairly quickly when I ring the doorbell.

His flat is on the top floor and is everything I had been dreading, and more. It is all ashtrays, booze bottles and books, plus a sofa and a couple of armchairs that like Bill were bulging in all the wrong directions. The books are everywhere. They look as if they'd spread out from the ceiling-high shelves like some sort of self-perpetuating fungus. It is ten in the morning and Bill offers me a Gin and Tonic. He's barely changed in five years: a bit more flab maybe, a more flegm-

Mrs Midnight

filled cough. I ask if I could have a tea or coffee.

He looks at me as if I'd demanded quail sandwiches and an avocado pear, but wanders into the kitchen to light the gas for the kettle.

"Does that gypsy woman regularly camp out on your doorstep?" I asked.

"Who?"

I went to the window to point her out to him but she's gone.

Bill managed to make some proper coffee in one of those percolator things, but it was still filthy. When I mentioned what I was here about, Graham and the Ripper connection, he became all excited. What is it about Jack the Ripper and some people? He started pacing round the room, talking enthusiastically and pulling books out of the shelves.

"Ah, yes. Well of course Dr Graham is known to Ripperologists, but he comes fairly low down on the list of possible suspects, mainly because we don't know much about him. But this new stuff you've dug up is fascinating. Perhaps you and I could collaborate on a new Ripper book about it?"

Not wanting to put him off at this early stage, I merely shrugged. "You called him 'Doctor' Graham?" I said.

"Yes. He was a doctor. Struck off, if I remember rightly. Of course being a doctor is always a plus when it comes to Ripper suspects. Anatomical expertise, you see. Knowing how to cut up bodies." He is leafing through a rather squalid looking giant paperback entitled *The A to Z of Ripperology*. "Where are we? Ah, here we are! '*Graham, Dr Simpson S. Date of birth unknown.*' That ought to be easy enough to find out. '*Medical practitioner with eccentric theories. Devised a treatment known as* zoophagy *in which patients were treated by being fed organs from still living animals, by means of vivisection.*' Bloody hell, that's absolutely disgusting!" Bill, the ripperologist, seemed genuinely shocked. "'*Wrote a book on the subject:* A Treatise on Brain Food, Or the Benefits of Zoophagy Explained...' Et cetera, et cetera. '*Struck off the register for misconduct towards a female patient. Thought to have been suffering from the early stages of tertiary syphilis...'* Ah! Listen to this! *'Became an entertainer known as 'Mrs Midnight' who performed with a troupe of trained animals. The times and locations of his appearance at various East London music halls were said to have coincided with some of the Ripper murders, but this has not been confirmed. It is believed that he died in 1889 or 1890 in an institution for the insane, having been injured by fire in an accident.'* He gets two bleeding daggers out of five on the Suspect Rating. Wait a minute, there's a book referred to here in the bibliography: *Quacks and Charlatans, Alternative Medicine in late Nineteenth Century England* by Harrison Bews. Might be worth a look."

He then asked me why I was so keen on the Old Essex project. I tried to sound genuinely enthusiastic, but I think he saw through it.

After a pause he said: "The thing these restoration nuts don't get is that some old things are best left buried and unrevived. Just because it's old doesn't mean it's good; quite the opposite sometimes. I come from down that way myself, and my old Dad wouldn't go near the Old Essex. He never really told me why, but he did say that just after the war they tried to turn it back into a theatre or something. I don't know what happened exactly, but he said it was a disaster."

That afternoon I rang Jill and proposed that we should meet for dinner in the evening at my local gastro-pub, the Engineer in Primrose Hill. I thought dinner at my house might seem a bit forward for her. She accepted.

Sometimes I'm a good judge, though that's not what people say about me in *I Can Make You A Star,* but I thought Jill would like the Engineer and she did. The food's well cooked and imaginative, all organic of course and that sort of rubbish; but it's classy and modern without being pretentious and overpriced. She seemed in her element there.

You know how when you meet someone and you go away and start fantasising about them; then when you meet them again it's a terrible let down? With Jill, it was the opposite. She was even better. I don't want to go on about it but everything about her was somehow clear: clear skin, clear eyes, clear laugh. She dressed nicely but obviously didn't worry much about her appearance. Her hair was mousy coloured, not dyed.

Immediately I wanted to start talking about her and me, but I knew this would be fatal, so I told her about my researches. She gave me her full attention and seemed thrilled by the information I gave.

I said: "You don't think it's all a bit sordid and sinister?"

"Good grief no! Fascinating stuff. It all helps to raise the profile. There's no such thing as bad publicity. You of all people should know that."

I could tell she was teasing me which I liked, but it was in the way you tease a favourite uncle, not a friend, or a lover. Still, I had done well, so I told her grandly that there were a couple of books I thought I would look out at the British Library which might help. She stretched out her hand and touched mine.

"You know, when somebody suggested you to help raise money for the Old Essex, I didn't like the idea. I thought you would be, well... I mean, your reputation, the kind of programs you do..."

"I know. A case of Pride and Prejudice on your part."

"Well, sort of. Not that I'd exactly describe you as Mr Darcy."

"You wound me, Jill."

We both laughed, but she had wounded without knowing. Then we discussed the practicalities of fund-raising events, television air time, recruiting other 'names' to support the cause, and all the rest of it. I realised that by now it was far too late for me to bow out of the Old Essex project, even if I wanted to, but I couldn't because it would mean losing her. Then at the coffee stage, she said something, though I can't remember how it came up. Mature people are supposed to take these things better than the young, but I don't think that's true.

She said: "By the way, you may as well know, I'm engaged to Crispin."

"Crispin de Hartong?"

"That's right."

"But you can't!" The words were out before I could stop myself. She seemed amused rather than shocked by my reaction.

"Why not?"

"Because he's a pretentious pillock."

"Actually, he's really rather sweet when you get to know him."

There was something very steely about the way she said that. I had offended her, so I apologised. Then I told her gently that in my very humble opinion I thought she deserved better.

"Thank you for your fatherly concern," she said coolly.

"I hope I'm more than a father to you."

"What do you mean by that?"

Quickly I said: "And what does *your* father think about it all?"

"My father is dead; my mother lives in Leamington Spa," she added, as if that explained the situation.

"I see."

She giggled. I laughed. The rest of that evening would have been pleasant in a trivial sort of way if I hadn't felt this great weight on my chest, brought on by her announcement. It was only then, I think, that I admitted to myself how much I felt about Jill. It often happens that when you confess to yourself, your feelings come to be like a physical pain. Call it heart ache if you like; I won't. Since I stopped working for the tabloids I've tried to avoid clichés like the plague.

Shortly after eleven I put Jill into a taxi outside the Engineer, and kissed her chastely on the cheek. This was not like me at all. Then I walked slowly back to my house. I took a long way round so that I could think, but I didn't really think at all. My mind was too full of Jill, and what a pillock Crispin

Mrs Midnight

was.

I have a little Georgian terraced house in Princess Road. It was one of those ones with railings along the front and steps going up to the front door. I was quite some way off when I noticed that someone was sitting on my steps. It was no more than a squat black shadow in a long dress from this distance. A ridiculous hope that it might be Jill vanished almost as soon as it came. The figure was motionless. Perhaps someone had just dumped some black bin bags on my doorstep, but no; the form was too precise. It must be a tramp and I would have to give her or him something before they cleared off. The thought enraged me. Hadn't I enough problems already?

As I approached I could see more clearly what it was. It was dark of course but there was enough light from the street lamps for me to tell. It was a tramp of some kind, a bag lady, except that she had no bags. She was big bulky old woman in a rusty black dress. Over her head and shoulders was a plaid shawl, greenish in colour I thought, but so dirty I could barely make out the pattern. It was only when I had come right up to her that I could see the face under the shawl and even then half of it was in shadow.

It was an old face, jowelled and wrinkled with pale pendulous cheeks and a puckered, lipless, dog's bottom of a mouth. I could not see the eyes clearly as they were shadowed by the thick overhanging brow, but I sensed that they were looking at me fixedly. Something about the heaviness of the chin and the thickness of the nose was making me suspect that the figure in the dress was not a woman at all but a man. This was confirmed when it thrust out a hand, palm upwards, from the folds of the plaid shawl. It was a big, heavy, dirty man's hand and there were great scars on it like old burn marks.

He wanted money. Well, that was simple enough. I fished for pound coins in my pocket. Even so, the idea of coming close enough to this thing to give them filled me with loathing. I stretched out my hand to be able to drop the coins into his while remaining as far as possible from him, but just as I was

Mrs Midnight

about to let the money go he gripped my wrist.

It felt like a handcuff of ice. I screamed like a girl. I felt dizzy; I suppose I must have passed out; drink I suppose, but it had not been my imagination because when I came to I looked for the coins. They and the bloke in the dress had gone.

From that moment I became a driven man. The following morning I went to the British Library and ordered up *Quacks and Charlatans*, as well as *A Treatise on Brain Food*. In the BL catalogues I noticed that Simpson Graham M.D. was also credited with another book entitled *Mother Midnight's Chatechism*, so I ordered that as well.

Research is like fitting together the pieces of a jigsaw puzzle. *Quacks and Charlatans* had only a few pages about Graham, and was completely ignorant about his Music Hall Career, but it gave me this:

'*He had been a brilliant if erratic medical student and early showed an almost insatiable desire to make his mark in the world... Dr Graham developed the idea that ingesting organs, in particular the brain, from a living animal was extraordinarily beneficial to human health. Several times he gave a demonstration before an interested and alarmed public in which he trepanned a fully conscious dog or cat, an operation which can, if skilfully done, be executed without much pain to the subject. He would then proceed to dip a spoon into the brain pan and devour the contents until the wretched animal finally lost consciousness. Many colleagues poured scorn on his unorthodox methods, but very few of them objected from an animal welfare point of view... After his disgrace, he continued to give lectures and demonstrations on what he called* zoophagy *(the eating of a still living being), often doing so in female dress for no apparent reason. Doubts as to his sanity naturally grew and he was finally consigned to an asylum.*'

I only skimmed though *A Treatise on Brain Food, Or the Benefits of Zoophagy Explained* by Simpson Graham M.D. Something about the very act of reading it, even in the

Mrs Midnight

antiseptic surroundings of the BL seemed poisonous. I did gather from a cursory glance that Dr Graham was no stylist and did a lot of boasting. All the same, I couldn't help noting down one passage which comes towards the end of this tedious little book.

'If we could only overcome the contemptible prejudice against using our fellow human beings in such experiments I am convinced that the benefits would be extraordinary. At present criminals, condemned by law and society, are either executed or left to languish in unhygienic conditions, an unconscionably wasteful practice. How much better for us, and indeed them, if their living, palpitating organs and brain cells were to be used to refresh and rejuvenate a select few. With the skills that I have perfected, the suffering of the reprobates in question could be kept to a minimum; or indeed prolonged and exacerbated, if required, to point a necessary moral lesson. By ingesting these living substances and fluids the health and sanity of our finest men (and women) of genius would not only be enhanced but also greatly prolonged. Through this use of 'living brain food' as I term it, human lives of two or three hundred years might in the future, I sincerely believe, become a commonplace.'

The third book, *Mother Midnight's Chatechism* was subtitled *Zoophagy Explained to the Young*. Graham did not claim authorship on the title page, and I am not surprised. It is printed on cheap paper and decorated with crude, muddy woodcuts. Nearly all of it is in verse. It begins:

'How can you be big and strong?
Hear then Mother Midnight's song...'

Then there were a number of stories or anecdotes told in verse.

'Edward ate a living mouse
And he learned to build a house;
David downed a wriggling rat,
And so he grew big and fat...'

Concluding with the moral:

Mrs Midnight

'Make your meal off breathing things
And become as great as kings.'

The final set of verses tells the story of a boy called Alfred who catches his sister out in the act of cheating him at cards. Thereupon he ties her to a chair and proceeds to cut her open with his 'trusty knife'. It was all told in a light-hearted almost humorous way that was very difficult to gauge. How serious was the man being?

'Then he cut a slice of liver
While she still did quake and quiver...'

I wanted to be sick, so I started to skip this stuff, but I know it finished:

'When he'd eaten all his sister,
Do you think that Alfred missed her?
No, for all her wit and vigour
Had been used to make him bigger.
All his wants she could provide him
By being safely there inside him.'

I'd had enough, and I left the British Library in a hurry, nearly tripping over an old bag lady in the courtyard outside. Then my mobile started to ring. It was Bill Beaseley. He seemed far away and his voice kept breaking up.

"Danny, I think I've found something which may... I'll send you a..." The phone went dead. I tried calling him but the line was engaged. On an impulse I rang Jill and asked if she would like to come to the recording of the final of *I Can Make You A Star* the following night.

"Great!" she said. "Can I bring Crispin too? I'm sure he'd be fascinated."

I bit my lip and told her I would have two tickets biked round to her that afternoon. I could have sold them on eBay for silly money.

The following morning a rather grubby envelope arrived for me by first class post. It could only be Bill Beaseley. Sure enough, inside was a photocopy. (Bill was one of those Luddites who refuse to use PCs and e-mails.) On the back of it

Mrs Midnight

he had scrawled:

'*Page from a book called* The Complete Ripper Letters, *containing all the letters that were sent to the Police about the Whitechapel murders in both facsimile and transcript. This just may be the clue that clinches it!!! But don't forget, we go 50/50 on any book deal. All right, mate? Bill*'

The facsimile showed a few lines written in a big scrawly handwriting on a scrap of paper. I got the feeling that the writer was trying to make his handwriting look rather more primitive and uneducated than it actually was. The legend above the facsimile read:

'*Note addressed to 'Inspector Frederick Abberline at Scotland Yard', which arrived 3rd October, 1888, three days after the double murder of Stride and Eddowes. It was dismissed as a hoax at the time as, though the message had been written in blood, it was found to be the blood of a cat.*'

Here was the message:

'*I have eaten some of the lights out of them girlies as you will see. I'd send you a morsel, Mr Abbaline [sic], only it'd be long dead and won't be no use. Still we may meat, some time, but you won't know me from midnight as I'm not wot I seam.*'

That night was the Big One. Well, you all saw the final of *I Can Make You A Star*, this year, didn't you? The tenor in the wheelchair won it because of the viewers' phone-in votes, even though the judges and I thought it should have been the blind juggler. Anyway the audience ratings went through the roof. Jill and Crispin came round afterwards for the champagne do with all the celebs. Jill was excited by it all and just thought it was a hoot, but Crispin was being very snotty and stand-offish, I'm glad to say. I kept my eye on them and when I noticed that they seemed to be having a little argument I came over. He was bored and wanted to go home apparently, but she wanted to stay. So I touched her bare arm and took her to meet some of my famous friends, purely because they might help out on the Save the Old Essex campaign, you understand. She loved that.

I was feeling pretty good the next morning, even when the doorbell rang shortly after seven-thirty. Those bloody tabloids, I thought, they'll be asking me to confirm some stupid rumour, or they want a picture of me looking rough in the altogether. I took care to dress carefully before I opened the door, but it wasn't the press, it was the police.

"Good morning, sir. Could we step inside for a moment...? Do you know a Mr Bill Beasely of Flat C. 31 Congreve Street...? Well, the thing is, sir, Mr Beaseley was found dead last night... Murdered, sir... There was a notebook on the desk and it was open at a page on which your name and address had been written... I wonder if you could possibly account for your movements last night..."

They actually asked me where I had been that night! I told them that my alibi was pretty impeccable as I had about twenty million witnesses to my whereabouts. Oh, says, the Inspector, all sophisticated, we thought those programs like *I Can Make You A Star* were prerecorded. No, I said, you can check, it was all live, every fizzing second of it. I believe in live. If it isn't live it hasn't got that something.

I asked for details about poor Bill and they seemed happy to oblige. His skull had been split open with a meat cleaver apparently and it looked as if some of his brain had been removed. That scared me, I must say, but I said nothing. They asked me if Bill had had enemies. No, I could not think of any enemies, but Bill had been a crime reporter, you know.

The next day I let the press have it, and by the time the late editions of the *Evening Standard* were on the streets, there was a nice little spread on the inside pages:

I CAN MAKE YOU A STAR MAN CLAIMS: 'I HAVE SOLVED RIPPER MYSTERY'

Well, not exactly, but near enough by press standards. I had given them a pretty coherent run-down of the evidence, and they got most of it right. The one thing I'm afraid I hadn't told them about was old Bill's part in my discovery, but I thought what with his murder and everything, it would just make things too complicated. Still, I did feel bad about it for a while.

I had rung Jill naturally, and she seemed delighted by the news coverage.

"I'm beginning to think you're a bit of a star too," she said.

"You are too kind, Miss Bennett."

"By no means, Mr Darcy." That was progress.

I discussed with her the television feature on the Old Essex and the Ripper suspect that I was arranging for the local London TV News and the possibility of a full-length documentary. Three days later Jill, Crispin and I were down at the Old Essex with a camera crew. I had specially asked Crispin to come along as our 'architectural expert' which pleased Jill.

Once again it was raining, but not as heavily as the last time. We decided to film indoors first and wait for it to clear to do the establishing shots outside in the street. I did my stuff to camera about this wonderful old building and how it was steeped in the rich history of the East End, and then Crispin did his architecture bit. I wasn't going to tell him that his material was bound to end up on the cutting room floor. He wasn't bad, but he was too fond of his own voice.

Then there was a lightening in the rain so Jill and the crew went out to do the establishing shots. Crispin and I voted to stay indoors and drink the skinny lattes the P.A. had got us from the nearest Starbucks.

So there we were, the two of us, alone in the auditorium of that great dirty old Cathedral of Sin. It was so quiet; you could almost hear the dust falling through the shafts of grey light. Somewhere in the deep distance background traffic rumbled in a 21st century street, but it was miles and ages away. Crispin started to look at me very intently, so I looked back at him. He was not bad looking, I suppose, in a rather girly way, with his shoulder length blonde hair and his pretty mouth. The looks won't last, though, I thought. I'm dark with good cheekbones. I may be forty, but I'm built to last. I go to the gym.

Mrs Midnight

"You really are a little shit," he said. I was astonished, but I said nothing. Crispin went on. "You may as well know; you haven't a chance with Jill. She is, as you would say, 'out of your league.' You do realise that, don't you?"

He was expecting me to react, to say something, but I didn't. I just went on staring at him. He reckoned without the fact that I didn't get where I am today without being a bit of a psychologist. After a pause, he started up again, but not quite as confident as before.

"I know all about your efforts to impress her. Visits to the British Library; dinners at gastro-pubs, tickets to that truly ghastly show of yours. It won't do you any good, you know. She isn't remotely interested in you, never will be, and shall I tell you why—? Good God, what's that?"

"What?"

"Didn't you see it? Some sort of flicker of light, there on stage, just behind the pros arch."

No. Nothing. Then, yes, there *was* something. By the proscenium arch, I saw a yellow light flicker, like a candle flame. Someone was holding a lighted candle on the stage of the Old Essex. Then it began to move and we saw the outline of the thing that carried it. It was a big old woman with a long dress and a shawl over her head. Her back was to us. She looked like a huge huddled heap of old clothes. Slowly she began to shuffle away from us upstage.

"Excuse me!" said Crispin, in his best public school prefect voice. He was talking loud and slow as if to an idiot child. "Excuse me, I don't know who you are, but I don't think you're supposed to be here. This is a listed building, you know! Excuse me!"

Then he started to move towards the stage.

"Christ, where are you going?" I said.

"I want to know what the hell's going on," he said. "Come on!" I couldn't stop him, so I just followed.

He climbed up onto the stage and I warned him about the floorboards. Dammit, there was a great hole in the middle of the stage; but he ignored me and I climbed up after him.

It was a funny thing. That great shambling lump of an old woman kept ahead of us the whole time as we threaded our way over piles of junk and rubble. We weren't able to catch up with her, but she was always in our sight. It was almost as if she was leading us somewhere. Crispin called out to her several times, but she simply did not react. She shambled on with her flickering candle.

When she got to the back of the stage she turned right and went through a narrow brick archway. There was now no light apart from the candle and our torches. Once through the archway we were in a backstage corridor. It was all brick, black with age or fire, To our right was a stone staircase up which we could see a flicker of candle and hear the heavy footsteps of the old woman ascending, accompanied by long groaning breaths.

Surely now we could catch up with her, so we plunged up the dirty, lightless stair, barely considering now what we were doing or why.

At the top of the steps we found ourselves in another dim, black brick corridor. And we were amazed to see that the old woman, now practically bent double and so headless to us, was halfway along it, about twenty yards ahead, hobbling away. We shouted at her, but on she went regardless.

The corridor smelt of something oily and old, and when I touched the wall by accident a black tarry substance stuck to my hand.

At last we were beginning to catch up with the woman when she suddenly stopped in a viscous looking puddle, turned and then started to climb yet another staircase to her right. When we arrived at the bottom of this flight we heard her steps cease and saw that she had halted ten steps up, her back to us. The groaning breaths were beginning to sound like some dreadful kind of singing. I thought I could recognise some words of the old Music Hall song:

"Why am I always the bridesmaid,

Never the blushing bride?
Ding dong, wedding bells,
Only ring for other gells..."

With little shuffles she was turning slowly round to face us, and I knew now that my worst fears would be confirmed. As she moved she let the plaid shawl slip from her head to reveal a greasy white cranium planted with wild tufts of white hair, sprouting like winter trees in frost on a barren landscape. Half of her face I had seen before. There was the heavy brow, the wild grey eye, the great blob nose, the thick mannish chin, but the other half was a mangled mess, an angry chaos of fiery scar tissue, utterly unrecognisable as a face at all. Mrs Midnight lifted the candle to his head so that we could see it all.

"Why am I always the bridesmaid,

Never the blushing bride...?"

Then he hurled the candle down the stairs towards us. I thought it would extinguish itself in the oily pool at the bottom of the steps. But it did not. It guttered for a moment, then a great tongue of flame leapt up from the pool and began to lick at Crispin's jeans. There was a roar and the next minute he was engulfed in flame. I took off my jacket and tried to smother the fire, but he was screaming and fighting me off. The only thing to do was to hurry him back down the corridor which was now spitting little gobs of flame from every tarry crevice. Before we had reached the stairs leading down to the stage, Crispin collapsed. First I beat out the fire on his body with my jacket, then picking him up in a fireman's lift I carried him downstairs. Behind me the flames were roaring like an angry ghost.

I had got down onto the stage level with Crispin on my back. I thought we were home safe so I began to run across the stage, but I had forgotten how rotten the boards were. There was a crack and suddenly we were falling into a pit. Crispin broke my fall a little, but I felt a sharp pain in my shoulder and one leg appeared to be useless. We were in the dark. I could see nothing, but there was a reek of corpses all around us.

Mrs Midnight

The Fire Brigade eventually heard our calls and we were rescued. They told me later that Crispin and I had tumbled into a cellar where they had also found a large number of dead cats in various stages of decomposition. What was odd, they told me, was that so many of the cats had suffered injuries to the head. Some of them looked as if the tops of their skulls had been surgically removed. I did not want to know.

I had broken several bones in my body and needed a couple of operations, so I wasn't going to be pushed out of the hospital in a hurry as usually happens. I'm afraid Crispin was rather worse off. As well as other injuries, the fire had burned the beauty out of half his face. I genuinely feel bad about that.

I have a private room at the hospital, of course. In the evenings Jill, my angel, comes to see me with grapes or something else I don't really want, but I feel better for her coming. I want to say something to her so much, but I can't because I'm frightened of being turned down, rejected.

Get off! We want the bingo, not you, yer boring boogger!

And then, just recently, I have woken up in the early hours of the morning to find the great bulk of Mrs Midnight crouched by my bed. From the folds of the plaid shawl Mrs Midnight will take a kitten, still alive and mewing, and out of its trepanned head Mrs Midnight will scoop a quiver of grey jelly with a teaspoon.

"This is your brain food," says Mrs Midnight. "Eat up!"

THE MAN WITH A HOLE IN HIS HEAD

Marcus Gold

It isn't nice to wake up with a splitting headache and find yourself lashed to a kitchen chair, with nylon cord biting into the flesh of your ankles, wrists and thighs. As consciousness – and pain – flooded back, Ritzy Jacobs realised he was in trouble – right up to his nostrils.

To underline the fact, the face of his least-favourite enemy swam into focus. Krobo King was a West African, big in the drug scene. His fleshy mouth was twisted into an evil smile, and his eyes were bright with hatred.

"Bastard!" hissed Krobo, and jabbed his fist into Jacobs' face. Ritzy tasted blood where his lip had been jammed against his teeth, and waited for the pain to get serious. "You're a turd, Jacobs, and you' going where all turds go."

"Keep yer cool, Krobo," mumbled Ritzy, blood trickling from his mouth. "I'll put it right if you gimme a chance."

"Don't talk crap. Nuthin' you can do will put it right. You dissed me, man, and in a way that's real bad for my street cred."

"What can I say?"

"Say? Nuthin'. Fuck all. Zilch. You dead, man!"

"Hey, Krobo... Please." The word stuck in his throat, but it had to be said. "Please – hell, I was stupid, that's all!"

Krobo King balled his fist, so that the heavy signet ring on his middle finger stood proud. "Shut up, punk," he hissed, and hit Ritzy lazily but viciously, so that the ring laid his cheekbone open. Ritzy groaned and closed his eyes. He wasn't a hard man. Crafty, ruthless, streetwise yes, but not tough in the old-fashioned sense. He'd always used hired hands for the physical stuff.

But Krobo was different. He'd been taken for fifteen grand, and wanted to settle the matter personally. Krobo did his own dirty work, and was reputed to enjoy it. Ritzy Jacobs swallowed noisily, fear of what might be to come blotting out even the pain from his battered face. Krobo glanced across the room.

"Hey, Welcome. You got that putty?"

"Sure boss." One of the two other men present spoke for the first time. He was a powerfully built Caribbean with Rasta dreadlocks, and a face that looked as if it had been around the small-time boxing circuit more than once.

"Stick a lump on his head."

"Eh?"

"On top of his head, moron."

Mystified, the man called Welcome scooped a handful of putty from the tin, and slapped it onto the bound man's scalp. Then he stepped back, wiping the tacky residue from his fingers.

"Where I come from, we have a way with thieves," whispered Krobo. "In fact," he added, "we have several ways, but for those who steal from their brothers, we have a special way."

"I'm not your fuckin' brother, Krobo. Don't give me that!" Ritzy tried to crack hardy, but it was an effort.

"I use the word in the sense that we shared a common interest, Jacobs. An interest you betrayed. I've got to show people that no one can rip me off and get away with it. And I must do it in a way they'll remember."

Ritzy stayed silent. Whatever Krobo intended, it wasn't going to be nice. But maybe it would be survivable. Maybe the pain would go away with time, and he would be able to live again. Maybe even plot his revenge. He felt the sweat trickle down from his armpits to the waistband of his trousers, growing cold as it did so. All true feeling had gone from his hands and his feet now, leaving just a dull throbbing in time with the beat of his heart.

"The sledge, Honkers!" Krobo stretched out an arm, and the fourth person in the room, a man with bloodshot eyes and a slack mouth picked up a fourteen-pound sledgehammer from

The Man With a Hole in his Head

against the wall, and shambled across with it. Honkers was another small-time criminal, an addict with a craving who would do anything to assuage it. Smiling malevolently, Krobo took from his pocket a new six-inch nail, and held it up to the light as if to admire its perfection. Then, with care and precision, he pushed it into the putty until Ritzy felt the point prick his scalp.

"No!" screamed the bound man, who suddenly realised what was coming. That it was far worse than he had imagined. "For God's sake... No!" His voice became an incoherent babble. "Please, please, Krobo – I'll do anything – anything you want! Christ, it was only money – I'll pay you back – ten times over... honest..."

Krobo King stretched back his lips to display a set of large, perfect teeth, and hefted the hammer.

Even Welcome was looking pale. "You're jokin', boss, huh?" he croaked. "You ain't really gonna do it?"

Krobo giggled. "Where's your bottle, brother? I thought you was hard."

"Let me just blow him away!" Welcome reached under his bomber jacket for the bored-through starter pistol he carried.

Krobo smiled even wider, and shook his head. He poised the hammer an inch above the nail, and like a golfer lining up a putt, took aim. For a few long seconds, no one in the room breathed. Ritzy's terrified eyes nearly popped out of their sockets as they were drawn upwards to look at the instrument of doom poised above him.

Krobo swung the hammer rhythmically, accurately. The head of the sledge buried itself in the putty with a soft thud, and Ritzy's scream ended in a weird gurgling sound. The chair rocked and toppled over. Krobo skipped nimbly aside to avoid his shins being barked, and the squashed lump of putty split and fell away, leaving the head of the nail standing about an inch proud of the victim's scalp. A few beads of blood, not much, glinted amongst the black strands of Ritzy's hair.

"Jesus!" croaked Welcome when he had opened his eyes.

"I think he's dead," growled Krobo. "Pity, I'd've liked to have the bastard live a while. Get rid of the mess, will ya?"

"Where?" asked Welcome, swallowing vomit.

"Anywhere. On the street. So people know what happens when you cross Krobo King."

"What about the law?"

"Fuck the law. Dump the hammer. Ain't no prints on the nail. Not now anyway." Krobo laughed at his little joke and walked out of the room, wiping his hands on a silk handkerchief. Welcome bent to cut the cords that bound Jacobs to the chair. His hands shook, and he could hear Honkers retching in the toilet. Krobo was a friggin' hard bastard, no one could argue that.

It was dawn, and the body lay where Welcome and Honkers had dropped it, in the alley off St. Michael's Hill. A stray dog approached, sniffing, and the bundle in the gutter groaned. The dog decided it had business elsewhere, and loped away.

The cleaner brushing the steps of Bristol Royal Infirmary looked up to see a drunk stumbling along the pavement towards him. As the figure came closer, he could see there was blood on the drunk's face.

"You…" he was going to add: 'all right, mate?' but the man crumpled at his feet before he could finish the sentence. Then he saw the silver head of the nail, and scuttled into the building to fetch help.

The two surgeons prepared to remove the nail from Ritzy's skull. The blood had been cleaned away, the hair shaved off the crown of the patient's head and a flap of skin lifted to bare the cranium. "He should live if we can control the haemorrhaging quickly," said the senior surgeon. "It'll be interesting to see just what damage has been done."

"The X-rays suggest surprisingly little," said his colleague. "Industrial accident, was it?"

"Nope. The police think it might be the consequence of what is commonly called a gangland vendetta."

The Man With a Hole in his Head

"Really?" The junior surgeon pulled a face. "Nasty way to settle an argument."

"Apparently it is not uncommon in certain parts of the world. Standard treatment for a thief who robs his own people. Are you ready?"

The younger man nodded, and the senior surgeon grasped the head of the nail with what looked remarkably like a pair of carpenter's pliers. "Well here goes. Hold the head very still. Nurse, have those swabs ready."

One or two of the theatre staff went distinctly pale as the nail was drawn from its resting place with the sound of soft suction, and a slight grating of metal on bone. But serious haemorrhaging *was* prevented, and after a period of tidying up, Ritzy Jacobs was wheeled into the intensive care unit with his head bandaged and a drip in his arm.

"You're a lucky man," said the neurologist on the day Ritzy was due to be discharged. "As far as we can tell, you are more or less one hundred percent fit again – neurologically speaking – except, of course for the pain threshold. You might never feel pain again. You might find that a bit of a problem."

"There's worse," said Jacobs, philosophically.

"Don't underestimate it. Pain has a purpose. You could burn yourself, cut yourself, or maybe develop a cancer and not know about it until it's too late."

"I'll be careful. Thanks, Doc."

"Come in once a month for a year or so. The nurse will give you an appointment card."

Ritzy ran his fingers over his new Frankenstein hairstyle in the taxi going back to his flat. The operation scar was small – just a dent in the top of his scalp, under which was a tiny metal plate. The surgeon had joked about unscrewing it whenever a service was necessary. The police had been to see him of course, but he had told them nothing.

What he needed now was money. Enough money to hire some help. Enough money to hire a couple of seriously hard men from out of town who wouldn't worry about tangling with

The Man With a Hole in his Head

Krobo King. That kind of help came expensive, and it would take time. But however much time and money it took, he was going to square the account. Then perhaps the nightmares would go away. The nightmares where a grinning black man was hammering nail after nail into his skull. Nightmares from which he awoke screaming, and the shock of which lingered long into the following day. Yes, Krobo King had much to answer for, and the new Ritzy Jacobs wasn't the jaunty, devil-may-care character of the old days. When the nail pierced deep into his brain, it altered his nature more than the BRI psychologists realised.

The first thing Ritzy did when he came out of hospital was to give his girlfriend, Arabella, a beating for playing the field whilst he'd been away. He'd hit her before, but this time it was really nasty. She was the first person to realise how much he had changed. He told her he was going to London for a while, and left her the keys of the flat, but told her she had better watch herself because he was coming back. She promised she would, and she *was* good for a couple of months, because she was afraid of the new Ritzy Jacobs who seemed to take pleasure in hurting her.

Ritzy soon carved himself a niche in the lower echelons of the London drug scene, partly because of his natural sharp wits, and partly because he rapidly earned a reputation for being a hard man. Minor criminals have a great respect for 'bottle'.

The first of two incidents that gave Ritzy his reputation occurred when he strayed into a Lambeth pub which was in another mob's territory. The boss of this 'manor' broke a tankard on the counter, and 'glassed' Ritzy full in the face. Instead of collapsing in agony, Ritzy stood his ground, and with the blood pouring down his shirtfront, pulled a knife, and ripped it into his assailant's lower abdomen. The bossman was in hospital considerably longer than Ritzy, and lost his enthusiasm for gangland warfare. Ritzy took over his patch.

The second happened a few months later when business was

The Man With a Hole in his Head

really beginning to roll. Two plain clothes officers of the Drug Squad took Ritzy down an alleyway one night. The working over they gave him became a legend, and they were rapidly transferred. But the underworld knew Ritzy Jacobs hadn't talked, and his reputation rose even higher.

When Ritzy decided to return to Bristol, his face was considerably scarred, and his right arm, which the Drug Squad had broken in two places was nearly useless. But his bank balance was healthy, and he ran a drugs network that was on its way to becoming the biggest in the South of England.

Only one thing gnawed at his bowels. All the time he had been grafting and risking life and limb in London, he had been fired by the thought of the revenge he would wreak on Krobo King when he had the means to do it. Now the opportunity was snatched away from him. Avon and Somerset constabulary had raided Krobo's City Road flat, and found a quantity of cocaine awaiting distribution. Krobo was sent down for seven years, with deportation to follow.

So the hatred smouldered, made more intense by frustration. Krobo was untouchable in prison, for he had been a long time in the drug network, and had powerful friends. When, after five years, he was escorted aboard a green-and-white 747 of Nigerian Airlines at Heathrow, Ritzy was watching from the spectator gallery, but there was nothing he could do except grind his teeth. Where Krobo was going, he had connections in high places, and a white hit-man would stick out like a sore thumb. Ritzy's attempts to subvert one or two of Krobo's fellow nationals had been rejected with a grimace and a shudder, even though the money had been big. It looked as though Ritzy would just have to nurse his burning hatred and live with his nightly torment.

And so it was. At night he suffered, by day he knew no pain – not when he inadvertently rested his hand on the hot plate of an electric cooker – not when he crashed his Porsche at ninety-plus on the M4, breaking half his ribs and leaving his left foot

The Man With a Hole in his Head

in the wreckage – not even when the cancer cells first began to multiply in his colon.

Then fortune played into his hands. Krobo King showed no signs of wishing to return to the shores of the country where he had made his pile, but he had a perverse regard for the English, and in particular for the English public school. He sent his only daughter, Prudence, to an expensive girl's academy in Devon, and Ritzy Jacobs got to hear about it.

The worst moment – so far – in Krobo King's life occurred when an airmail package arrived from the UK. The sidekick who had been sent into the yard to open it, (Krobo was a careful man), returned with a puzzled look, and a small box containing a human finger. A little finger, slender, with a polished nail. The accompanying letter told him that the finger had belonged to his daughter, and more would follow unless he returned to Bristol for 'discussions' with a Mr Ritzy Jacobs.

Krobo sent a stalling letter whilst his contacts in England tried to get him more information. The next parcel contained a ring finger, and on it a gold eternity ring he had bought his daughter for her last birthday. He set off for Lagos, but had difficulty getting visas for two of his bodyguards. He sent a cable from the Ikoyi Hotel saying he might be delayed, and received a cold reply stating that he had better hurry, or a third digit would be on its way.

In a mood that combined burning hatred with cold fear for the fate of the child he cherished, Krobo arrived at Heathrow determined to make an upstart Jewish bastard pay dearly for daring to throw down the gauntlet in this manner. He was met by a couple of his old St. Pauls mob with a car boot full of assorted weaponry. As they pulled out of the short-term car park, there was a shattering explosion.

When the outcome of his plot was conveyed to Ritzy, he nodded but did not smile. In truth he was a bit sorry that his enemy should have gone so suddenly, without pain, without the terror *he* had suffered. Still, it was done. The underworld would know, and would respect him even more. And perhaps

The Man With a Hole in his Head

the nightmares would go away.

"What shall we do with the girl?" asked one of his lieutenants.

"Ach, let her go," said Ritzy in a rare moment of compassion. "Tell her if she keeps her mouth shut she can go to a private hospital, and have a first class ticket back to Lagos."

"How can we be sure she won't talk?"

Ritzy Jacobs' face darkened ominously. "Tell her that if she does, what's happened to her so far will seem like parlour games compared with what I'll do when I get my hands on her again."

The next few years saw Ritzy Jacobs' fortunes blossom. He was able to pull back from the day-by-day operations of his drugs empire, and invest the profits it generated in legitimate businesses. On his fiftieth birthday he retired from criminal activities, and began to work at establishing himself as a respectable entrepreneur and man of substance.

Then his luck began to run out. The damage to his face, his useless arm, his artificial foot, had been impediments – but the sort you could live with. He had enjoyed an uninhibited sex life, travelled wherever the fancy took him, eaten well and enjoyed the best of wines. But inevitably, his body clock started to run down, his infirmities to grow more intrusive by the day. Worst of all, the insidious cancer, unheralded by pain, had taken hold, undiagnosed until it was too late. Ritzy Jacobs was suddenly faced with the prospect of degenerating into a chronic invalid; impotent, incontinent, pathetic.

But he still had guts – even if they weren't working very well – and even he wasn't the type to wait philosophically for the candle of life to gutter out. He put out the word that he was looking for the best treatment money could buy. An answer came from the High Haven Clinic in Southern California, an institution which smugly acknowledged that it catered exclusively for the very wealthy in order to 'push back the frontiers of surgical science'.

Ritzy Jacobs embarked on his last great adventure in a mood of anger and cynicism. The anger was not assuaged when he learned that the High Haven tariff was three thousand dollars a day – before treatment began. The cynicism was mollified by the amazing sophistication of the Clinic's equipment, and the confident welcoming words of Vidal Van Kleef, the proprietor and senior surgeon. "We can do anything that's known to medical science, and maybe a few things the rest of the world hasn't heard about yet."

Two days later, when Ritzy had undergone the full gamut of physical tests, X-rays, body and brain scans, Van Kleef told him the score.

"Mr Jacobs," he murmured, "you are in terrible shape."

"Do I need to pay a small fortune to be told that?" rasped the patient.

"But one of your disabilities may turn out to be a blessing in disguise," the surgeon continued. "Do you think you could stand surgery without anaesthetic?"

"Sure," said Ritzy, with a grim smile.

"Prolonged surgery?"

"As long as it takes," snapped the patient. "Look, I don't feel pain, and I ain't squeamish. You wanna cut me up, you cut me up. I'll lie still, I promise. Just build me a friggin' body I can live in."

Vidal massaged his chin, and lapsed into a long silence. When he spoke, his voice was low but distinct, as if he were making sure he used exactly the right words.

"You know, Mr Jacobs, I think we have in you a very, very special opportunity. A patient with whom the frontiers of surgery could be pushed back a long way. But although you do not feel pain as the rest of us feel pain, what I am going to suggest might be even more than *you* can take."

"Could it now," growled Ritzy. "What's the bottom line?"

"I could give you a whole new body."

Ritzy was silent for several seconds.

The Man With a Hole in his Head

"A whole new body?"

"Exactly. It's not something we have ever been able to contemplate doing under anaesthetic. It would simply take too long. Hours and hours of delicate surgery just to connect up the nerve endings and suchlike. Not to mention the plumbing."

"Plumbing?"

"The blood supply and airways."

"I see. But in my case you could take as long as it needs, eh?"

"If you can stick it out."

"I can stick it out."

"I wonder. The shock would be immense, even without the pain."

"Try me," whispered Ritzy Jacobs. "I'm going to kick the bucket if you don't do something, ain't I? So just try me!"

"Okay," said Van Kleef. "But there's one other thing. It'll cost maybe a million bucks."

"C'mon," growled Ritzy. "You're gonna make a fortune for yourself if you pull it off. Half a million is all I pay."

The surgeon smiled. "You've got guts, Mr Jacobs. Five hundred grand it is then. In advance, I'm afraid."

Ritzy nodded. "That figures. I'll brief my accountant, and he'll pay as soon as you're ready to begin. I suppose you've got to find a suitable – er – donor, first?"

"Sure. It may take a few days, but we've a lot of contacts. I'll go ahead with the other arrangements."

The preparations leading up to the surgery were detailed and complicated. It had to be planned to the minute, because, as Van Kleef explained, flesh and tissue degrade very rapidly. Crucial to the operation was a large supply of suitable blood, and of course a body, fresh, healthy, relatively undamaged, and – until the moment of death, with that same group B blood coursing through its arteries.

It took about ten days for one to turn up. A man of thirty-three with an inoperable brain tumour in a Chicago hospital.

The Man With a Hole in his Head

Just conscious enough to bequeath, validly, his mortal remains. A man whose wife and two kids would be left without a dime if he said 'no' to Van Kleef's offer. It was a big offer, and he didn't. An executive jet was placed on stand-by at Chicago airport, and Van Kleef's assistant moved into the hospital with the equipment necessary to keep the body medically viable once the brain had ceased to function. At 01:30 hours on the following Friday, the man was declared clinically dead, and an hour later the jet was hurtling through the night sky on course for Los Angeles.

As soon as the plane was airborne, Van Kleef went to see his patient.

"Your new body is on its way," he told Jacobs. "Are you ready?"

"Sure, when do you want to begin?"

"Now. There's a lot of preparatory work to be done."

Ritzy swallowed hard. There was a churning sensation in his stomach. Would he still feel it, he wondered, when his stomach wasn't there anymore? What would happen to the spittle he swallowed then? They would void it, of course... There would be tubes and siphons and pumps keeping the vital fluids circulating. All the same, it was best not to think about it.

"I'm going to give you a drug to relax you a bit," said the surgeon with a smile. "Of course we'll screen what's going on from your field of vision and give you some music to listen to, but from time to time we may want your help."

"Help?" grunted Jacobs.

"Just to check the working parts as we put them in."

The narcotics and the soothing music fed to Ritzy through the earphones clamped to his head, made the early stages of the operation just about bearable. There was no agony in the usual sense of the word, but losing one's ability to experience pain is not the same as losing one's sense of feeling. Although the messages sent back to his brain were not interpreted in the normal way, Jacobs' nervous system still functioned. There were sensations not easy to describe or endure, and he found

The Man With a Hole in his Head

himself struggling against a panic that threatened to engulf his whole reason.

From time to time, Vidal Van Kleef would move to Ritzy's side of the smoked glass screen that prevented the patient seeing what was happening to the rest of his body, and offer words of comfort and reassurance. Sometimes, other members of the surgical team would loom briefly into his view. That was how he saw her first, a slim black woman, only her eyes exposed between a mask and a surgical cap. Big liquid eyes, with long lashes, that seemed totally absorbed in the work being done, the sculpting of flesh and bone that was happening on the other side of that barrier.

And then the eyes looked directly at him, and he realised with sudden horror that they were not dispassionate at all, but bright with malevolence. Ritzy Jacobs was no stranger to evil, but knew at once that the owner of those eyes bore him a hatred deeper than anything he had ever known. But why, he wondered, as the alarm bells clattered in his head. Why, in the far west of the USA, in a city he had never visited before, should anyone hate him so? Then before his drug-hazed mind could grapple with the mystery, the woman lifted her right hand to adjust her surgical mask. Two of the fingers of her rubber glove had been clipped off and sealed with tape. Then he knew, even before Van Kleef leaned across with a little speech of introduction.

"This is my assistant, Prudence King, Mr Jacobs. One of the finest young surgeons out of Africa. She'll – oh shit!" He turned to the nurse who had been sitting silently beside Ritzy's head. "Quick, oxygen – and give me that hypo!"

When the theatre lights swam back into focus, Ritzy found he had an oxygen mask clamped to his mouth, and a row of anxious faces looking down on him. Out of the corner of his eye he could see Van Kleef thoughtfully studying a hypodermic syringe.

"We're going to take a break, Mr Jacobs," said the surgeon soothingly. "Everything's gone very well so far, but it has obviously been a bit much for you. Your – er – new bits and pieces can go back on ice for a few hours, and then we'll finish the job. In the meantime, this'll help you rest." He smiled as he finished speaking, and inserted the needle smoothly into his patient's neck.

What was left of Ritzy Jacobs wanted to say: 'Please, for God's sake get that woman out of here,' but he couldn't articulate the words, and a huge weariness was pressing down on him.

"Don't worry," Van Kleef's voice seemed far away now, "Miss King will be beside you all the time."

Ritzy tried to scream 'NO!' but all that came out was a whimper.

Then fell the darkness.

Except for the hum of the machinery that was circulating his blood, and the rhythmical sucking of the air-pump that had replaced his lungs, the operating theatre was quiet when Ritzy Jacobs regained consciousness. At first he thought he was alone, but then he became aware of someone behind him, out of his field of vision, someone working on his head, touching, scraping, probing deep into his skull.

"Who – who is it?" he croaked. "What are you doing?"

"Ah," came the reply. "So the sedation is wearing off. That's good, I wanted to talk to you." The voice was soft and musical, the accent faintly redolent of Lagos or Accra.

"I want you to call Mr Van Kleef," said Ritzy, trying to make his voice carry authority.

"So I shall," said the woman behind him. "But first I have work to do."

"What do you mean, work?"

"You tortured me, and killed my father, remember?"

"I'm – I'm sorry I had to hurt you," muttered Ritzy, "but your old man had it coming for what…"

"Shut up!" snapped Prudence King. "I am the judge now – the judge, the jury – and the executioner if I choose!"

The Man With a Hole in his Head

"You wouldn't kill me, would you? Being a doctor and all that?"

"I would do so with pleasure," hissed Prudence. "I've killed you many, many times in my mind when I've seen men I've wanted stare at my mutilated hand... and shudder... and turn away. Can you imagine the problems I had getting accepted for training as a surgeon? And worst of all is the pity. 'Lovely girl', they say when they think I can't hear. 'What a shame she has that deformity!'"

"I thought," whispered Ritzy, "that you doctors took a hippo – hippo something oath."

Prudence King laughed softly. "Oh yes, the Hippocratic oath. I've thought about it since you were brought here. It forbids me to kill you, but positively encourages me to cure your unfortunate affliction, and do you know, I think I can! I've studied your brain scan with great care."

"My affliction?" Ritzy Jacobs almost managed a brief chuckle. "Which one, for God's sake?"

"Your inability to feel pain, Mr Jacobs. Your inability to feel pain!"

"You – you must be joking. Why, if I felt pain, I couldn't..."

"I'm in this team because of my dexterity with fine suturing in confined spaces, Mr Jacobs. My missing fingers are actually a help sometimes, because my hand is so small. The fiddling inside your skull, which you can no doubt sense as we talk, is me doing a certain amount of reconstruction."

"You can't! It would be diabolical!"

Prudence King laughed, and it was the most chilling sound he had ever heard.

"All you are at the moment, Mr Jacobs, is a head connected to a spinal column. Oh, but that doesn't mean you won't feel the legs and arms and other parts you haven't got. You will feel them all, I can promise. And when Vidal starts trying to give you new flesh and bones, the sensations should become *very* interesting. Of course, you won't survive to enjoy your new body – eventually the shock will kill you."

The Man With a Hole in his Head

"You bastard!" croaked Ritzy. "You want to push me into telling Van Kleef to terminate the operation, don't you? Okay – you win. Call him. I'll tell him I don't want to go through with it."

"Will you really?" Prudence King murmured softly. At that moment she was engaged in a very delicate bit of microsurgery. Suddenly her patient's head jerked, and a howl of agony burst from his lips. She straightened her back, and picked up a scalpel from her tray.

"I think a little attention to the vocal cords is necessary at this stage," she added, moving round into his line of vision, and smiling. He felt a stab of pain as the thin blade entered his throat, but his scream was very brief.

STARLIGHT CASTS NO SHADOW

Ian C. Strachan

Captain Mondarez arrived, yawning, as we were bringing the two plastic bags out of Unit Twenty-eight. He only shrugged when Gibson asked him about radioing the authorities.

"The nearest police is forty kilometres away." He took off his cap and ran his hand over his black hair. "And after all – two Indians? It is not worth troubling about, eh? I will detail some of my men to help you dispose of the... the bodies."

But as he turned away I heard him mutter in his own tongue: 'Reduced to bones in a night! It is not natural, that.' I didn't think it was natural either, but there was no getting round the fact that it had happened, and we had two bags filled with bones to prove it.

The two Indians, a man and a woman, had come to our camp late in the previous day. Their canoe had overturned, they said, and all their supplies lost. We gave them enough food to last them to the next village and they started off again along the highway that ran all the way to distant Chimbarazo. But they must have returned as darkness dropped over the plain, to spend the night in Unit Twenty-eight. And now, some eighteen hours later, they were just two skeletons. No, it certainly wasn't natural.

The six labourers grew more and more uneasy as the day passed. Like the soldiers, they were from the city, and had been showing signs of unhappiness since we came out to that flat empty landscape. That night two of them vanished, taking with them some of our tools.

Mondarez cursed the sentry and despatched a search party, which returned empty-handed at noon.

At first light on the following morning, the skeletons of the four remaining workers were found beside their camp fire. Mondarez was now visibly concerned: two wandering natives, alive or dead, might be of no account, but the deaths of four of the men he had been ordered to protect were something else.

"The sentry speaks of a shadow," he told us morosely, "a great dark shadow moving silent over the ground. But there was no moon last night, and the stars cast no shadow. And then, what kind of animal is it that consumes men in silence, and leaves only bones? No, no, it is all nonsense."

The shadow, whatever it was, had apparently been seen to move from the direction of one of the mobile homes. The dead men had been sleeping between our tents and the soldiers' bivouac, which was alongside the road.

"Unit Twenty-eight," Jiffy Foyle pointed out thoughtfully. "Where we found the first two. What say we make a search instead of starting work?"

He and Jan Hergol took forty of the units while Tommy Gibson and I went into each of the other forty, but when we met again at the tents none of us had anything to report.

"A waste of time," Jan declared. "The creature evidently comes here from somewhere across the prairie. Also, the units cannot conceal anything that is big enough to eat men."

The mobile homes were simply oversized caravans with an outer skin of aluminium over a steel frame and an inner wall of thin laminated plastic. Inside, they were partitioned to form a lounge at the front, a kitchen, a toilet with a shower and a bedroom at the rear.

They had been imported from the States and were to house the staff of the nuclear power station that was being built on the bank of the river, some four miles along the highway. There had been some unexpected hold-up in the construction of the plant, a minor radiation leak it was rumoured, but that wasn't our worry. All we had to do was make the units ready for connecting up to the water and electricity supply when it arrived, and plumb in the drainage.

"I vote we borrow guns from Mondarez tonight," suggested Foyle, "and wait up in Twenty-eight to see what comes along. We've got torches, and we'll be awake and ready for it, not like these poor devils. What d'you say?"

Starlight Casts No Shadow

Tommy Gibson replied sourly that he had been taken on to do a job of work, not to go hunting dangerous animals in the dark. Jan sided with Jiffy, and a futile little argument arose. I took the same view as Gibson: if there was any shooting to be done, let the soldiers do it, I said firmly.

In the end Foyle and Jan opted to sit up all night in the mobile home nearest the workers' camp, Number Twenty-eight, while Tommy and I slept as usual in our tents.

I didn't sleep much, though. I lay for a long time listening to the sentries – Mondarez had posted four instead of one – pacing round and pausing to talk, and eventually I saw the tent wall brighten as the sun rose.

I got up, sticky-mouthed and unrefreshed, to find Tommy Gibson sitting smoking his pipe beside the remains of the fire. He was staring hard at the half-open door of Twenty-eight.

He turned his head as I emerged and grunted: "Right. We'd best be getting over there."

Something in his voice brought me fully awake. "What's happened?" I asked. "Have you seen something?"

He tapped out his pipe, got up stiffly and said: "It's what I don't see that's worrying me. No sound, no movement. Jiffy was always one for getting up with the sun."

We walked across and went in. A skeleton lay on the floor of the tiny kitchen, and another was sitting propped against the wall in the front room. This one was, or had been, Foyle: we could tell that by the heavy gold ring on one of the finger-bones. A rifle lay nearby, its safety-catch on. Gibson picked up the torch and tried the switch. "Dead," he observed. "Been on all night."

His outward calmness vanished and he made for the door. "I've had enough of this," he said over his shoulder. "I'm going to make Mondarez radio for transport out of here."

He ducked his head under the top of the doorway and I heard his boots thudding away on the hard earth.

As I stood in that sun-heated room I became conscious of that indescribable sensation you get when you know you are being watched. So strong was it that I turned and bent to look out of the big front window. All I could see was the shining rows of mobile homes standing in the baking sunlight. Nothing moved. I looked down and was confronted by the grinning thing that had once been Jiffy Foyle. I snatched up the rifle and almost ran out of there.

I saw Captain Mondarez and began to walk over but half way I halted, struck by a sudden realisation. I turned and looked at the units behind me, one by one. When I reached the others I said:

"Tommy, have you noticed anything about the units? Something that should be there and isn't?"

"This is no time for guessing games. What you on about?"

"No birds," I told him. "And no lizards, no bugs on the walls or ceilings. Remember the noise of the birds on the roofs when we first started here?"

He stared, first at me and then at the nearest units. "Hey, that's right!"

Mondarez broke in impatiently: "What is all this foolishness? Birds, lizards, black shapes on the ground at night – this is the talk of old women. There is nothing in these homes to hurt one."

"I'm not so sure," said Tommy, half to himself. "I wouldn't go back in Number Twenty-eight for half a million dollars, and I bet you wouldn't either."

I don't think he meant it as an offensive remark in any way, but Mondarez chose to take it like that. He drew himself up – he wasn't a tall man – and his face turned first red and then white.

"So – you insult me, you question my courage, yes? Then I will show you different. I shall explore the trailer with thoroughness – and maybe then you will make apologies."

And he loosened his revolver in its holster, pulled a jack-knife from a pocket, and strode to the door of Twenty-eight.

We heard his boots stamping from room to room, and then there came a noise like ripping cardboard.

Starlight Casts No Shadow

"By God, he is taking the place apart right enough," said Gibson, and laughed nervously.

Then there were two shots. I saw the dust spring up from the roof as the bullets went through it, and then we heard a cry. It was like no sound I had ever heard before or since: a choked, rasping cry.

Tommy Gibson said: "God in Heaven!"

Something the size of a man appeared at the door and tumbled to the ground. For a wild moment I wondered if Mondarez had somehow been engulfed in molten tar, for the glistening black shape lying there seethed and bubbled. Then I saw what it was that covered him and I brought up the rifle and snapped off the safety-catch.

Gibson pulled at my arm. "What are you doing?" he shrieked.

I fired three shots and the heaving black object ceased to move.

Then as we watched, it flattened, flowed out and down, spread along the ground to the wheel of the mobile home, and drained away like black water. A heap of gleaming bones with a few buttons, a buckle and a pair of boots among them lay in the sunlight like some lunatic still life painting.

Two troopers and a sergeant ran up, guns at the ready. Tommy, who had recovered his composure to some extent, explained what was wanted and the sergeant snapped out an order that sent the soldiers running back to the camp. They returned carrying three crates.

Tommy read the stencilled lettering on one and nodded. "Phosphorus grenades," he said grimly. "Aye, that'll do it."

The sergeant positioned all his men around the unit, each man armed with two or three grenades. Then he ran past the doorway, tossed in a grenade, raced back to us.

A sheet of yellow-and-red flame shot out of the door and the windows cracked and fell out. In seconds, the caravan was a solid mass of fire. A man shouted, pointing, and we saw a long black tongue extend itself from beneath the unit. A grenade bounced in front of it, exploded in a ball of flame and smoke, and the black column dissolved.

Five times these black shadows on the ground surged out, and each was destroyed or driven back by a grenade. Only one reached out as far as the ring of men, and a soldier screamed like an injured horse before the flames blossomed up and drove it back. The mobile home's frame collapsed in a tangle of twisted steel, and only the smoking earth showed that an inferno had raged there.

The trucks came for us in the evening and Tommy and me threw our gear into the back of one and climbed in. The tropical night fell with its usual abruptness as we sped along the highway, the lights of the following truck shining in on us.

"Did you ever see such monsters?" marvelled Gibson. "Three-quarters of an inch long – you wouldn't have thought it possible."

I unscrewed the cap from the bottle of Scotch I had found in Captain Mondarez's tent and drank.

Tommy went on: "Something to do with that leak at the plant, I'll bet. Did you see that soldier's leg where the brutes reached him? You could see the bone."

"Shut up about it, will you," I told him. I held out the bottle but he shook his head, his face very white in the headlamps' beams.

"They must have been in the space between the walls of Twenty-eight," he said. The truck's wheels rumbled on the smooth highway, the canvas behind me rattled.

"Came out at night through the ventilator grilles and..." he said. It was like listening to a fever patient's delirium. "They never made any noise – poor Jiffy and Jan. Nor the others didn't, either."

"You can't make a noise," I pointed out, "when your nose and mouth and throat are filled with soldier ants. Now shut up about it, all right?"

I made for the nearest port soon afterwards, signed on with a freighter bound for the UK and let the good sea air blow the horrors out of my brain. But even now, in cold damp England, I still shudder whenever I see ants run on the garden path, and I remember the day I stood in that oven of a mobile home with two skeletons for company and millions of deadly ants concealed all around me in the walls.

LEIBNIZ'S LAST PUZZLE

Craig Herbertson

Outside the Dome restaurant, I paused on the steps; at my side, Mulholland. He rested his cane against the crisp leg of his plus fours then drew a cigarillo from a small silver case. Absently he offered one to me and on my refusal lit his own.

It was one of those moments that I believe only happen amongst men. The brisk, night air, the distant laughter and clinking glasses, the rain-washed, empty streets all offering a temptation to walk home in solitary contemplation. Yet we both paused in that masculine companionship, which neatly combines a mutual appreciation of the absurdity of the universe and an empathy with one other. Mulholland, smiling whimsically, tasted a breath of smoke and watched it curl out to meet the streetlamp glow.

"Fancy a pint?" he said. "Oxford bar is only across the way. Quiet. We can have a bit of a talk."

I pondered Mulholland's transformation as we walked to the pub. Gone the weak and cowardly schoolboy with the skinny legs and the stutter: Gone the gawky clothes. Instead, here he paced up the street, a man approaching fifty with the step of a twenty-year-old, his clothes elegantly tailored, his voice assured and commanding. The only certain means to know that he was once that maligned boy – the lewd wound where his left eye had been.

Almost as though Mulholland sensed my gaze, he paused then drew a patch from his wallet and placed it over the missing eye. "Bloody school reunions," he said with a laugh. "Still we saw off that bastard, Gray."

I knew then that my tacit support of Mulholland at Bellport High, so long ago, had remained in his memory; and the farce of a reunion meal had cemented a new-found camaraderie.

"Bit of a puzzle that Gray," I said as we walked.

"Yes, he is. Yet I suppose I have to thank his sadistic games

Leibniz's Last Puzzle

for getting me out of Bellport."

After losing his eye in the Gray escapade, Mulholland had moved to a public school. From there, Oxford to study Anthropology. Then, apparently on a whim, he had taken up Egyptology and had joined a couple of digs with our old deputy head. After a masters in Divinity, he became a missionary in the Far East.

"When that fell through," he said blithely as we pushed open the bar door, "I took up big game hunting."

"Big game hunting," I spluttered. "Bit of a contrast from saving souls?"

"Oh, I wasn't quite the missionary you might imagine. I was dabbling in the black arts all through my education. I had my eye on something and the church seemed a dandy way of covering my tracks."

I contemplated the occult as we settled into the snug of the Oxford. It seemed a far cry from the simple wooden chairs and unpretentious surroundings that momentarily lent Mulholland an archaic charm. I cradled my pint of 80 Shilling. Mulholland made to light a second cigarillo, then remembering the proscription said, "Writer now, Horror? Plenty of preparation for that at Bellport High." I laughed but then Mulholland's voice took on an earnest tone: "You mentioned 'puzzle' earlier and that got me thinking. I have a little tale that you can perhaps use. Must do the usual; change a few names, tart it up, but I'll tell you it, if you like."

I nodded and Mulholland began to unravel the tale that came to be known as 'Leibniz's Last Puzzle'

*

We were in the year above Norton at Bellport. You remember Norton, the school chess champion? Prefect, cricketer, endearing fellow. You probably don't know that he had a German pen pal, something of a mathematical genius. His name crops up everywhere in chess circles, conundrum clubs

Leibniz's Last Puzzle

and the like.

Norton and this fellow, Lubecker, met up at the Leibniz Universität, in Hannover and became best of pals. They were working on some significant treatise in applied mathematics – mind-bogglingly clever stuff; utterly beyond the likes of you or me, but for some reason it all fell through and the two of them left the University and came over to Blighty. Caused a sensation in academic circles – rumours of a homosexual affair, which in itself was nothing – but of course, giving up such promising careers on an apparent whim...

In any case, they left immediately for a camping trip; that much was known to their erstwhile colleagues. In fact, their destination was the north-east coast of England, specifically the Yorkshire Wolds. As far as the academic circles of Europe were concerned, they simply disappeared from the ken of man. But not, as it transpired, from the ken of good old D. Mulholland. It was late November – and here you have to ask yourself, whatever were two men doing out in tents in the deep of winter – when I received a letter from Norton. I was to come immediately. There would be expenses as an incentive, but you know, I would have gone without any mention of money.

There was something in the tone of the letter. Can't quite describe it, but you could tell that Norton, normally fearless, was a bit on edge. And then, of course, he asked me to brush up my research on occultism and in particular the sixteenth to eighteenth century. There were more specifics – this was the time of the witchcraft madness and certainly, a bit later, the ghastly period when even the cathedrals came under threat. Norton was aware of my interest in the occult and I suppose he banked on me being anonymous enough, external to his academic penumbra and trustworthy. The specifics will become clear as we go.

Intrigued, I took a train down to the address he'd given. When I arrived, there was no one to meet me at the station, no taxicab, no village bus and the usual sense that one has entered an utterly foreign country. Fortunately, Norton had prepared me in advance with a small map and a picture.

Norton's pal, Lubecker – he seemed to be the one with the readies – had rented a cottage somewhere off the beaten track. It was apparently, one of those small places surrounded by nothing but dry stone dykes and bleak hills. As I began the long hike I could almost imagine lonely tribes of Brigantes out on the moors doing whatever unpleasantness Celtic tribes did back then. Parts of Yorkshire can be a bit eerie and this was living up to the image in style. A light snow wefted through the sky but it wasn't sufficiently strong enough to lie. It was damned chilly.

By dusk, I arrived at a small beck and perched on a low promontory, was the cottage. It was possibly bleaker in aspect than the surrounding hills.

Norton had warned me that he and Lubecker only occupied the place at odd intervals while the main work, whatever that might be, was going on some distance away in the hills – hence the tents. Whatever it was, they insisted on at least one of their little team being present on site. When I arrived, the cottage was empty. They were both out somewhere in the growing dark. The back door was open. I stumbled around a bit and found a candle.

It was a typical bachelor mess in dire need of a woman's hand: Dirty plates lying around on the floor of the kitchen, rubbish piled high in bags, empty whisky bottles, muddy boots and digging equipment in the hall. But equally typically, there was a wide open doorway that revealed a small room at the back, devoid of furniture with the exception of a very large oaken table. Placed on this table were neat diagrams and an ordered stack of books and papers. The walls of the room had a built-in bookshelf or two filled with a collector's bonanza and I reflected even then, that it was lucky that no one of significance knew where Lubecker and Norton were hiding or the whole library, lock stock and barrel, would be out gracing the tables of every dodgy book dealer.

Leibniz's Last Puzzle

Naturally, I looked first at the bookshelves. It was an eclectic mix but there were five clear strands – archaeological fieldwork, endless reams on games, puzzles and conundrums, a lot of German texts about the history of Hannover, some of the dullest mathematical books imaginable and a small section on concave and convex mirrors. In reference to the latter, I found an early edition of Ibn al-Haytham's *Book of Optics*, worth a small fortune. I had read it with interest at university.

After musing over the contents of Ibn al-Haytham's masterpiece, I turned to the desk. A cartographic board revealed a maze of scribbles, equations, lines and planes. Geometric devices of unfathomable variety set alongside some Tilly lamps. These quaint lamps were positioned around some small mirrors not unlike those described in the *Book of Optics*. Under the flickering light of the candle the table looked a little like some awful dwarfish discothèque. This appearance was not unaided by an exquisite pocket chess set whose pieces seemed like so many tiny dancers. The reflections of the chessmen in the distorted mirrors lent a kind of surreal carnival atmosphere to the whole diorama.

I didn't like to fiddle with the antique lamps but I found a few more candles and set them about the place. Then I unearthed a clean glass and poured myself a Glenlivet from a half-full bottle. It was in that relaxed posture, with my boots off and my feet up on the table, that I suddenly saw the letter. I confess I took my feet off the table quick enough.

You see, I recognised the handwriting from my studies. It was that of Leibniz, the German philosopher; the chap who amongst many things, invented calculus. And it was either an extremely good fake or, quite unbelievably, an original. I rose to my feet in astonishment.

What with the flickering lights, the fatigue and the silence it would have been quite easy to assume that I was hallucinating, but you know me, I'm not the type. Still, even I had doubts. Problem was I couldn't even touch the thing because I had no gloves. I could only look at the two pages open before me.

Leibniz's Last Puzzle

They were written in old French and *Fraktur* that pedantic German script, neither of which is much of a speciality of mine but there were all sorts of interpolations and comments in Latin, which is a nap, if I say so myself.

I had studied Leibniz at University, of course, and as chance would have it, was something of an expert. The thing that had so impressed me? The title on the letterhead: '*Episcopus*'. I didn't recognise that title and I knew them all – curse of a photographic memory. I was staring at an unknown Leibniz, priceless not only in monetary terms but also in its possible enlargement of our understanding of history and philosophy and a lot more besides.

Carefully laid alongside the open page, a small notepad had the word 'bishop' written in various styles and languages and a little picture of the chessman clearly drawn from the set. Beside that there was a scrawl of translations. The more I looked at the open page, the more I thought the writing was genuine. And it wasn't *a* letter. It was a series of letters and presumably all in the same revered hand.

At that point a voice said "Yes, it's the real thing," and there was Norton behind me, clad in dungarees and heavy boots, his boyish face somewhat careworn. Nevertheless, he was smiling with genuine pleasure and he held out his hand.

"Leibniz?"

"Yes the great man himself and a reason we invited you to the party"

"I can't see why, Norton. Selling this would probably ensure you and your friend a wealthy retirement. That is, if it is yours to sell."

"Doubting Thomas." Norton filled a glass with the malt and took a sip. "It's ours alright. I found it, of all places, in a Burgdorf flea market."

"Lucky you. Don't suppose your old colleagues at Leibniz Universität know much about it?"

"Hardly. They will. But only when we're ready. In fact, as you have doubtless surmised, no one knows much about these

Leibniz's Last Puzzle

notes except you, me and Lubecker."

"Notes? I thought letters."

"It's a mixed bag actually. Some correspondence, notes, other bits and pieces. In fact, that invaluable piece of parchment is the tip of a rather large iceberg."

"Interesting. And it's just us three. Much as I value our friendship, Norton, I can't imagine a reason why you would let me in on one of the finds of the century."

"Because," said Norton – and here he looked distinctly weary, "without you we can't crack it."

No amount of badgering would make Norton come out with any more. He insisted that telling would do no good. He would simply show me in the morning. We finished off the whisky. Norton advised me there was room on the couch until they could fix something up.

After Norton retired, I stayed up for a good hour. At one point, I heard something; could have been a scream but I suspect it was a peacock or a dog. I opened the front door and had a look about. The air was chill. There was nothing but bleak hills, silence and the awe-filled sense of centuries unfolding like so many seconds. And then faintly, on the periphery of my senses I thought I heard a cathedral bell. Which was quite impossible, of course.

Lubecker never appeared. Presumably, he was up working in the hills.

Lubecker was still absent at five the next morning when I scrambled into my all weather gear. Norton had made Earl Grey tea with a dash of lemon and there was Alpen cheese and some of that hard German bread that lasts forever. I mentioned the scream, which Norton dismissed immediately as the peacocks who still inhabited the environs of a derelict mansion in the next valley. The cathedral bell made him stop. He looked up at me with those intense pale-blue eyes. "Sound carries here," he said finally, and gave a strange smile.

While he was off getting ready, I had another look at the table. I found some gloves and was able to handle the Leibniz notes. It is difficult to express the feelings that accompany this kind of exercise. Hernando Cortez might be able to tell you as he looked across vistas of unknown continents or perhaps that virgin boy unhooking a bra for the first time. There was no time, however, for me to indulge in bibliophilic fantasy. Norton was in the doorway with a walking stick and a rucksack.

"You can pore over that at your leisure, Mulholland. But we best take a bit of breakfast to Carsten."

Strange to hear his first name. Academia was gossiping like mad about the famed Herr Lubecker. I wondered what he was like.

We walked up the low valley in the morning mist; the sun just peeking over the hills behind a bank of clouds. It began to rain lightly almost as soon as we left and I was glad of the foresight to bring my wet weather gear. It took us just under an hour to walk up the hill; the last section a bit of a scramble that revealed a slight plateau before a steep crag and a deep cleft between two promontories. It was an unusual sight. Below us a deep wooded gully, less than a mile in dimension and this narrow rift bridging a tree-filled gap of perhaps seventy or eighty yards. Massive trees edged the ridge on either side and lent the secluded valley a certain wildness unusual in the Wolds. I would have called it beautiful but something intangible held me from saying that. Norton nodded. "You felt it," he said ominously.

We climbed down a rather steep slope, the last part a drop of some twenty feet, but easily negotiable. Then we walked a little further, hugging the cliff face, and here a low shelf appeared. It was very flat but felt as unnatural and misplaced as that racetrack at Mount Olympia. Though shrouded by trees and bushes, it was clearly manmade. I said as much to Norton.

"Yes," he said. "Another reason I wanted you in. You're sharp, Mulholland. Now what do you make of this?"

I have to stop here and say that much of what is termed 'The Occult' is a species of nonsense better left to melodrama and the funfair. Occult research is a highly practical affair to most of its credible aficionados. You won't often get an occultist saying 'I felt something strange' or the like. It's an experimental 'science' you see. However, on this occasion – as I looked at what appeared to be the ruins of a dry stone dyke or possibly an old sheep pen from the late eighteenth century – 'strange' is about the only epithet that came to mind. There was no apparent reason why this crumbling jigsaw of moss-covered stone should promote such a reaction, but it did. I looked at it all again.

Behind a couple of birches, I could see a section that had been recently dug. It helped establish context. The pattern of falling stones suggested a high wall where we were standing, with its exact counterpart some fifteen yards away facing us and then another longish wall that ran parallel to the low cliff; in all making the shape of block print C.

I bent down for a more careful examination. Norton stood gazing over my shoulder in expectation. I picked up one of the stones. It was badly eroded but I could make something of it. "Baphomet," I said. "It's only the legs and the tip of a wing but I would stake money on this being a representation of that energetic old spirit."

"Your money would be safe," said Norton smiling. "The other figures and representations are emblazoned on this scattered stone."

I surveyed the tracing of stones through the bushes with a critical eye. "I would say you had half a Masonic temple here, young Norton."

"You would be right."

"But where's the other half?"

I mentioned the strange feeling that had swept over me on first looking at the stones. Even as Norton replied, the feeling intensified to a kind of dread.

"Over there," said Norton quietly. He pointed to the far side of the deep ravine. I was already looking across the gulf having anticipated his reply.

I sat down, drew out a Havana, cut and lit it. I placed my chin in my hand.

"You don't mess about when you discover things, Norton," I said after a space.

"To be fair," he replied, "it all emerged from the notes. My old French is tolerable, but Carst... Lubecker's is rather good."

"Norton. I can understand your finding this place, but you do realise exactly what we are facing here?"

"Quite. They either built the temple in two parts so that central gulf would be some kind of symbolic catalyst, perhaps a spiritual receiver. Or some cataclysmic event tore the ravine from the earth and split the temple down the middle."

"And?"

"I'm afraid it's the latter, Mulholland: Some cataclysmic event – and Lubecker is over the other side of that ravine trying to determine exactly what."

It may sound extraordinary but here was I sitting on the finds of the century, the like of which would keep a chap in an obsessive trance for a lifetime, and yet all I wanted to do was meet Norton's *parfait*, Lubecker. There were mysteries and puzzles jostling for attention and I understood that, perhaps because of his relationship with the man, Norton felt that the full exposé would only merit dénouement in his presence. It was with a pang of regret that I left the ruined temple. But it had kept for hundreds of years. Hopefully, it could wait a little longer.

There was no easy way across the ravine. The bottom was a soup of ancient bramble under which nettles, frogs, toads and bones – of what I hoped were sheep – were all scattered amidst the rotten mould of leaves. It was incredibly dark. The pitch of the ravine cut out the light in an almost unnatural fashion. Botanically speaking, there should be no brambles in such a place but I supposed that a force that could rip up hills could do what it liked with ecology. Under the auspices of ravaged temples a bit of gloom and absurdity might be anticipated and

Leibniz's Last Puzzle

at least the rain had ceased.

Norton and Lubecker had cut a path through the brambles. At times the makeshift path went under vast bowers of them and I imagined the effort it must have taken to do this simple piece of labour. The route up was fairly tough but it was helped by some rather large blocks of masonry from you know where. As we reached the opposing ledge, Norton cautioned me to silence.

"Lubecker will be working and we must be careful how we approach."

The site was almost a mirror of that left behind. But to the west, there was a large tent that I nearly missed, camouflaged, as it was, with bushes. The tent, just tucked under a slight overhang, was illuminated by an inner light and one could vaguely discern the shadows of two men, one seated, one standing. I raised my eyebrows. Norton advanced. The world seemed like a tightrope walker about to tumble. For some reason I went before Norton and under the tent awnings pulled back the flap to reveal a sight that I will never forget.

Lubecker was sat on a camp-stool, his face a picture of studied concentration, so intent, that I could only term it a meditative trance. All around him were Tilly lamps revealing a stack of papers on a desk to the rear of the tent: A stack so large that leaves of paper had fallen from its heights and were strewn across the tent floor; leaves covered in archaic symbols, cabal, Aramaic, Greek and Latin but most predominately, a virtual cornucopia of mathematical equations. The lamps also emblazoned a large table and fell upon the strangest thing I have ever seen; on the table before Lubecker, the object that I had mistaken for a man.

You might have seen those anatomical drawings in the medical books or perhaps that dreadful body sculpture that was paraded around Europe. Try to imagine that. Add what you see under a very good microscope, an eclipse and lots of moving mayflies trapped in a glass. Laugh if you like. I can get no closer to an explanation of that dreadful thing. It stood, about

Leibniz's Last Puzzle

half the size of a man, surrounded by bits and pieces of itself. Lubecker was holding a part of it in his hand.

For the thing was not complete. It is possible to say what it was *not*, it is possible to say what it *might be* but the one certainty is that it was far from complete. The pieces of it were stuck together like a very unfinished three-dimensional jigsaw. And some of the pieces, though in the correct place, and this the truth, were simply hanging freelance in the air.

Lubecker gave us one glance. He was a hard looking man, dark hair cropped close to the skull, gaunt cheekbones and five days beard. He looked powerful, with a kind of latent ferocity, and perhaps it was just that he was clearly a bit occupied, but he didn't look like a man to argue with. The glance said it all. Norton tiptoed in. Left the breakfast box on an empty chair and then we both left in a silence that lasted all the way back to the cottage.

It was past lunchtime when we returned but neither of us displayed much interest in food. Norton cut some logs and got a fire going. We retired to the 'map' room. Norton cracked open a bottle of Smokehead. I relit my cigar.

"How long has he been at it?"

"Well, it's been months since we discovered Leibniz... one tends to lose track of time."

"I can imagine."

"The puzzle itself—"

"You call it a puzzle? I was thinking in terms of alien lifeforce, thing from the deep, creature of another dimension, devil incarnate"

"Yes, it is a puzzle, Mulholland. It's possibly all those things you suggest and more, but fundamentally, it's a puzzle." Norton took a sip of the Smokehead and placed the glass carefully on the table. "Lubecker, as you are aware, is perhaps the foremost mathematician of his time. There are a few others but... well... Lubecker is just Lubecker. If that thing were Satan and his host of dark angels, Lubecker would still have to solve it... Lubecker and I..." He flushed here. "Well, we're

Leibniz's Last Puzzle

very close—"

"Norton," I said quickly, "that thing could well *be* Satan and his several hosts of dark angels. If Lubecker unlocks the puzzle, we might be talking immortal souls. I presume that you want me to stop him?"

Call me arrogant, as many do, but I really thought that was why Norton had called me out. I was shocked when he said: "Damn it no. You have to help him solve it."

Then I understood. Or at least I think I did. Just say you were a great ladies' man and you were in love with a beautiful girl. You wouldn't be terribly happy if someone said you can't have her but you can take any number of those plainer girls. It's the necessary condition of great lovers, the *need* to obtain *that* lover or live or die in unhappy circumstances. So, it looked like Lubecker, potentially the finest mathematician of his time, didn't simply *want* to solve the puzzle, he *needed* to solve it.

Bit of a dilemma for poor Norton; no slouch himself at adding up and clearly keen on his German colleague. It was all or nothing and in the last analysis, he hadn't been able to contribute as much help to his friend as he wanted.

Norton began to fix up a good student's meal at the fire. Pasta, chopped raw onions and dried tomatoes laced with Parmesan. I offered to help but he asked me to start on the notes. It was no task. Lubecker had prepared a translation of the French and presumably had little problem with his archaic but native German. I kept jumping back between his translations and the papers. Occasionally, Norton would glance over. Once he quietly filled my glass with Glenlivet.

Some say I have an eidetic memory. I'm not sure but I am a quick reader and I remember things where others don't. I skim-read most of the tracts by the time the pasta was boiled. I won't plague you with unnecessary details.

Leibniz was a polymath – he did everything, from the design of a more efficient wheelbarrow to the invention of differential calculus. But Academia often neglects mention of Leibniz's

Leibniz's Last Puzzle

first job as an alchemist. The occult remained, for him, a perpetual fascination. These letters put the seal on all that. The first batch was to his cabalistic friend, Van Helmont and they more or less confirmed what we all knew: Leibniz was steeped in occult learning. The rest of the letters were to an unnamed group. The language was highly symbolic, riddled with cipher and allusion. But we knew now that our merry party had seen the symbolism come to fruition on that spirit blasted gully. Leibniz had designed the temple to specifications for some English breakaway lodge, probably the owners of the ruined mansion in the next valley. No doubt, some fragments of their bodies were strewn amidst the nettles over the gully and what little was left of their souls inhabited the peacocks in the grounds.

The remaining stuff held the most fascination. It was in essence, a treatise on puzzles. Everything from the Egyptian Dogs and Jackals game to backgammon. But it was more than that. It was written with an unusual twist of humour, much in the style of Aleister Crowley, the Great Beast. One couldn't help feeling that Leibniz was laughing somewhere out of earshot.

Norton placed the food on my lap. We both ate mechanically in silence.

Finally, Norton said, "The title '*Episcopus*'. Interesting?"

"Very. Nothing in the text refers to it."

"Did you cope with the maths?"

I laughed. "Not a bit."

"It differs slightly from what is generally known of the man. There are some tangential steps in infinitesimal calculus. Quite brilliant. We would regard them as dead ends now I suppose."

"Perhaps not." I raised my eyebrows.

"You have something?"

"I can't read this damned French properly. Look at the second word of each line in the first chapter though. The choice of the words seems intuitively wrong to me."

Norton threw his plate to the floor. For a few seconds he

Leibniz's Last Puzzle

poured over the words. Then he began writing in French. "You're right," he said finally. "It's a diastic. In the first sentence, the first letter makes the first letter of the first word, the second, the second letter and so…" He scribbled away for a bit. I could see him think rapidly in two languages.

Then in a fit of disgust, he threw the paper into the fire. "Damn," he said. "It would have been too easy just to tell us."

I waited for him to calm. He took another shot of whisky and slowly began to write again. Then he handed me the paper.

'One English, one French; each the same, each derived from the same Latin mother, yet not one part in common.'

"Well, that's simple enough, Norton" I said. "Bishop. In French, '*évêque*', both derived from the same Latin root."

"Yes, but where does it leave us?" Norton rose to his feet. "It's been months, Mulholland: Months of sudden inspirations and blind alleys. Transcribing and transliterating notes; research in Leipzig, Hannover. The temple took us an age before we even stumbled on it. The dig itself was endless. I can't tell you how long it took to find the chamber on the second shelf. When we got down there was a tiny room. It seemed… unnaturally preserved. The remains of a man sat in a chair slumped over a small table; his skull rested among the scattered pieces of this damned puzzle: The puzzle that he died trying to solve. And Carsten… He's up there and I can't stop him."

Norton was at breaking point. He carried on in a voice bordering the hysteric. "Mathematics, Mulholland. The beautiful science. The elegance of numbers and their relationships. Every paradise can become an asylum. I'm losing—"

"Sit down, Norton. You're going to snap unless you find some inner reserve. Already you're talking nonsense." I poured us both a glass of Glenlivet, thought again and made it a double. "There is only one issue here. Forget everything else. Forget the temple, the letters, the research. There is only the puzzle. You could make your fortune on what you already have – you'd make more than a footprint in the sands of time with half of this stuff – but your friend Lubecker has fallen for the oldest trap in the book. He's been offered something he doesn't have and now he believes he needs it. The puzzle mustn't be solved. It's got to be destroyed."

Norton got out of his chair quick enough. He looked half-mad. I suspect he was.

"Destroy it and you destroy him." He clenched his fists and fell back into the chair.

After a moment, Norton rose to his feet. From a small cupboard, he took a large box, scarred and pitted with age. It had all the appearance of an Arabian container for chessmen, something of the Alhambra about its design. You could see immediately that it belonged to the puzzle.

"We could go back this evening," I said.

"Mulholland, it just won't work. Carsten has a mind like a computer – a beautifully constructed machine; the balance of its parts is infinitely delicate. If anyone can solve the puzzle, it's him. He's been at it five days and night…"

"I didn't see much, Norton but that figure was very far from complete. I'm very intuitive and my intuitions tell me he's going to fail."

"Then help him for God's sake, Mulholland."

Well, not much a man can do really. Appeals to friendship, loyalty, the old school – not many to common sense. I have always been a sucker for the underdog and the tryer.

"Give me a look at those papers, Norton," I said. "Somewhere in this encyclopaedic cribbing, you must have found something. I want to see what you have on the puzzle itself. What about the box, for example. Is there a relationship between the box and the pieces? Just how many pieces are there?"

"Leibniz states there are forty-seven pieces." He handed me the box. "We found forty-eight. Presumably he miscounted."

I looked keenly at Norton. "Miscounted? I would think adding would be a bagatelle for someone who could juggle

Leibniz's Last Puzzle

quadratic equations."

"You never know," said Norton, "sometimes the mundane details are lost on genius."

"Forty-seven. That's a cabalistic number of significance. There might be something in that. Perhaps even deliberate misdirection. Let me see the rest."

I paced around the room a bit to get the blood moving. "There's something intriguing about the two halves of that temple. Something telling. No, no, it's all in the title of that treatise. Damn you, Norton it's called '*Episcopos*' – 'Bishop' but it's all about bloody mirrors. Why?" I stopped pacing. Norton stared at me with his pale blue eyes. "A genius might slip up over a number or two but this is Leibniz we are talking about. He wouldn't have mistitled a whole treatise on mirrors, nor would he have interpolated a secret diastic into the text unless…" I paused and then it hit me. Norton saw. He knew. He leapt to his feet but couldn't bring himself to speak. I drew myself up.

You'll think this ridiculous, especially when the story plays out, but I *did* know. Perhaps my dealings with the occult had given me more of an insight, I was certainly no mathematician. I couldn't have solved the puzzle myself if you'd given me a hundred years but now I knew how it *could* be solved.

"Right," I said. "I have it."

"Thank God," said Norton. "But what have you?"

"Not sure it's God we should be thanking, young Norton but one thing is certain. I am divulging nothing until you bring Lubecker down here. He needs a decent meal, a bit of a rest and we'll approach the thing together."

Norton argued. I think he wanted it all over with at once and I'm pretty sure he didn't want to disturb Lubecker through fear, or perhaps because he thought he wouldn't come. But I was adamant. I can be a rock when I choose and on this occasion, I was adamantine. I wouldn't even accompany Norton. Deep down, I wanted to give him a bit of companionship out in the darkness; the whole area around that temple stank of darkness, but I thought it better he brave out his friend alone. Eventually, Norton accepted it and I was left to stare at the fire.

About eleven o'clock I walked out the front door. Far away the peacocks were crying in the night and as though it were all prearranged. I heard the bell again. This time I knew it was no cathedral. It was a temple bell, a summons of some kind, and I guessed now for whom the bell tolled.

I was lighting up a second cigar when the footsteps sounded over the hills and I saw two shadows approach. I congratulated myself that I had managed to contrive a success when Lubecker came towards me in an aggressive pose.

"You better be correct, Mr Mulholland." His accent was mild but his voice brimmed with restrained violence. "I was on the threshold of the solution and…"

"Rubbish," I said firmly. "You were going around in circles."

He paused as though weighing up whether thrashing the life out of me would be useful. He decided not. "*Es tut mir lied.* I have…"

"No need to explain. Come in. Put your feet up beside the fire."

We huddled around the fire. I had already boiled up a kettle and some hot cocoa was just what the doctor ordered. Norton took an age to persuade Lubecker to sit down. The German looked like a zombie. The strain was clearly kicking in. He refused any food with a look of disgust. Eventually Norton got him in the easy chair and stood behind him, massaging his neck and shoulders. I thought I better put him out of his misery.

"It's quite simple really, Herr Lubecker. What you have is some infinitesimal calculus on your hands. I couldn't solve it if you gave me a thousand years but I believe you can. I don't do maths, only intuition." He nodded. "All that I insist upon is that you have a nights rest."

"No!" he said. "You must understand—"

Leibniz's Last Puzzle

"Oh, I'll tell you the answer or at least the road to the answer, but give me your word you will sleep on it tonight. You know it makes sense." He nodded again reluctantly.

I threw a log on the fire. The flames burgeoned and sent shadows flicking across Lubecker's drawn face.

"It's all in that simple diastic," I said after a space. "I assume Norton pointed it out on the road back. *'One English, one French; each the same, each derived from the same Latin mother, yet not one part in common.'*

"The word of course is bishop, *'Bischof* auf Deutsc*,* I believe, but the treatise to which it refers is on mirrors and nowhere is this bishop mentioned. Why?

"It's all about mirrors, my dear Lubecker. By placing a convex and concave mirror on either side of the object, you will have two different illuminations from the same root yet neither will be connected to each other. You will then be able to see the puzzle in itself and as an object of both repeated reflection and reflections in two mirrors. Your abundance of mathematical knowledge will take over and utilising this you will create the 'bishop' – the esoteric figure or, as it is termed in some cases, the first, the leader or foreman. The bishop, of course, is that damnable figure."

Lubecker leapt to his feet. I could see him visualising reversed infinitesimal equations in his head; that wonderful brain making a host of neural connections that had been obscured because he had attempted, in effect, to solve the puzzle 'upside-down'. It was an epiphanous moment.

I knew better than to say anything. He was straight over to the map room, playing with the mirrors and drawing circles and equations everywhere.

I turned to Norton who looked less enthusiastic. I said softly, "In occult terms, Norton, there are far too many 'coincidences' here. There are too many echoes of this triad. You two, the *parfait*, and me the catalyst, the chasm that divides two sides of a temple, the two mirrors making their ethereal contact with the thing in between. This puzzle is a triatic equation and its solution has me intensely worried. What is this 'bishop'?"

Norton had no answer. He couldn't take his eyes off the older man whose hands were now flickering over the table.

Much later, in the deep of night, I heard the door open. Lubecker had given his word but under the dreadful compunction of those infinitesimal equations, had broken it within three hours.

I heard his footsteps retreat into the night and again I heard that phantom bell.

*

Mulholland put his whisky down. The Oxford bar had emptied and we were alone with our thoughts. "Can you use it?" he said.

I laughed. "Perhaps," I replied, "but it's not quite finished is it?"

Mulholland smiled quietly. "Come," he said. "We might as well walk back together."

A fog had settled. The New Town streets were deserted and silent. "I'll tell you what we'll do," said Mulholland. "Stop at mine tonight. You may as well kip on the couch. That way, I can show you the puzzle."

It was at this point that I thought Mulholland must be joking. There's a kind of gulf between hearing a bizarre and impossible tale of terror and then having the severed head or phantom coach put in front of you. I had believed Mulholland when he told the tale but now I didn't quite believe him anymore.

We paced up the streets in silence and then reached his Georgian house on St. _____ Square. He threw open the door, advanced through the darkened hallway to a small anteroom surrounded with bookshelves whose regiments of leather tomes glistened by the light of a fading wood fire. There he produced some Glenlivet and then with an almost flippant disregard for theatrics, placed an unusual box on the table before us.

Leibniz's Last Puzzle

"That's it," he said. "Leibniz's last puzzle. Quite something."

I can't adequately describe that box except to say it was about the size of a brief case and apparently made of shimmering wood. Suffice it to say I am reduced to Mulholland's description of the ruined temple. It felt strange, *very* strange. I took a long sip of whisky. Mulholland lit a cigarillo. Embers glowed in the dying fire.

"Norton got me up fairly briskly in the morning," he said finally. "We'd both had a bad night as one hell of a storm kicked up in the early hours. When we got to the tent we found Lubecker – not a mark of violence on him but he was dead and slumped over the table with the pieces of that puzzle scattered everywhere. I had a terrible job getting the body back to the cottage. It was absolutely clear that we couldn't leave it there and naturally, Norton was so distraught he could hardly function. Anyway, the deed was finally done. We had to walk to the village – no mobile phones or email in those days – we eventually raised the police and they came to the cottage. There was a fair amount of suspicion kicking around, village police, outsiders and all that. Although they never thought to search the hills – thank God – they asked a lot of questions and poked around a fair bit. So much so that I was fairly certain that we were going to be up for murder. Not a pleasant prospect.

"In the police cells – and yes it did go as far as that – Norton and I were kept apart. We waited a day or was it two? I could hear Norton weeping most of the time but couldn't do much about it. And then Norton was standing there with a police officer who looked rather strangely at me. I can recall the conversation perfectly although at the time I misheard the officer's reply when I asked if they'd established a cause of death.

"You see, I thought he said 'heart attack', which would have been feasible. But Norton corrected me later."

"Not a heart attack," he said sombrely. "They opened

Lubecker up and his heart was simply missing; as though it had never been there."

"Naturally, the police hushed the whole thing up. That kind of thing can get you in an asylum and perhaps all sorts of records went to secret government offices and lots of things were changed, but I'm not sure they even did that. It was only later that I realised something quite significant.

"You see Lubecker's heart had disappeared. I can't emphasise that enough: *Disappeared*, literally transported from his body. I got to thinking not of how that could happen but where it could have gone." Mulholland stubbed out his cigarillo. "I think you have guessed have you not? That unknown man whose skeleton still rests in the little chamber beneath the temple? He hadn't died trying to solve the puzzle. He died *solving* it. If you look at the pieces, you'll find there are not forty-seven now or, indeed, forty-eight but *forty-nine*." Mulholland smiled. "But then I really wouldn't look at the puzzle."

It was hours later after a succession of double malts, that Mulholland got to his feet. He intimated that his man would serve a late breakfast and bid me good night. I sat for a while after he had gone to bed. I looked to the couch with its comfortable blanket and then back to the puzzle box that Mulholland had inadvertently left on the table; Leibniz's last puzzle.

I confess it held something of a magnetic attraction.

HANGMAN WANTED: APPLY IN WRITING

Paul Finch

The voice on the line was deep, resonant and extremely well-spoken; 'BBC English', if Gargan had ever heard it.

"Mr Gargan?" it said.

"Yeah," Gargan replied, puzzled. Only a few people had *this* number.

"Mr Joel Gargan?"

"Who is this?"

"You replied to my advert."

"Oh... yeah." Gargan sat upright on the shabby bed.

"Are you serious?" the voice asked.

Gargan swung his legs to the floor. He was fascinated to know more, even if he didn't necessarily intend to commit himself. "What does it involve exactly?"

"You must have a reasonably good idea from the way the ad was worded?"

"Well..."

"I've made it quite clear what kind of service I'm requesting." The voice remained polite, even deferential in tone, but there was a firmness just below its surface. "So... are you serious?"

Gargan stuck the mobile under his unshaved jaw as he stubbed out his cigarette. "Yeah... I'm serious."

There was a pause, then: "*Who* are you?"

"I gave you my name and telephone number in the application."

"Let me rephrase it. *What* are you?"

Gargan stood up. He idled across the small, cheap room. Beyond its dusty window, grey rain fell on the alleys and tenements of east London. "I'm unemployed. Not to mention broke."

"Jobs aren't so hard to find these days, Mr Gargan. Is there something you're not telling me?"

Hangman Wanted: Apply in Writing

Now it was Gargan's turn to hesitate. This was always the part where the wheel came off. "I... I have a criminal record."

On this occasion however, just for once, the interviewer seemed unperturbed. "I anticipated that. Are you in trouble with the law at this moment?"

Gargan gazed down on the litter-strewn backstreets. Why else would he be ensconced in a low-rent rat-hole like this? "Yes... I am."

Again there was silence. This one lingered.

"I take it that means I haven't got the job?" Gargan finally said.

"On the contrary. It makes you eminently suitable. However, I recommend that you take a couple of days to think this thing through first."

Gargan was jolted. Did this mean he was in with a chance after all? A chance for what, though? And how much would it pay? Peanuts was no good, not to a man in his position.

"There *is* money involved?" he blurted out.

"Of course. I'm looking to employ you, not ask you a favour."

"How much money?"

"Just take a couple of days to think about it, Mr Gargan. Then I'll call you back. Oh... by the way," and now the tone altered, a hint of steel seeping into it, "just in case you're actually an inquisitive policeman, let me advise you that I'm talking to you on my mobile and that I'm currently out and about in my car, so any attempt to trace me by cell-site triangulation is doomed to fail. Likewise, the PO box you originally wrote to is now defunct. Putting someone on it would be a waste of time."

And the line went dead.

Gargan wasn't sure what to think. He hadn't expected any response to his letter at all, let alone a response *this* quickly – three days later. He'd only answered the ad because he was at such a loose end. Even now, he wasn't sure if this would come to anything – in fact he suspected that it wouldn't – but it certainly seemed fortuitous that he'd been scanning those classified columns when he had. Even among the personal escort services and housewife home-videos, it had jumped out and hit him in the face. And in truth, how could it not have done?

*

They finally met at the junction of Grosvenor Road and Vauxhall Bridge Road on the north bank of the Thames, on another cold and drizzly March afternoon.

Gargan was standing with a copy of the *Daily Sport* visible in the left-hand pocket of his faded Wrangler jacket. In addition to the jacket, he wore a plain white T-shirt, ragged jeans and a pair of once white but now coffee-coloured plimsolls.

"You're quite what I was expecting, Mr Gargan," came a voice from behind.

Gargan spun around, and saw a lean man of average height, perhaps sixty years old, approaching along the pavement. The stranger had collar-length, sandy hair, now running to grey, and wore white slacks, a beige sports jacket, and under that a neat white shirt buttoned to the throat. His face was pale and pudgy, but surprisingly genial.

"And what would that be?" Gargan wondered. "A hooligan?"

He was tall – almost six-three – and strongly built, with a shock of unruly black hair and a thin hatchet-face. He'd always looked like a roughneck, even as a youngster.

The sandy-haired chap smiled and shook his head. "Someone who could use a bob or two."

And that was certainly true.

Gargan held out a hand. "You're Mister...?"

"You can call me Styles," the man said. "That isn't my name, but you can call me that. Now, if you'll excuse me?" At which point he began to pat Gargan down, evidently searching for a wire.

"Still think I'm a copper?" Gargan asked.

"There's every possibility. Not that it really matters, even if you are."

"Why would that be?"

The man straightened up again. He seemed satisfied. "Despite the wording of my advert, I'm not actually committing a crime here. Let's walk."

They headed south across Vauxhall Bridge.

"So... you *don't* want a hangman?" Gargan said.

"Oh no, I *do* want a hangman. In short, Mr Gargan, I want you to hang *me*."

Gargan wasn't as stunned as he might normally have been; he'd been expecting something bizarre. "You're one of those fetishists..."

"No. Not that. I want you to hang me until I'm dead."

Gargan halted, looked round at him. "You're kidding, yeah?"

"Not at all. In fact, that's why I'm not actually committing a crime. I'm not trying to recruit someone to commit murder. I'm looking to find someone to assist my suicide."

"That isn't a crime?"

"Not the sort of crime I could be sent to prison for. In any case, jailing me would be a relatively fruitless exercise. I'll be slipping off this mortal coil in about six months as it is."

"Come again?"

Styles strode on. Gargan followed.

"I'm ill, Mr Gargan. I have cancer, and it's going to kill me."

"Pardon my saying it, but you don't seem very upset."

"I'm not. There's nothing left for me here. My wife died three years ago, of the same disease. I yearn only to be with her in the Hereafter."

Gargan made no comment.

"You find that amusing... the notion of a heavenly Hereafter?"

Gargan was non-committal, but, as far as he was concerned, the many scars he still bore from his traumatic childhood – both physical and mental – didn't bode well for the belief that a force of celestial good existed in the world.

"Personally, I *know* there's a Hereafter," Styles said. "I was born and raised a Roman Catholic. And I've remained one – a devout one, I should add – all my life. I have absolute faith that death is not the end, just the next stage."

"If you're such a good Catholic, surely you're worried that if you take your own life, the next stage – as you put it – might not be so pleasant."

Styles smiled. "That's why I intend to employ you. I can't just kill myself. According to the conservative tenets of my religion, to do that would consign me to hell. But I believe in a loving God rather than a vengeful one, and I'm quite certain that most suicides are judged fairly and probably given a reprieve because they committed their mortal sin while of unsound mind. When I finally meet my maker, I expect the same treatment…"

There couldn't be any doubt about that, Gargan thought – the 'unsound mind' part.

"I do feel, however," Styles added, "that it will help my cause a little if someone else actually does the deed."

They'd now crossed the river and arrived at Vauxhall tube station. They descended to the platforms.

"Well, that's all nice and dandy from your point of view," Gargan said, "but, whatever you *want* to call it, it's still going to make me a killer."

"Technically, it will make you an accomplice to suicide, which is, I admit, an imprisonable offence. However, for taking this risk, you'll be very substantially rewarded."

"How much are we talking?"

"Three million pounds."

They'd now emerged onto the south-bound platform of the Victoria Line, and passengers were hurrying back and forth. Even so, Gargan froze mid-stride. He gazed at Styles.

Styles smiled again. "Don't look too surprised, Mr Gargan. I'm a well-off fellow. I made my fortune in property during the boom years of the nineteen-eighties. But unfortunately I'm not going to live to enjoy it." Fleetingly, and for the first time, a wistful look came into his eyes. "I've now sold my company and realised all my assets. I've had to settle a few accounts of course, remunerate other people who've served me in the past, so I'm not quite as wealthy as I was. But everything I have left exists in the form of hard cash – three million pounds' worth."

"You don't have children, any dependents?"

"My wife and I were not blessed."

Gargan's head was spinning. It seemed unlikely, in fact he didn't believe it. But just thinking about so much money made the Earth move. "So how do I get the cash once you've been... once it's done?"

"That's taken care of. All I need to know at present is that you're still interested?"

"For three million quid, yes... absolutely."

Okay, he might not believe it, but what had he to lose?

"Good," Styles said. A train came in behind him. "So, are you free next Wednesday?"

"I'm free any time."

"Excellent. Meet me at this place." Styles handed over a slip of paper. "At two o'clock in the afternoon precisely."

Gargan glanced at the paper. An address was scribbled on it.

The train's pneumatic door hissed open. Styles turned and climbed aboard.

"Wait," Gargan shouted. "I mean... do I need to bring anything with me?"

Styles stood in the doorway, considering. "A pair of gloves, I suppose, which you'd be advised to wear from the moment you set out. But that's all."

"Wait... look, how's it to be done?"

"Mr Gargan... you'll have only one task to perform, and it will be very simple indeed."

"It seems too simple." Suddenly Gargan's innate animal-cunning came to the fore. "I mean... three million, for doing next to nothing?"

"That all depends on your moral standpoint. No matter how simple I make the procedure for you, you *will* be taking a human life. Not everyone finds that easy. *You* may not when the time comes."

That made sense, of a sort.

"You trust me though?" Gargan asked. "I mean, you trust me to do this... and you don't even know me?"

"Stand clear of the doors please!" a guard bellowed down the platform.

"At present Mr Gargan, all I'm trusting you to do is turn up at a certain place at a certain time. From that point on, until the very final second, you'll be fully in my control. Believe me, I didn't become a multi-millionaire by leaving things to chance."

At which point the door slid closed.

Gargan was left alone on the platform, still in a daze.

There had to be a catch somewhere. The guy himself – how could he be so cool? He was going to die. But then Gargan remembered relatives of his who'd also been diagnosed with terminal cancer, and how they too had eventually become resigned to the idea, mainly because they'd had no alternative.

Either way, an earner was an earner and, curious circumstances or not, Gargan had never been one to pass that sort of thing up.

*

Gargan, gloved as per his instructions, was standing in the entrance to a boarded-up shop directly across Tottenham Court Road from Goodge Street tube station, when he first heard the phone start to ring. He glanced around irritably, but saw no one in his immediately proximity. He checked his watch. It was three minutes past two. Shouldn't that weirdo have made contact by now? And then he thought about the phone, still ringing shrilly behind him.

Hangman Wanted: Apply in Writing

He turned, and amid a heap of newspapers stuffed into an old, piss-stained sleeping-bag – an object he'd first taken for a tramp – he saw someone's mobile. It was silver, looked brand-new; the tiny blue light on it flashed indignantly as it rang.

He snatched it up and answered: "This is Gargan."

"I know who it is," came the familiar voice. "Now listen. From here on, you do everything I say… to the absolute letter. Or the deal's off. Understood?"

"Yeah. Course."

"I hope I am." Styles sounded distinctly less affable than he had done previously, but then this was the day on which he expected to die. "As I said before, I'm not engaged in a major criminal enterprise here, but I can't afford to have my meticulous plans interfered with by the police. So from now on you will use only *this* mobile phone. Switch your own off, and place it in your jacket pocket. If you make any attempt to take it out again, the deal's off." He paused. "I'll be watching you, Gargan. Not all the time, but you won't know when I am and when I'm not. So, by the same token, if you speak to anyone at all the deal's off."

"Got you," Gargan said.

"Proceed on foot to Euston Station. And be quick. Time isn't on your side."

Gargan switched his own phone off and shoved it out of sight. Keeping the new one close to his chest, he set out at a brisk walk. Quarter of an hour later he was inside Euston's cathedral-like concourse, every part of it crammed as usual with travellers awaiting connections. The hubbub of voices was deafening; however, as soon as he arrived, the new mobile began to ring.

"Go to the automated ticket machine," he was instructed. "I've reserved a ticket for you on the two-thirty to Letchworth. The code for that ticket is A6927BN. Once you've collected it, get on the train and remain on it until I tell you to get off."

Gargan threaded his way through the bustling mob. According to his watch, he only had five minutes before the train departed.

"Remember," the voice said in his ear, "I'm watching you. Once the train is moving, I'll follow. If at any point I suspect that I'm not the only one following – for example if I see a helicopter – the deal is off."

"A helicopter?" Gargan scoffed. "Do me a favour."

But the line was now dead.

A short while afterwards, he was seated on a half-empty, mid-afternoon train as it slowly wove its way north through the London suburbs. Gargan had never been to Letchworth, nor knew anyone who had. To him it was like Luton or Milton Keynes; just another one of those faceless, soulless 'new towns' that had sprung up all over the Home Counties in the last fifty years. It struck him though, that, en route, he was likely to pass numerous commuter stations, all unmanned and, at this time of day, unused. In that respect, any one of them would be ideal for this situation. He was just approaching a fourth one of these, when the phone rang again.

"Get off at this stop, Gargan," he was told. "If anyone else gets off with you, the deal's cancelled."

Gargan did as instructed, and was relieved to see that he was alone.

He stood there as the train pulled out. Several minutes passed. He glanced at the mobile, contemplating a call-back, when a car horn suddenly started to sound on the other side of the building. He made his way through, and from the front saw a large, metallic-green Daimler waiting at the end of the adjacent road. As soon as he spotted the Daimler, the horn ceased to sound.

Gargan hurried over to it. As he reached it, Styles climbed out, now dressed appropriately in a black suit, with a matching black shirt and tie. There was a suitably grim expression on his face.

"Helicopters?" Gargan said. "It could be you're overestimating your importance."

"Maybe," Styles replied, and again he patted his employee

Hangman Wanted: Apply in Writing

down. "But the one thing I never overestimate is the government's willingness to meddle in other people's private affairs." He stood back up, apparently satisfied. "Shall we go?"

They climbed into the car. Its interior was lush in the extreme, smelling of suede and newly-varnished leather. Soon they were gliding along narrow country lanes.

"I don't suppose," Gargan said, "it would be presumptuous of me to ask what it is exactly that you're expecting me to do?"

"Just what I hired you for. To hang me."

"Perhaps this isn't a good time to tell you... but I don't know the first thing about hanging."

"Then allow me to enlighten you." Styles turned the car onto an even narrower lane, hemmed to its verges by dense undergrowth. "Hanging is, far and away, the most humane method of execution practised in modern times. In the electric chair, people are frequently burned alive. In the gas chamber, eyeballs have been known to rupture. Lethal injection can result in chemical entombment, and may take as long as eighteen minutes to kill. Even the guillotine is now believed slower than previously thought; according to new scientific evidence, heads severed even by the quickest, cleanest blow can live – see, hear, think – for as long as twenty seconds afterwards. But hanging isn't like that at all – not drop-hanging, the method perfected by we British some ninety years ago."

He almost seemed to relish the prospect of what lay ahead of him.

"You see, Gargan... when a person is correctly drop-hanged, he precipitates downwards over a scientifically measured distance, which has taken into account his exact weight and height. When he hits the bottom of the rope, his head is jerked sharply upwards with mathematically predetermined force, causing an immediate fracture-dislocation of the spinal cord and instant deep unconsciousness. Though it may take him a short while to actually expire, he'll know nothing about it."

Hangman Wanted: Apply in Writing

Styles glanced sideways. "And that's very important to me. I'm ready to die, Gargan, but I'm not ready to suffer. Not in any shape or form. That's why I've taken so much care about this. There'll be no slow strangulation for me, no agonised choking and kicking. If I was prepared to face all that, I might as well just go through my natural death. And I'm not, believe me."

It was another twenty minutes before they reached their destination, an apparently abandoned farm in the middle of wild, uncultivated woodland. Styles pulled off the road, and parked behind a row of ramshackle outbuildings. Overhead, a mountainous pile of slate-grey cloud was threatening further rain. The encircling trees were filled with opaque shadow.

For the first time Gargan experienced a pang of uncertainty. It had been difficult enough getting his head around this thing, not least because he'd be the one left to pick up the pieces if something went wrong, but three million reasons had finally convinced him otherwise. However, now that he was here, at the place where it was actually going to happen, he felt genuine trepidation.

He climbed from the car and glanced around. The farmbuildings were dilapidated, every door and window boarded. That still didn't mean there was nobody here.

"You've checked this place out properly, yeah?" he said.

"Of course," Styles replied. "There's no one within five square miles."

They approached an old barn, another gaunt, neglected structure, though in this case a shiny new padlock had been fixed on its closed doors. Styles produced a key, removed the padlock, and they went inside. It took a moment in that dusty, unlit interior for Gargan's eyes to attune, but when they did he went cold. In the very centre of the open space before him stood a gallows.

A proper gallows.

A *real* one.

Though by the whiteness and apparent freshness of its

Hangman Wanted: Apply in Writing

timber, it had only recently been constructed.

Gargan approached it, awe-stricken.

It was essentially a platform, raised ten feet from the ground by four well-braced legs, with a flight of wooden steps to one side of it. The trapdoor in its middle was clearly visible, as was a complex unlocking device, which emerged through the top in the form of a single upright lever. Above the platform, a length of rope was suspended from a steel beam. Its noose hung directly over the trapdoor, at roughly knee-height.

"Jesus," Gargan breathed.

"It's perfect in every detail," Styles said. "I weigh twelve and a half stones, in which case I must drop exactly five feet and eleven inches. I *will*... the rope has been minutely measured. The old-fashioned hangman's knot is absent, you'll notice. Instead, the noose has been formed by passing the free end of the rope through a brass eyelet, which must be placed directly below my left ear. When the trapdoor opens, it will take me an estimated third of a second to fall the requisite distance, and when I do, the blow struck against the side of my neck will immediately separate my fourth and fifth cervical vertebrae. I won't feel a thing."

He half-smiled, though it was noticeable that sweat now glinted on his brow. "You see, Gargan. I told you it would be simple. All *you* need to do is pull a lever."

"And you're sure you want to go through with this?"

"I haven't come all this way for nothing."

"Neither have I." Gargan turned to face him. "So before we do anything else, let's talk about the money."

"Yes, the money. It's quite safe. It's currently locked in a secret room, somewhere in London."

"What do you mean a secret room? How do *I* get hold of it?"

"The address of that room is written on a piece of paper, which is wrapped around the key to that room. As I speak, that key is in my left shoe. You may take possession of it when the job is complete."

Gargan wasn't sure about *this* development. He'd expected the money to be here.

"What's to stop me overpowering you right now and taking possession of that key while you're still alive?" he wondered.

"Perhaps *this*." And a revolver appeared in Styles's hand.

Gargan tensed. "You bastard!"

"Just a precaution, Gargan… to make sure you keep your side of the bargain. I'll be training this revolver on you from now on. It will only drop from my hand when my neck breaks."

Gargan gazed down at the gun, at the ugly blot of its muzzle. Eventually he shrugged. It was nothing to him. He fully intended to help Styles kill himself, if that was what the crazy old bird wanted. "Let's do it," he said, moving towards the gallows. "I'd like to get this thing over with."

"Gargan," Styles said from behind.

Gargan glanced back.

Styles had lifted the gun and was pointing it directly at him.

He fired.

Fortunately, he was a less able marksman than he was a property tycoon. The gun – an old Webley – gave a mighty kick in his hand, pegging the bullet far to Gargan's left.

Gargan still threw himself to one side. "You barmy… *what the hell are you doing?*"

Styles shook his head, his expression solemn. "You can't think I'd just let you hang me… not without my resisting."

"What?" Gargan was incredulous.

"Unless I resist, and most strenuously… with deadly force in fact, I may as well be committing suicide. If I don't try and kill you, Gargan… to prevent you killing me, I'm going straight to hell."

And he fired again.

Gargan threw himself the other way. The slug only just missed, ricocheting from the concrete floor with an ear-piercing *whine*. "You bloody lunatic!" he screamed.

But Styles had finished talking.

Hangman Wanted: Apply in Writing

Shot after shot followed, the hired man racing madly back and forth, on each occasion evading death only by centimetres. Fortunately, of course, the Webley could only discharge six times before it needed to be reloaded, and the moment Styles dug into his pocket for fresh ammo, Gargan hurled himself forwards. His fist caught Styles on the point of the chin, sending him reeling backwards and toppling to the floor. As Styles lay stunned, Gargan kicked the revolver away, reached down and snatched him by the collar.

"You really want to hang, you demented bastard? Okay... no problem."

He dragged Styles to his feet, and hauled him brutally across the barn. At the foot of the gallows-stair, Styles dropped to the floor with all his weight, but sheer rage had made Gargan stronger even than normal; for a couple of seconds then he'd tasted death himself, and he hadn't liked it. First, he used his belt to bind his struggling captive's hands behind his back. Then, in a frenzy of sweat and gritted teeth, he lugged the guy up the steps, at the top of which he wrestled him onto the trapdoor, where he looped the noose around his neck, and with a single yank of his hand, tightened it under his ear.

Styles tried to free his hands, but realised it was futile, at which point he immediately ceased to resist. He simply stood there, rigid, blinking. He swallowed hard – then, under his breath, began to pray.

"Pack that in!" Gargan shouted, moving behind him and falling to one knee. "Before we do anything else, we're going to see what other surprises you've got in store for me."

Styles gave no opposition as his left shoe was torn off.

Gargan turned the shoe upside-down, but no key fell out. He fingered the inside of it, to no avail. He forcibly removed the right shoe, but this one too was empty.

Breathing heavily and deeply like some wounded wild animal, Gargan rose to his feet.

"I hardly have a penny in the world," Styles said in a small voice. "Let alone three million pounds. I *did* have money once, but it's all gone… on doctors, private hospitals. Mainly for my wife, you understand. But there's nothing left now."

"You lying, manipulative old…" Gargan's face was fiery-red, bloated with fury.

Styles shrugged. "In all honesty, how *could* I pay you to kill me? I'd be buying my own suicide, which would be as bad as carrying it out myself. In fact, doing it like this, I've not only avoided that, I've gone one better. Since we got here, I've actively resisted you. I've fought you every inch of the way… I've ensured that my soul will be safe."

"You still expect me to kill you?"

"Oh, I *know* you're going to kill me. I've conned you, Gargan. I've raised your pathetic hopes and cruelly dashed them. You surely want to pull that lever now more than ever before."

Gargan bared tight-locked teeth. "You know what, Mr Styles… you're right. I *do* want to kill you, and I *am* going to." He backed off the trapdoor.

Styles watched him, the eyes almost popping from his pallid face.

But Gargan didn't move towards the lever. "Before I do it, though, I'd like to tell you a bit more about myself."

"The longer you dally here, the greater the risk."

"I told you I was in trouble with the law." Gargan tongued the razor-blade to dislodge it from the roof of his mouth, and spat it into his hand "But I didn't tell you why."

*

Evening Standard, March 2009

Fresh rumours are linking the unidentified male body found in Throcking Wood last weekend with bankrupt property tycoon Simon Styles-Bartlett, who has been missing from his home address for the last six days.

Speculation is mounting that the body, which detectives say

Hangman Wanted: Apply in Writing

had been subjected to a savage and extremely prolonged attack, may be the latest victim of the so-called 'Wolverine', the unknown assailant now believed to have tortured and sexually murdered five gay men in the Greater London area.

A police spokesman refused to comment.

IN THE GARDEN

Rosalie Parker

It really is a lovely day.

I'm not used to sitting in the garden, basking in the pleasant weather and enjoying the fruits of my labour. I spend most of my time here weeding and pruning, so I'm grateful for the opportunity to laze around for a change, watching the flower heads bob gently in the soft breeze, listening to the drowsy hum of the bees as they gorge on the comfrey blossoms.

You'll have noticed that where we're sitting, beneath the high wall, is concealed from view. None of the surrounding houses overlook us. We can lounge in perfect peace while we chat – and I'm in a chatty mood today. An afternoon of rest after all my work. Yesterday's showers mean that even the vegetable plot doesn't need watering.

It never ceases to amaze me how the garden, cold and as good as dead just a few months ago, has burgeoned into lush green life. Is it only two years since I hacked back the old lilac tree behind you there – and look at it now! Tall enough to peep over the wall, its vigour restored by the judicious elimination of unproductive wood.

You're not a gardener, are you? So perhaps you don't know that once a garden is established, much of good gardening is about removal rather than planting, honing what you have to produce a pleasing effect, sacrificing the particular for the good of the whole. Gardening is a creative pastime, but the result is always a work in progress; unlike a painting or a piece of music a garden is never fixed in time.

I couldn't see the attraction when I was a child. My mother would sometimes ask me to help weed our extensive vegetable beds, and it seemed a thankless task to me. I didn't understand or appreciate the work that went into it, just the end result, which I viewed as entirely natural and given. Perhaps that's how you see it now? As an adult I have learned to appreciate

In the Garden

the satisfaction of managing nature, but as a child the garden was simply my world, the arena of my imagination, the setting for my elaborate games.

In those games I would order existence to suit myself. One day I'd lead expeditions, exploring the rainforest in search of wildlife to sell to zoos, the next, the tamer of a wild bronco stallion, galloping on my hobby horse round and round the corral until the animal became tired and more responsive to my commands. My favourite game involved my brother as my trusted chimpanzee servant as I ruled, queen-like, over a large household. I expect many children have played similar games in gardens over the centuries, rehearsing unrealistic expectations of their adult lives. The green shoots of our imagination are soon blighted by the late frosts of adolescence.

Before we moved here I'd never owned a garden larger than a postage stamp, and at first I was daunted by it. I tinkered around the edges, snipping a twig here, pulling a weed there. But gradually I've become more confident, until now, I feel, I have ordered it how I want it, within the limits of the time available and the amount of money I've had to spend. I think you'll agree that it pleases the eye – is well designed, both ornamental and practical. The oriental poppies are over now, and I have tidied them away, but they are one of my additions, along with the ferns and hostas in the shade of the southern wall. I removed the rowan tree that overshadowed the goldfish pond, and dug the vegetable beds over by the pear tree. The chairs we are sitting on I found in an architectural salvage yard. Despite the occasional attack of aphids and the despoilations of the wind that blows down this valley, I have charmed – and coerced – nature into doing my bidding.

Stephan doesn't spend much time working in the garden; he regards it as my domain, which suits me. As you know, he prefers to tinker around with car engines. Each to their own. In the summer he comes out here to eat his meals in the sun, and he feeds the goldfish every day. I think he appreciates the garden, although he's been so busy recently he's not spent

In the Garden

much time at home. We have achieved a hard-won symbiosis, he and I, which is as satisfying to me as it is, I have always thought, to him. We rub along well together, which is more than you can say for most couples. You're probably too young to understand.

I wouldn't want you to think that I am totally obsessed by my garden. I do have other interests: reading, for one, and my voluntary work. But gardening is the way I unwind; it soothes away the cares of the day, and keeps me fit. I've never been one for the gym – by the look of you I expect you go regularly. When you get to my age you have to allow for a bit of running to seed – middle-aged spread – as you know, we don't have any children to chase around after – although I must say that Stephan somehow manages to keep himself in trim.

We did try to have children, but it wasn't to be. I'm not one for test tubes and hormones and what have you. I think it's best to accept the hand you're dealt on that score. I thought about adoption or fostering, but Stephan wasn't keen. He said, 'I don't want to look after someone else's kids', which is, I suppose, an entirely natural response. This would've been a good garden for children to play in, though, wouldn't it? With all its nooks and crannies. There are plenty of places to hide and you could play cricket on the lawn.

I love columbines – don't you? So willowy and delicate-looking. And so easy to grow; they sow themselves everywhere. In fact I spend quite a lot of time digging up the seedlings so that they don't completely take over. For such a fragile looking plant it's very invasive.

Some plants are like that; you have to take them in hand. Others – that delphinium there for instance – need nurturing and protecting – from slugs and the wind – otherwise they'd never flower at all. And the lilies, so showy and fragrant, so worth the wait! I have even had some success with roses, although blackspot is a perennial problem. Each flower in the garden has its season – its time and its place – and the picture changes from week to week – day to day, even – so you never

In the Garden

grow bored. Well I don't, anyway. I feel I am here to nurture each plant and encourage it to perform to the best of its ability.

The blackbird is singing again I hear – such a chirpy bird and so unafraid. Of course they're a devil when it comes to fruit! I protect the current bushes and the strawberries with netting, but they always manage to get in somehow. I have come to accept a certain amount of depredation, but how far should you allow it to go before taking more stringent measures? And just how rigorous should those measures be? Most people would think nothing of spraying aphids with insecticide or poisoning slugs and snails, even trapping a mouse. Is it the size of the predator that determines our response? To my way of thinking you should not be squeamish when protecting your own.

The shotgun belongs to my uncle: I've borrowed it to shoot the rabbits that have been eating my vegetables. Not strictly legal, I know – I don't have a firearms licence – but it's the only way I can think of to get rid of them. My neighbours have become used to the occasional shot and they're sympathetic because the rabbits are menacing their gardens too.

I'm always on the lookout for new ways to adorn the garden – I did well at the salvage yard, not only finding these chairs and the table, but also the wrought iron bench through the archway and the stone mermaid fountain in the fishpond. I thought as soon as I saw you that you would be an adornment to any setting, so slim and young and pretty – I could understand what Stephan sees in you – but you're a bit of a disappointment close up.

In fact you don't look too good at all now – bloated and blue around the edges, and with the flies crawling into your eyes.

Like the honey fungus in my soil, the blight in my crop, I have dug you out, and now I must burn you. The neighbours are used to my bonfires, and will think nothing of it. Stephan is coming home from his work trip this evening and unless I get on with it, you will still be sitting here, corrupting my garden. I thought that I had found the way to end the situation, but after

In the Garden

our chat I can see that you're going to be another work in progress. If I am not careful and clever about disposing of you, you could still spoil my design. I have to maintain constant vigilance to keep everything in the garden rosy.

THEIR OWN MAD DEMONS

David A. Riley

Nobby pulled up by the canal in his Transit van. Rain swept across the road and forced the few trees along the tow path to sag beneath its onslaught. A dull headache from the eight pints of beer he'd drunk last night in the Bell and Compasses hurt his eyes as he switched off the wipers. Instantly the depressing scene was hidden as rain beaded the windscreen. A couple of moments later the passenger door was tugged open and Stinko Parkinson pulled himself in.

"Filthy friggin' 'orrible weather," the old man spluttered, shaking the hood of his parka – a parka so greasy Nobby was surprised the rain hadn't simply slithered from it instead of soaking in.

"Worse thing is, you dirty old bugger, we can't even open the bleedin' window to let in some air. Soddin' hell, Stinko, don't you ever have a bath?" Nobby smirked. At six feet three and a good twenty years younger than Stinko, he couldn't care less how much he upset the man.

"Where're we off to?" Stinko asked between puffs, as Nobby kicked the van into gear and manoeuvred it down a short stretch of muddy potholes back to the main road.

"What d'you care, so long as you get paid for it?" Nobby swore as the van stalled. He restarted it with quick, jerky movements.

"It's about time you got yourself a decent van. Look well if it lets us down when we can't afford it to."

"I'll worry about that. It's never let us down yet, has it?"

"Yet!" Stinko laughed. "There's a first time for everythin'. The way this thing's actin' it won't be long afore it packs in for good."

As the van lurched onto the road, Nobby's lips twisted from his teeth. The filthy old bugger was starting to get under his skin. One more word and he'd lamp him, he thought. Good

Their Own Mad Demons

and proper. He glanced at him sideways. And wished he hadn't, as his nose was filled with the sour smell of unwashed clothes and stale urine that surrounded the man. Despite the rain Nobby lowered the side window a couple of inches and breathed in the air that blew, rain-flecked, at his face.

"What're you tryin' to do, friggin' well freeze us to death?"

"If you didn't stink so much I wouldn't need to." Nobby pressed down hard on the accelerator and the van bounced faster down the road, overtaking a Mini which he forced maliciously towards the kerb. "Get out of my way, you stupid cow!" he shouted at the driver, a suddenly sallow faced woman who swerved even more to avoid his bumper.

Ten minutes later they pulled up at a junk yard. Piles of cars loomed over its corrugated iron fencing. A sign above its open gates read:

Joseph Burger & Co
Scrap Metal Merchant

Joe Burger himself, as fat beneath his flashy pale grey suit as an oil-rich Arab, stood by the prefabricated office near the gates, talking to one of his younger – and dimmer – employees on how he wanted his wine-red Mercedes, parked nearby, cleaning and polishing, his stubby arms waving instructions. Seeing the Transit van he frowned, dismissed the young lad with a nod of his head, then strolled self-importantly over, hands in his pockets.

Nobby climbed out to greet him.

"Never mind the niceties," Burger silenced him. "I've a job for you and your smelly friend. Come into the office. Stinko can wait in the yard. I'll leave it for you to explain the details to him later."

"Righto, Mr Burger. Okay," Nobby jabbered. "Whatever you say."

"Exactly." Joe Burger led him into the office. "Sit down." Seating himself behind the desk that dominated most of the

Their Own Mad Demons

room, Burger reached inside one of its drawers and took out a gun. It clunked heavily as he dropped it on the desk. "It's loaded. Five rounds. Though with any luck you'll not need them."

Nobby stared at the revolver, his thin face pale.

"You've used one before?" Burger asked.

Nobby shrugged. "Once," he said, reluctantly. "A few years back."

Burger laughed. "No need to be shy. You'd be surprised how much I know about you. I make a point of finding out as much as I can about my employees, especially those who can be relied on to carry out *special* tasks."

"You wouldn't be wantin' me to kill someone for you, would you?"

Burger laughed again. "If I wanted someone killing I wouldn't ask you. The gun is for your protection. An insurance, if you like. A dissuader. Something to stop those I want you to meet with some stuff from getting too greedy and thinking they can have the cake and the ha'penny. Though it's not a cake we're talking about. And it's a damn sight more than a ha'penny too." The fat man leaned back in his chair till it creaked and his sparse but shiny, well-groomed hair touched the wall behind him. "You've heard of the Gortons?"

Nobby scratched his ear. "Sure, Mr Burger. Hard nuts. One of them was doing time when I got sent down a few years back. Big headed bastard. Bloody well ran the prison. Or thought he did."

"He probably did," Burger said, "if half I've heard about them is true."

"Is it them I'm meetin'?"

"It isn't Mickey Mouse. I'd hardly be talking about them now if there wasn't a point, would I?" Burger retorted.

Nobby stayed silent, though he wished one day, when he didn't want the greaseball's money so much, he could meet him somewhere nice and quiet where he could get on with kicking his balls into pulp without interruption. The picture in his mind of Burger's blubbery lips dripping blood as he begged for mercy, helped to keep Nobby's face from showing too much resentment.

"I want you to go to this address." Burger passed him a slip of paper. "Pick up the stuff that's handed to you and take it to the second address. There you should be handed a parcel of money. There'll be twenty K in it. In fifties. Check it. And don't get any funny ideas about scarpering. You're neither clever nor fast enough." He patted the gun. "I've more than this I can lay my hands on. And others who would like nothing better than a chance to sort you out."

Nobby shook his head. "You needn't have any worries about that, Mr Burger. What you pay me's enough."

"So it should be," Burger added, bluntly. "There's an extra five hundred in it for you and your friend. For the risks. Though there aren't that many. The Gortons are a bad bunch to do business with, but they're not stupid. They'll know I've taken precautions."

Nobby glanced at the gun, unsure how serious Burger was. The gun looked old, and there was rust on the barrel. And although he had used a gun before, that was eight years ago when a sawn-off shotgun he'd been given by Biffer Tompkins went off by accident at a sub-post office in Endon, shattering a display of Kinder eggs and putting the wind up Biffer, who legged it for all he was worth. Nobby had only gotten away by sheer luck. In the stunned silence that followed the blast a stupid old git had snatched at the gun. He'd squawked when the barrel burnt his fingers and caused enough confusion, as he jigged about nursing his injuries, for Nobby to dash outside, jump in the van they'd left by the corner and drive off as fast as he could. Biffer had been less fortunate. Racing across a road two blocks away, he was stupid enough to run in front of a passing police car, rolled across its bonnet and concussed himself on the road, earning himself two weeks in hospital and seven years in Walton, with time off for good behaviour. Just how much of this Burger had found out, he didn't know. What

Their Own Mad Demons

he did know was that guns were a lot less reliable than most people thought.

Reluctantly he picked up the revolver. He stowed it in his overcoat, then went on to pick up the paper as well.

"When d'you want us to meet 'em?" he asked.

"In two hours time. It's all been arranged. Just make sure you keep your eyes skinned." Burger smiled as he rose to his feet. "Come back with the money and I'll pay you out."

Nodding his head, Nobby walked from the office and back to the van.

*

"I don't friggin' like it." Slumped like a wrinkled heap of misery beside him, Stinko stared at the rain still lashing itself across the windscreen. "I don't friggin' like it at all."

Regretting having told the old man about the gun, Nobby shrugged as he drove down the road, only minutes away from their rendezvous with the Gortons, the five large cardboard boxes they'd collected slowly swaying in the back of the van.

"It's too late to worry about that," Nobby said. "We're almost there."

Stinko snorted. "If I'd known what kind of job we'd be gettin' I wouldn't've come. I've heard o' them Gortons. They're a bad lot. They wouldn't think twice o' doin' us over and takin' the lot, van and all."

"Just let 'em try." Nobby patted the gun in his pocket.

"Pah! And what d'you think you'd do? Pretend you were John Wayne? I know what you'd bloody well do, you soft pillock. You'd have more chance of shootin' your own friggin' foot than one o' them Gortons, especially if they've shooters o' their own, which the bastards friggin' well will have, mark my words." He picked out a shred of tobacco that had stuck to his tongue from his roll-up. "Yon gun that fat Yid gave you will probably blow up in your friggin' face anyway, if you're daft enough to fire it."

Their Own Mad Demons

"Fuck you!" Nobby's lips twisted, baring his teeth, in a mixture of anger and nervousness.

Stinko smiled. "Say that to the Gortons when they're bustin' your legs for a bit o' fun."

Mouthing a response, Nobby indicated right, then drove down a short, winding road that took them between a few hundred yards of dismal-looking fields, before arriving at a boarded-up redbrick office block at the entrance to a quarry. Not used for years, the quarry's walls rose towards a fringe of grass high above. Behind the building, hidden from the road, Nobby saw a large grey car and a pickup van. A group of men stood, sheltering from the rain, inside the open door into the building.

Nobby drew up a few yards from them, leaving the engine in neutral as he turned to Stinko.

"Hop out and open the doors so they can see what we've brought."

Two of the men strode towards them. One of them, his thinning hair plastered to his scalp by the rain, jerked a thumb towards the back of the van.

"Check them out for us, Joey," he said to the other man. His broad smile, twisted beneath a misshapen nose, had a worrying lack of humour. Instinctively Nobby touched the gun in his pocket, moving his fingers around it. The man's face was hard. Too fuckin' hard.

"You got the cash for us?" Nobby called from the van.

"It's here." The man opened his coat and pulled out a brown paper parcel.

What spit still remained in his mouth drying up, Nobby said: "Mr Burger told me to check it first afore we handed anythin' over."

"He did, did he?" The man's smile broadened humourlessly. "Would you like to climb out and check it?"

Nobby glanced at the men inside the building. They were watching intently.

"Well?" the man asked.

Their Own Mad Demons

Nobby shrugged. A heavy, debilitating tension coiled inside his stomach. His fingers slid around the gun. "I can check it just as well in here," he said.

"You can fucking well check it outside," the man grated. His brittle eyes stared straight at Nobby's. "Do you know who you're talking to?"

"I – I were told by Mr Burger—"

"And who the fuck cares what Burger says? You can tell him from me that Reggie Gorton lays down the rules, not Joseph fucking shit-face Burger. When I deal with people I expect them to act with respect. Not treat me as if I was no more than a back street barrow boy." The man's fake smile reappeared. "Are we going to finish this properly? With respect? Or are you going to stay in that van as if you didn't trust me?"

Nobby glanced at the men still inside the office block.

The other man, Joey, returned with Stinko.

"The stuff's okay," Joey said. A razor scar puckered his cheek as he grinned. "This old bugger don't half pong, though. Burger'll be hiring bag ladies next as receptionists for his fucking scrap yard."

Nobby glanced at Stinko, who was shuffling his feet in agitation. His eyes looked scared. And Nobby wondered if Joey had said something to him while they were at the back of the van.

Undecided, Nobby half pulled the gun from his pocket. He didn't like the place they were at. He didn't like its isolation. And he didn't like how many of Gorton's men were hanging around.

What was that fat Kike up to messing around with people like this? Reggie Gorton was known to be a friggin' psycho, who'd had more bodies put away over the years than anyone else in the city. And never been nailed by the police either, even though everyone knew about him.

Nobby turned as the rest of the men strolled towards them, positioning themselves in front of the van.

Their Own Mad Demons

Reggie Gorton cocked an enquiring glance at Nobby. "Are you getting out or not? I haven't all day to piss around in the rain."

"Okay," Nobby said. "I'll take the parcel. I don't need to check it. I trust you."

"That's big of you. That's fucking well big of you indeed, my friend." Reggie turned to his men, grinning. "I like that," he grated. His grin undiminished, he jerked the van door open. "Get out and do what your boss told you." He thrust the parcel into Nobby's arms. "Count it. Here."

Releasing his hand from the gun, Nobby dropped to the ground. Rain splashed across his face as he grasped the parcel, his fingers shaking so much he almost dropped it.

"Alright, Mr Gorton." His fingers fumbled with the edges of the paper as he ripped it open.

A click made him pause and he could feel his balls crawl into his groin. A sawn-off, double-barrelled shotgun, no more than three feet away, was pointed at his face. A sour taste filled his mouth as he stared at the end of its barrels. Holding the gun, Joey grinned as the parcel fell from Nobby's hands. Instinctively Nobby snatched at it, his mouth gaping when he saw the sheets of newspaper that scattered across the ground.

Reggie laughed. For the first time there was a hint of humour in it, as behind him Stinko moaned sickly.

"Good lads," Reggie said. He strode towards Nobby, patting him on the back. "It's good to see Burger's not improved with age. Still too tight to hire anyone better than a pair of deadbeats to do his dirty work." Reggie turned to his men. "Get that stuff shifted. And carefully. Some of it's fragile."

Joey waved his gun to the left. "Over there, string-bean," he said to Nobby. He nodded his head towards the office block. "Both of you. *Shift!*"

He followed behind as the men reluctantly made their way towards the building.

"What're you gonna do to us?" Stinko asked in a pathetic whine which even Nobby couldn't help but despise. "You're

Their Own Mad Demons

not gonna hurt us, are you?"

Joey laughed. "You shouldn't take no notice of what you've heard about us. We don't go in for things like that. Not to people who behave themselves and do as they're told," he added, prodding Nobby in the middle of the back with the shotgun. "Even though some buggers sometimes try their best to get up our noses."

Nobby stumbled as they went inside the office block. Its mildewed, graffiti covered walls were cracked from neglect, and scabs of plaster lay across the concrete floor. Broken doors hung from their hinges, giving glimpses of deserted corridors and empty rooms. Leaks through the roof had left puddles on the floor. Dodging them, the men crossed the room, Joey behind on their heels.

"That's far enough," he said at last. "Sit by the wall." Obviously enjoying himself, the gangster waved the shot gun from side to side, emphasising the seriousness of his order.

His lower lip trembling, Stinko sidled down till he was crouched on the floor. His hands in his pockets, Nobby stared uncertainly about the room. It smelt of death.

"I told you to sit down," Joey repeated.

"And then?" Nobby asked.

"If you behave yourselves, nothing. If you don't..." Joey flexed his finger on the trigger. "There's room enough to hide a body or two in this place."

Stinko tugged at Nobby's coat. "Do as he says, you daft bugger. Can't you see he means it?"

Joey nodded. "And I do," he said, smiling, the razor scar shining on his cheek.

Putting his back against the wall, Nobby slid to the cold, concrete floor, though his fingers were already tight around the gun in his pocket. Its barrel was aimed at Joey's stomach, not ten feet away, unsure even now why he knew he had to do it. Somehow, for some reason, he knew neither he nor Stinko were going to get out of here, no matter how obedient they were. Once they'd done everything Joey told them to do he'd

Their Own Mad Demons

shoot them.

Nobby's fingers curled around the trigger in his pocket, slowly, carefully, his heart beating faster till he was sure he would have a coronary if it didn't slow down soon. His face felt flushed as beads of sweat dribbled from his hair.

"You look as if you're about to shit yourself," Joey said with a smirk. "You don't trust me, do you, string bean?" Balancing the barrel of the gun in one hand, he pointed it at Nobby's head with a nonchalance as frightening as it was false. Nobby's fingers tightened on the gun in his pocket. In his imagination he could already hear the shot gun blast that would scatter his head in a stew of brains, bones and blood across the wall behind him.

"So help me," Nobby started to mutter, his thin lips trembling with tension as his finger pulled one millimetre more on the trigger in his pocket. His coat ripped forwards as the gun exploded, bursting a blackened, smoking hole through the cloth as it spurted out fragments of charred fabric through the air.

Joey's face jerked forwards in a violent nod as he was thrown back, doubled, his gun going off reflexively as it whipped skywards, blowing a yard wide, almost circular hole through the ceiling. Mewling, he rolled over and cracked his head on the ground, his legs twitching. A deep-throated, hideous moan gurgled from his mouth as his hands clutched at the blood on what remained of his stomach.

Nobby jumped to his feet. He grabbed hold of Stinko and shook him.

"Come on! We have to get out of here before the bastards get us. They don't know who's been blasted yet. They'll think it was us. But it won't be long before they realise it wasn't."

Stinko stared at the man on the floor. "Why d'you do it?" His voice sounded desperate. "They'd have let us go after they'd taken the stuff."

"And maybe not," Nobby muttered. "You know these Gortons. They're mad bastards. I did what I had to do. Let's

Their Own Mad Demons

get out of here while we can. We've no other choice. Unless you want to see what kind of thanks Reggie Gorton'll give you."

"After what you've done, you daft bugger, they'd kill me."

"Then you'd better get a move on, hadn't you?"

A quick glance through the doorway showed they had no hope of escaping that way. Their van was too near the other vehicles, all of which were surrounded by Gorton's men, two of them carrying one of the cardboard boxes to their pickup. Reggie Gorton was staring at the building, drawn by the gun blasts, and seemed on the point of coming over to check things himself. Nobby knew they had only seconds to get out of here.

"Come on. Quick!" he told Stinko. He strode past Joey, still mewling like a cat that had been run over by a car. Ignoring him, Nobby pushed through a door onto a long corridor flanked by more doors, all of them shut. At the far end a sharp bend led to an empty warehouse. Broken windows lined its outer walls, too high for them to reach. At the far end, next to a steel, roll-up door, was a smaller one made of wood. There was a narrow strip of light down one side of it.

"It's open," Nobby said. "Come on."

"Half a mo' there, Nobby. I'm not as young as you. I need a second to catch my breath." Stinko's feet stumbled; his bristly face mottled with purple blotches. His lips looked blue. "You're killin' me," he panted.

Nobby grabbed at his arm, gripping it hard as he tugged him along.

"If we don't hurry, Reggie Gorton'll be killing you for real, you daft old sod."

Already they could hear shouts echoing through the building behind them as if from a great distance away, though Nobby knew better. He tugged at the door. It sprang open and slammed against the wall. Outside they could see the road leading out of the quarry past fields turned a misty grey in the rain. None of the Gortons were in sight. Probably they were all in the office block now, Nobby thought, some of them seeing to the man he'd shot, while the rest would be starting to search the buildings, looking for them.

"Back to the van," Nobby said. "If we can get to it before they find us we'll get away from them."

Stinko shook his head. "We'll never get away from them. They'll hunt us down wherever we go after what you did, Nobby. We'll never get away. Not for good, we won't. You've doomed us, you bastard. You've doomed us both."

Nobby took hold of his collar. "Quit your whining. We'll get out of here."

Throwing the man to one side, Nobby dashed through the rain. Skidding to a halt at the edge of the building, he peered around the corner. Satisfied, he called Stinko on.

"They must have gone inside. Now's our chance."

The noise of the rain helped drown the sound of their feet as they ran to the van, Stinko wheezing and coughing behind him. Reaching it first, Nobby was relieved to find the keys were still in the ignition.

"Get in!" he urged, not waiting till Stinko was in his seat before starting the van up. The engine growled into life, backfiring twice. With a snarled: "*Shit!*" Nobby slammed the gears into first and the van lurched forwards.

As they drove off, one of the Gortons ran out of the office block brandishing a shot gun. Nobby thought it was probably the one that Joey had threatened them with, as the man was still trying to reload it by the time the van was well on its way to the open gateway out of the quarry. There was a bang, and a handful of pellets beat a half-hearted tattoo against the rear doors, shattering one of the windows, then the van was bouncing along the road.

"Look out!" Stinko shouted.

Too late Nobby tugged at the steering wheel in a desperate attempt to veer the van away from the ditch beside the lane. But the front wheel had already spun into it, jamming in the sudden dip and dragging the rest of the van sideways in a drunken skid. The steering wheel was whipped from Nobby's hands, almost dislocating his wrists. Cursing at the pain, he grabbed at the wheel, but the van had already tilted too far. Realising it would end up lying on its side if he let it move forward, its chassis screaming alarmingly, he slammed on the brakes. A violent shudder rippled through the vehicle.

"*Nooo!*" Stinko whined, his hands to his face as he cringed back as far as he could in his seat.

The vehicle creaked as it lurched back and forth, half of it overhanging the ditch.

Peeling his hands from his face, Stinko peered through the windscreen. Nobby grimaced. His mouth tasted coppery and foul and his bladder was all but ready to burst. Remembering the danger they were in, he reached for the keys and tried to restart the van. The only response was a long drawn whine from the engine. He tried it again, but the whine had grown weaker, and he glanced at Stinko, a sinking feeling in his stomach.

"It's not going to start, is it?" Stinko's voice sounded faint, a disheartened murmur. "The friggin' bastard's gone and given up on us, hasn't it?"

Ignoring him, Nobby reached in his pocket for the revolver. By now the Gortons would already be starting to pile into their own vehicles. It would only be seconds at the most before they came tearing through the gateway in pursuit. Not that they would have to go far to find them, Nobby thought.

"We'll have to get out of here," he said. "If we cut across the fields we can still get away."

Stinko stared through the rain that left the distances a dim blur of hills and trees on either side of the quarry.

"I can't," he murmured. "My heart won't take it. It'd kill me."

"Reggie Gorton'll kill you if you don't."

Stinko glared at him. Anger blazed in his vein-reddened eyes. "It's your fault, Nobby. You've gotten us into this. If you'd kept your head and not gone and shot that bastard back there they'd've let us go. You know that, you barn-pot, you friggin' nutter. You've gone and done for us."

Nobby grabbed him by the throat. "If you want to stay here, winging, do it. I'm off." He pushed the man back against his seat, then opened the door and leapt out of the van into the rain. His feet slithered on the wet grass as he pulled himself up out of the ditch and reached for the fence that ran along the edge of the field beyond for support.

Behind him, Stinko shuddered in the van. He looked down the road, his eyes wide with panic. Clumsier than Nobby, he pushed himself out of the van and struggled to climb out of the ditch, his gnarled hands slipping on the grass, his arms too short to reach the fence. He would have called out to Nobby for help, but the big man was already on the other side of the fence and had begun to run across the field, too far away to hear him now, even if he'd risk his own neck to come back to help.

On the road, a car skidded to a halt. Looking back, Stinko let out a yelp as he saw three men climb out of it. One of them pointed towards him. Even from here Stinko could see Reggie Gorton's face, livid with anger. Without hesitation Stinko tried to jump to the fence, his finger nails scratching at the wooden posts in a useless attempt to grab hold of them, till someone took hold of his arms.

Writhing and kicking, he was dragged up out of the ditch and back to the van.

"*Nobby, you bastard, I'll get you for this,*" the old man shrieked as he stared at the figure looming above him. The man who had grabbed him, hauled him round. Rain splashed Stinko's face, mixing with the tears in his eyes.

"We've got one of you, at least," Reggie said, leaning over him. "We'll soon get the other, however fast the bastard runs."

"Please, Mr Gorton, it weren't me," Stinko stammered. "It were Nobby. It were him as had the gun. I didn't know nothing about it."

Reggie smiled, his false teeth artificially even. "Joey was my nephew." The man's voice was a harsh monotone –

Their Own Mad Demons

remorseless – his eyes cold. "He was family." He bent down and stretched his hand out to pat Stinko's cheek with a strained gentleness. "Even in the eyes of the law you're as guilty as your partner, whether you pulled that trigger or not. You were there." His smile faded, the mask discarded. "You'll have the pleasure of finding out some of what your partner is going to get when we catch up with him. Perhaps that will help to compensate. Though I doubt it." He nodded his head. "Take him to the farm." He glanced at Stinko, their eyes meeting. "No one will disturb us there while we get on with things."

*

Nobby ran faster and further than he had ever run in his life – faster and further than he would have ever thought possible, outdistancing even the crippling stitch which for three miles all but doubled him up. Staying low to keep himself as much out of sight as possible till he'd left the Gortons beyond too many hedgerows and trees to be seen, he kept to the countryside as much as possible, too scared to take the easier routes along any of the minor roads he passed in case the Gortons drove along them, searching for him.

Travelling across country, he headed in the direction of Amesbury, five miles to the east. An ex-Mill town filled with dreary terraced streets of local stone and corner shops twenty years out of date, it offered little hope of security, except there were at least a dozen similar backwaters he could have headed for. Too many for even the Gortons to cover in one afternoon. Or so he hoped. Though this did little to help ease his fear when he walked down its streets, his clothes drenched and his shoes all but ruined. If the Gortons didn't get him, pneumonia would if he didn't get into some dry clothes soon.

His first stop was a back street pub across from the entrance to a closed-down mill. Choosing a side room at the far end of the grubby bar, he ordered himself a large whisky and a couple of bags of crisps.

"Do you have a phone?" he asked the landlord.

"Round the corner, by the Gents." Pursing his lips at the twenty pound note Nobby had given him, the man ungraciously trudged away for some change.

After he'd come back, Nobby downed his drink, then searched for the phone. The whisky had at least begun to kindle a comforting imitation of heat in his stomach, which would do for the time being.

Ten minutes later he managed to get hold of Marcia Fielding. He'd lived with her on and off for the last few years, when he could put up with her seven-year-old son. And when he wasn't going out with someone else. She was a reliable standby. Or as reliable a standby as he had ever had so far.

"What's wrong?" she asked. "My supervisor said it was important. I hope it is and you've not dragged me away from my check-out for nothing. The old bitch has been watching me like a hawk for weeks." Her voice nearly always had a grumbling tone to it, which was why she was only a standby. Nobby grimaced at the phone.

"Tell your supervisor your Gran's on her deathbed if that'll satisfy her. Tell her whatever you like."

"*If* you tell me what you want first," Marcia said. "What is it? The Law?"

"Nothing like that," Nobby said. "Some bother, that's all. The police aren't involved." Not yet, he thought, wondering how the Gortons would handle the man he shot.

"Who is it you're in trouble with? That bloke you sometimes work for? Burger, is it?"

"Naw, nothing to do with him," Nobby cut in impatiently. "Can't we leave the third degree till later? I need some help."

"Why else would you ring me after – what is it, Nobby? – three weeks?" she said sarcastically.

"I've been busy. You know how it is."

"I *know* how it is all right," she said. "What do you want? Money?"

He shook his head automatically at the phone. "Naw, I've

plenty of that. Enough for now."

"I'm glad to hear it." Her voice softened slightly. "What do you want?"

"I could do with somewhere to stay for a couple of nights, that's all. Just till things have cooled a bit." Or until he'd managed to arrange for somewhere safer to hole up, he added to himself.

"I suppose you could always stay with me," Marcia said, though he could hear doubt in her voice. "Where are you now?"

He told her. "Could you drive over and pick me up when you've finished work?"

"I'd have to arrange for someone to look after Peter."

"Ask your Mum. She always wants to look after him."

"Maybe."

Nobby leaned against the wall. "When can you be here?"

"Eight-thirty all right? I knock off at eight and it'll take me at least half an hour to drive all the way to Amesbury."

"That'll be fine."

"I hope so," Marcia said. "Just so long as this bother you're in doesn't get out of hand."

"No chance," he lied. "It'll blow over in a couple of days. You know how it is."

*

It was nearly nine by the time Marcia arrived, parking her ten-year-old Fiesta outside the pub while she went in to find him. By ten-thirty, after picking up a takeaway from a Chinese on the way, they were back at her flat on the outskirts of Edgebottom. It was in one of three tower blocks, with a view of the town on one side and the moors on the other.

A couple of hours later, a half bottle of gin drunk between them to wash down their takeaway, both Marcia and Nobby were asleep in her bed, Nobby too exhausted after the day's events to make more than a passing attempt at lovemaking.

Their Own Mad Demons

Even his worries about what the Gortons would do if they caught up with him had not been enough to keep him awake for long, though he'd left the gun that Burger had given him tucked away beneath his clothes on the bedside table beside him.

The bedroom was warm from the central heating radiator, its window closed against the winds that blew around the tower block, lashing it with rain. It was as secure a refuge as any that Nobby could have found at short notice – secure enough, he knew, till the Gortons found out about his link with Marcia Fielding and checked into it. By then, though, he would be well away from here – well away from Edgebottom too. Marcia's Fiesta was one reason he'd contacted her, though she did not suspect that yet. One of his last thoughts before he drifted into sleep was the hope he could be away in it long before she realised what he was after.

A clock tower somewhere far into town chimed two, unheard by either of the sleepers.

Up on the hills above Edgebottom the lights inside an isolated farmhouse still burned, though there were no eyes to see anything tonight as the gales swept by. There were sounds from within the farmhouse, though, sounds that sometimes cut through the howling of the wind, sounds which made the few sheep huddled by the dry stone walls that crossed the hills in haphazard lines look up and bleat disconsolately.

Not long after the distant clock struck two a scream rang out from the farm. A scream even louder, more shrill, more pain-wracked than any that preceded it. A scream that changed into an agonised whimper, then silence. Moments later someone laughed. It was harsh laughter. While a low intonation, too faint to be heard from outside the farm, went on and on...

Suddenly cold, Nobby woke. Shuddering all over, his skin prickled with an icy clamminess from head to foot despite the duvet that covered him. Startled, he stared into the darkness, his heart hammering. Holding himself as still as possible, he barely breathed as he listened to the winds and to Marcia's alarm clock ticking away on her side of the bed. For a moment he wondered if he'd heard someone enter the flat while he slept. Could the Gortons have gotten around to checking on people like Marcia so soon? His panicked mind rove over how they might have found out about her as he listened for something that might – just might – explain what woke him. When nothing moved for what seemed like hours he started to shift his arm from the duvet and reached through the darkness to where he remembered leaving the gun beneath his clothes. Feeling through them he closed his hand around the reassuringly heavy butt with a suppressed sigh of relief, gripping it tight.

Breathing deeply in an effort to ease the tension in his body, he suddenly frowned. Stinko? Recognising the old man's awful smell, he wondered how Stinko had found his way here. He couldn't mistake it. Stinko was not far away from him, he was sure.

Whipping the duvet from his body, Nobby rolled out of bed and padded quietly towards the door. He listened for a moment before gripping the handle. There was only stillness outside in the living room, no unusual sounds, only the wind, Marcia's clock and her own deep breaths in the bed behind him.

If Stinko was here only his smell betrayed him, spreading through the air with its distinctive odour of sweat and urine.

With a sudden, silent intake of breath, Nobby flung the bedroom door wide open. Clenching the gun before him he scanned the living room. Still sensing nothing besides the smell, he reached for the light switch. The sudden glare dazzled him for an instant, but not enough to prevent him from seeing there was no one there.

Quickly, he searched the rest of the flat: Peter's bedroom, the bathroom, the passageway filled with boxes, coats and bags of rubbish that led to the outside door. There was no one, apart from Marcia's son, asleep in his bed.

Had Stinko been here and gone? Nobby was unable to understand it. He'd known the old man long enough to realise he was incapable of breaking in and getting out again without making a mess of the outside door, yet it wasn't even scratched, its lock still fastened. His smell was here, though, as strong as before. Perhaps even stronger.

What the fuckin' hell was he up to? Where the fuckin' hell had he gone?

"Stinko? Are you there?" he called in a low whisper. "Where the frig' are you hidin' yourself, you daft old bastard?"

He looked into the kitchen. Its neon light cast a harsh clarity over everything inside. Yet, here too, Stinko's smell was strong.

Too strong.

It wasn't natural. Even for Stinko, the bugger would have to be pressed up against him for it to be as strong as this.

"Come on, where are you?"

"Who are you talking to?" Marcia stood by the bedroom door, rubbing her eyes with one hand and holding onto a flimsy pink dressing gown with the other. She frowned at the gun Nobby held in front of him, too startled to be able to hide it in time. "What the fucking hell are you doing with *that?*" Her face was pale and hard as she stared at him. "What kind of trouble are you fucking well getting me involved in, Nobby?"

He waved the gun casually. "It's not as bad as you think."

"Like fuck it isn't. Or do you always wander around in the middle of the night with a gun in your hand?"

"I could smell something odd."

"So odd you're prowling at three o'clock in the sodding morning with a gun?" Marcia sneered sarcastically. "You're going off your rocker, Nobby. You really are. They'll be locking you up in a nut-house next if you go on like this. *You smelt something odd!*"

Nobby clenched his fist, tempted to let her have a good old smack in the mouth. That'd teach the bitch to keep it shut!

"Can't you smell anything?" he asked instead, forcing his muscles to relax. If he hit her she'd scream till someone called the police. "Kind of sour and rancid?" he added. "Like old sweat?" Like Stinko, he could have told her if she'd met the man, which he knew she hadn't.

"There's no smell here. You're imagining things."

Nobby sniffed, Stinko's odour even stronger now. "It's here," he told her. "You must be able to smell it. It's friggin' awful."

"You're friggin' awful," she retorted. Ignoring the gun, Marcia crossed the room and picked up a packet of cigarettes from the arm of the sofa. Lighting one, she glanced at him sideways. "If I were you I'd see a doctor. Soon. And tomorrow you'd better see about getting yourself somewhere else to stay. I don't know what kind of trouble you're in, but you're not staying here. Not with a gun. No way, sweetheart."

She stepped back into the bedroom where she gathered up his clothes and dumped them on the floor outside. "I expect you to have gone by the time I get up," she said. With no further comment she shut the bedroom door on him.

Nobby stared at it for a moment, his emotions uncertain. A vein pulsed on his temple as he clenched his jaws, grinding his teeth. At any other time, at any other time at all, if he hadn't had the Gortons on his back, he'd have forced his way back into the bedroom and sorted her out good and proper. Instead, after a minute in which he forced himself to try and calm down, he started to get dressed. He'd teach her one lesson at least: by the time the bitch got up in the morning he'd be away from here in her car. There'd be sod all she could do about it. He'd already seen her keys, left where she tossed them when they arrived back earlier with their takeaway, in a glass bowl on the imitation beech wood unit by the door.

His repressed anger almost made him forget the smell. But it was too strong to be ignored for long. Stinko was here somewhere. But where? He scowled as his body grew cold inside his damp clothes. To warm himself and take his mind off the smell he went into the kitchen, where he fixed himself some coffee, fried eggs, bacon, sausage and toast. He found a bag, which he stuffed full of canned food. The bitch could restock the kitchen herself. That'd teach her to piss on him like she had, he thought.

An asthmatic whisper made him jerk round, dropping his food on the plate and almost making him wet himself. The thin hairs down the nape of his neck bristled as a shudder slid up his spine.

His name? Had whoever spoken whispered his name? It had been almost too faint to hear – yet close. Very close. As if whoever spoke was only inches from him.

"*You left me to them.*"

Nobby jerked round again.

"Stinko, you bastard, where're you hidin'? Come out or I'll friggin' well break your neck, you stupid old bugger..." His words trailed off. There was no one here, he was certain. There was no one anywhere around here who could have spoken. He felt sick and stupid. And afraid. Even more afraid than when Joey Gorton had been facing him, a sawn-off shot gun aimed at his chest. His hands trembled as he picked up the gun from where he'd left it by the plate.

"*They got me. When you left and legged it for all you were worth, they got me.*"

"Who got you, Stinko?" The tremors in his voice sickened him. He sounded pathetic. He *felt* pathetic, jabbering at nothingness – at a smell that all but smothered him – and a faint, asthmatic whisper. "Who got you?"

"*You friggin' well know who got me, Nobby. As soon as you'd gone they took me with them. Up on the moors. Oh God, Nobby, you shouldn't have left me. You shouldn't have let them get me, not so they could do what they did to me. It would've been better if you'd shot me.*"

Nobby rubbed his eyes, unable to ignore the whisperings, but even more unable to understand where they were coming from. "Where are you, Stinko? Where the friggin' hell are you hiding?"

"*Where?*" The whisper faded, then came back again. "*God knows, Nobby. Hell, m'be. Or worse.*" He whimpered for a moment. "*You shouldn't have left me. It weren't right, Nobby. Not when it were you as fired the shot that started it all off.*"

Wiping sweat from his face, Nobby said: "I can smell and hear you, but I can't friggin' well see you."

"*You'll never see me. Not till they've done to you what they did to me.*"

Fear catching in his voice, Nobby said: "What did they do to you, Stinko?"

There was silence for a long, long moment, and Nobby wondered if the old man, wherever he was hiding, was going to answer him or not. Finally the whisper rose once more, unnervingly close.

"*They made me what I am, Nobby. Bit by bit. Enjoying what they did! Enjoying every second of what they did to me, Nobby. Every sodding second of it!*"

"And now?" Sweat dripped onto his plate. "And now, Stinko? Tell me."

"*I've come to tell you they're gonna get you too.*"

Nobby tightened his grip on the gun. His eyes jerked from side to side in the hope of catching sight of where the old man hid, though he knew deep down there was nowhere in the flat he could be hiding. "What do you mean, they're gonna get me too? They don't friggin' well know where I am."

The smell, suffocatingly strong, suddenly closed in on him like a nauseous, impalpable gag, blocking his nose and mouth with its stench. Panic-stricken, Nobby clutched at his face. His fingers plucked at his skin in a futile effort to get rid of it.

"*They know where you are, Nobby.*"

Clenching the gun to him, Nobby stifled a cry of terror as he picked up the keys to Marcia's car, then ran for the door. Outside in the passageway he paused, listening. For a moment he thought he had succeeded in leaving the old man's stench behind, but it was there, wafting towards him seconds later, sickeningly thick. Gritting his teeth, Nobby dashed towards the lift. When he reached it his stomach sank yet again. The indicator lights above the lift doors were flashing as the lift

Their Own Mad Demons

rose up the shaft towards him. At three in the morning Nobby knew it couldn't be anyone except the Gortons.

A flight of steps led down a gloomy, concrete stairwell next to the lift. Clenching hold of the banister rail for support he hurled himself down it, leaping two or more steps at a time in his panic to get away before the Gortons found out where he was.

Marcia's flat was on the seventh floor. By the time he reached the last flight of stairs before the hallway he was starting to become dizzy. His breath rasped between his teeth.

Steadying himself, he peered around the corner at the bottom of the stairs, relieved to see the space between the stairs, the lift and the outside doors was deserted. Hardly daring to credit his luck so far – or the sheer incompetence of the Gortons – he ran towards the doors.

For a moment the breeze that hit him outside as he burst onto the forecourt dissipated the stench that had pursued him down the stairs. But it was a false respite. Between each gust, that briefly cleared the smell from around him, it returned as strong as before.

Trying to ignore it, Nobby ran towards Marcia's Fiesta. He unlocked its door and climbed in.

Even by the time he started the car and drove off no one had appeared in an attempt to stop him, though Stinko's smell was dense inside the car. Was it stuck to his clothes? Exasperated and bewildered, Nobby steered the Fiesta onto the road, accelerating away as quickly as he could. His relief at the ease of his escape quelled some of his fears over Stinko's bizarre whisperings and the inexplicable presence of his smell. Though he could live with the old man's whispers, the smell was something else. When he got a chance he'd get rid of his clothes and buy some new ones. That and a shower would take care of it, he thought, ignoring red lights along the way as he drove through Edgebottom. Taking the Blackburn Road, he headed towards the motorway. It was only two miles from here to the road that would take him to it. After that the Gortons could friggin' well do what they liked. They'd have a hard job tracking him to the far ends of the country, with at least a couple of hundred miles between him and the bastards, perhaps even more. He'd dump Marcia's car along the way, then take a train and lose himself completely.

If only that friggin' smell would ease up!

It made him sick, deep down in his guts. Opening the car window made no difference, as if the smell had attached itself to him. He could almost taste it. He grimaced in disgust as he wiped his mouth with the back of his hand, sweat beading his face.

"You're not gonna get away, Nobby."

He screamed, slamming his foot hard on the brakes. For a moment the car spun out of control all the way across the empty, rain-swept road, before shuddering to a halt next to the kerb, his hands clenched tight to the steering wheel as he bent dry retching over it till his throat felt raw and his chest seemed hollow.

"You friggin' bastard, Stinko," he croaked finally when the heaving of his chest had subsided. "I'll kill you." He pushed himself up from the steering wheel and glanced over his shoulder into the back of the car as if he expected to find the old man hunched there, hiding from him. But the back seat was empty.

Letting go of the steering wheel, he felt sweat drying cold on his skin as he stared at the empty seat behind him.

"Stinko?" He gulped, hardly daring to listen for the old man's reply. "Stinko, where are you? You're drivin' me mad. Show yourself to me." Urine trickled down his pants, hot against his legs. "Where are you, Stinko?"

"Where you let them take me when you ran away."

"I don't know what you mean. It weren't my fault they got you. Come off it, you stupid old bugger. What do you want off of me?"

"Help, Nobby. That's what I want off of you."

"What do you mean? I don't even know where you are."

Their Own Mad Demons

"I'll tell you, if you'll listen and do as I say."

"If I do, if I help you, you'll stop all of this... this stink? These whisperings?" Nobby cringed at the pathetic whine in his voice, but he couldn't help it.

"If you help me. If you don't, I'll stay as long as you live." The old man whimpered, dimly, somewhere far and yet not so far away. *"I want you to get them Gortons for me. They did this to me. They put me through hell."*

"The Gortons?" Nobby tasted fear in his mouth, fear so vile and coppery and strong it made even the stench he'd smelt so far seem sweet by comparison. "There's no way I can get them for you, you know that."

"You got one of them, didn't you? If you can get one, you can get more. You can get Reggie Gorton. He's the one as did it."

Nobby collapsed onto his seat. "Where are they?" he asked, his mind feeling numb.

"A farm. On the hills. Just drive where I tells you." Stinko paused. *"You got that gun?"*

Nobby said: "It's here." He patted the pocket of his coat.

"You'll need it." Stinko whimpered again as if in pain.

Nobby restarted the car. Slowly, he drove down the road, his reluctance to reach their destination fighting against his fear of what Stinko could do.

"Take the Rossendale Road onto the moors. There's a turnoff that'll take you to the farm. I'll tell you when we've reached it."

The road stretched dark and wild before him, what few lamp posts there were soon petering out before he'd driven more than a mile. Only dry stone walls and fields lay on either side, black beyond the beams of the car.

"What did they do to you?" Nobby asked, unable to stand the silence any longer.

"Did you never wonder why none of them ever got arrested for murder, even though everyone knows they've done it, again and again?"

Their Own Mad Demons

"Course I've wondered. I've kept my mouth shut, though. Like everyone else with any sense."

"*I know, Nobby. I know why. They were never done because no one ever found their bodies.*"

"No bodies?"

"*Without a body it's hard for someone to get done for killing 'em.*"

Nobby stared through the windscreen as its wipers jerked back and forth, momentarily clearing it of rain.

"What happened to them?"

"*You'll find out soon enough. But I'll tell you this: the Gortons are into more than robbery and violence and stuff like that.*"

"Such as?"

"*Such as rites as'd make old Aleister Crowley himself kneel down and pray to God for help.*"

"Rites?" Nobby struggled with the word. "What do you mean 'rites'?"

"*You stupid or something? You know what I mean. They're nutters, those Gortons. Nutters! They're into things only someone crazy would touch – because if you weren't to start with you'd be crazy soon enough later on.*"

Nobby stared ahead of him in silence, his brain unable to take it in. Struggling with what the old man had whispered, he felt a paralysing helplessness slowly take over as if he was still asleep and having a nightmare.

"*Turn right by that knob of a hill o'er there,*" Stinko whispered, so close to his ear he seemed almost in it.

Nobby swung the car onto a rutted lane full of stones and sods of grass that twisted the wheels of the car from side to side so violently the steering wheel was almost jerked from his hands and he had to hold on tight to keep control of it. He slowed to a crawl.

"*Turn the lights down. Dim 'em. Or they'll see you coming.*"

Nobby did as he was told. The surrounding moorlands seemed suddenly to stand out more clearly in the gloom.

Ahead he could see a distant farmhouse, perhaps half a mile away from him yet. Its windows glowed dimly in the darkness.

"Is that it?" he asked.

"That's it." Stinko's whisper was even more hushed than before. *"That's where the bastards are."*

Nobby looked over his shoulder. Dim in the gloom at the back of the car he could make something out, a shadow within a shadow, hunched and dark. His skin prickled and he felt an almost irresistible urge to scream, to blot everything out in a hysterical shriek.

"Steady yourself, Nobby."

He clenched his fists on the steering wheel, digging his nails into the palms of his hands till they hurt.

"I'm okay," he mumbled, though he knew that he wasn't. He was far from okay.

"Pull over. If you go much further they'll hear the car."

The engine died, leaving a silence marred only by the winds still blowing across the moors. Nobby reached for the gun in his pocket. He felt an overwhelming need for its reassurance suddenly, though he knew there were only three bullets left. Three bullets against how many Gortons? he wondered.

"Come on. Stir your stumps," Stinko whispered. *"Get a move on. It won't come to you."*

Nobby fastened his coat against the gusts of wind that buffeted him as he climbed out of the car. He bowed his head against the wind as he picked his way down the lane, his feet stumbling in potholes in its muddy surface.

Soon chilled by the dampness of his clothes, Nobby shivered as he hunched his shoulders. The only improvement was that Stinko's smell was barely noticeable in the open air as the wind lashed hard into his face, snatching the breath from his mouth – and carrying Stinko's smell away with it.

It took more than quarter of an hour to trudge the rest of the way to the farmhouse. A five-bar gate hung loose at the entrance. Sliding past, Nobby noticed a car parked across the otherwise empty farmyard. He recognised it as the limousine he saw the previous day in the quarry when they met the Gortons.

Ignoring the panic in his stomach, Nobby stole towards the building. For a moment he sheltered in the lee of its walls, before moving on and creeping towards the edge of the nearest window.

Nobby licked his rain-wetted lips, narrowing his eyes as he peeped through a gap in the curtains. Beams of light, directed from spot lamps positioned about the room inside, converged on the naked body of what had once been a man, hung from ropes fastened to hooks in the ceiling. For a moment the oddity of the body's stance puzzled Nobby. For some reason it looked wrong. Only after he had been staring at it for a few minutes did he realise why. The man's legs had been broken at the knees. Ropes fastened to the blood-covered ankles had pulled the lower part of the man's legs forwards. The same had been done to his arms, beaten into a bloody pulp at their joints and bent backwards.

Nobby could not see the man's face. His head was slumped forward on his chest. Probably dead, Nobby thought, as he grimaced at the ugly wounds covering what was left of his skin, whole sections of which had been flayed from his chest and stomach to hang like a tattered skirt about his waist. Blood had dried in crusts about the exposed sinews, fat, arteries and veins.

Even as he peered with horrified fascination at the corpse's head, Nobby was certain he knew who it was. He could not fail to recognise the grey hair hanging from it, glistening with sweat. He didn't need to be able to smell him to know it was Stinko. Nobby turned away, disgust and nausea – *and fear* – filling him. He leaned against the house, too weak to move. Stinko had spoken to him only minutes ago. Again and again he'd heard his whisper. And smelt his stench. Yet the man was hanging only yards away from him, mutilated and dead, his arms and legs broken and bent out of shape. Nobby shook his head blindly, his eyes shut tight. It couldn't be. It couldn't.

Their Own Mad Demons

Someone moved inside the house. He heard heavy footsteps creak across the bare floorboards, audible even through the window. Nobby recognised Reggie Gorton at once. He was staring at Stinko's body, a can of lager in one hand and a half eaten pie in the other.

What the friggin' hell was the bastard up to? Nobby wondered in disgust, tasting bile in his throat as, for the first time, he started to feel pity for what had happened to Stinko. What kind of tortures had the bastards put the old man through before he croaked? Nobby felt sick in his stomach as he thought about it.

"You see what I mean?" The old man's stench crept near him again.

Nobby shivered. "I see."

"And now?"

"Now what? Shoot him?" Nobby felt weak with fear. Fear at what he couldn't understand. Fear at the pain, the tortures, the hideous cruelties the Gortons were capable of inflicting on their victims. Fear of what would happen to him if they caught him now – or if he did what Stinko wanted him to do and failed.

"Shoot him, Nobby. If you don't, they'll get you. Sooner or later, they'll get you too."

Nobby shook his head, unable to act – unable to do anything.

"Shoot him, Nobby. You've got to."

"I can't." Sweat covered him. It dripped from his face, running thick with salt into his mouth. "I can't."

Stinko whimpered with frustration – and pain, as if he still felt the tortures he'd been inflicted with in the farmhouse. Nobby turned to the sound. Was there something there, waiting in the shadows? The impression was vague, so intangibly faint he couldn't be sure.

"Why?" Nobby asked. "Why have you come to me?"

Stinko must have moved closer, because his smell became suddenly stronger than before.

Their Own Mad Demons

"Look, Nobby – look and see!"

Nobby turned and stared through the window again.

Reggie Gorton was not alone in the room. Three other men stood there. One of them lounged nonchalantly against the open door into the inner hallway. They were talking, but Nobby could barely make out more than a murmur. For the first time, though, he noticed the signs and symbols daubed across the bare white walls – daubed in what might have been blood. They looked evil, with jagged curves and lines, more like implements of torture than letters.

Nobby felt as if he should cross himself, but too many years had passed since the religious teachings Father Donnelly at St. Mary's had tried to drum into him when he was a boy. Instead Nobby stared into the room with a sense of numbness, unaware at first that Stinko's smell had gone. No trace of it lingered now. When he realised this, Nobby sniffed suspiciously. Stinko had gone. But why had he deserted him now?

Staring through the window, Nobby saw that Gorton had finished his pie and was stood in front of Stinko's body, his head tilted back as he swigged the last of his lager. Emptying it, he crushed the can and tossed it to one side. He raised his hands towards Stinko. His thick fingers touched the old man's chest, its raw flesh glistening with blood that had still to dry completely. Tacky, it stuck to the gangster's fingers as he drew them from it and put them to his mouth, licking them clean. Vomit threatened to rise inside Nobby's throat, and he had to force the bile back as he gritted his teeth in disgust.

Reggie Gorton produced a knife from inside his jacket. It was curiously curved. For stripping skin? Nobby wondered. The gangster stroked it down the dead man's shoulder, digging deep into his flesh, before he reached out with his other hand. He pushed his fingers beneath the dead man's rib cage, nudging them upwards towards where the heart had to be.

Nobby felt blood drain from his face.

The body moved, twisting sideways.

Reggie Gorton pushed harder.

Their Own Mad Demons

And Stinko shrieked.

Even Nobby, outside in the wind and rain, could hear the old man's scream, as Stinko threw back his head and stared at Gorton, so much agony and despair transfixed on his ravaged, mutilated face.

But he was dead. Nobby knew it. He had to be dead. There was no way the old man could still be alive, not with so much skin peeled from him?

Besides, Nobby realised, he had heard and spoken with his ghost. He'd smelt it.

Stinko was dead. He couldn't be alive. Not now.

Yet he moved. And cried. And bled as Gorton worked on his body, cutting and slicing, peeling and plunging and removing objects from deep inside him.

Nobby felt for the gun. He pulled it from his pocket and checked that it still had three shells left in its chambers.

When he looked back again Reggie Gorton had succeeded in flaying most of Stinko's shoulder. The bared flesh glistened with bright red blood. Fresh blood.

"You friggin', fuckin' bastard," Nobby muttered to himself as he raised the gun and aimed with both hands, gripping it tight. "You friggin', lousy, stinkin' bastard." He pulled on the trigger. There was a loud, almost deafening crack. Flames shot from the barrel. Glass shattered, blowing inwards as Nobby felt the heavy jolt of the gun kick in his hands, his eyes transfixed on Gorton's head. Or what remained of it as the bullet, distorted by the glass it had smashed its way through, burst bones and brain from its path before erupting in a plume of spray from the other side.

Gorton stiffened, as if hit by a massive bolt of electricity, his left leg twitching as he fell to the floor with a resounding crash.

The other men stared for an instant at the shattered window, and Nobby was able to fire once more before they turned and fled the room. Using the gun, Nobby smashed the rest of the windowpane, before hauling himself inside. Ignoring the two

Their Own Mad Demons

bodies, he ran towards the door, but the hallway was already deserted. Outside he could hear a car starting up. Breathless, he rushed to the window in time to catch sight of the car in the farmyard setting off. He fired at it, though whether he hit anything he wasn't sure. The car surged forwards, smashing through the five-bar gate, before heading at breakneck speed down the lane.

"Fuckin' idiots," Nobby muttered. Seconds later there was a squeal of brakes. The thunderous explosion that came instants later was accompanied by a massive ball of flames that highlighted the fields in its glare.

He'd have to friggin' well walk away now, Nobby thought as he watched the smoke and flames where the gangsters' car had smashed into the Fiesta he'd left down the lane.

"You did well."

Nobby shuddered. His flesh ran cold as he turned to face what was hanging from the ropes.

"What were those friggin' bastards into?" Nobby asked, his voice little more than a hushed whisper as he stared at the obscure markings on the walls.

Stinko coughed what may have been a laugh. It was the best his ravaged, ruined body could do. *"Their own mad passions,"* the old man said. *"Their own mad demons."*

"I thought you were dead." Nobby strode towards him, though the sight of what was left of the old man made him sick to his stomach.

The old man moved his head a little. It wobbled on the flayed stalk of his neck.

"I thought it were your ghost that came to me," Nobby said.

"How d'you know it weren't? How d'you know I'm not dead?"

Nobby froze.

"Fools like the Gortons use people like Stinko to conjure and trap us in their tortured flesh. It wasn't the old man they were torturing here when you looked in." The figure straightened. Its limbs moved on their broken joints as if they

were meant to be that way. "*They knew all about me. They used me to help them.*" It sniggered wetly.

Nobby grunted as he started to back away from him. Stinko's face was changing. It was changing too much.

It was changing too fast.

"*They knew how to make me do what they wanted me to do. They knew how to keep me trapped.*"

The thing that had been Stinko hauled itself free of the ropes holding it.

"*You know nothing about me, nothing at all...*" It paused for a moment, a form of humour on its bloody face as it bent beside the body of Reggie Gorton, held one of his hands, then tugged at a finger, tearing it free like a child plucking fruit. It glanced at the finger, then slid it appreciatively into its mouth. "*No, Nobby, you know nothing about me... yet.*"

WINTER BREAK

Raymond Vaughn

It is winter, and the weather is cold and miserable. And so are the people in this house. It is December; a bitter month, the month all three of us were born, and we three are bitter people. Whilst the general populace is hoping for a white Christmas, we know that ours will be a shite Christmas. Just like all the ones before.

My father has always had a reputation for being tight. People have long called him Scrooge. And oh how amusing those jokes about moths escaping, on the rare occasions that he would open his wallet.

You don't know the half of it.

Winter brings his penny-pinching ways to the fore. To keep the heating bills down we aren't allowed any. 'Put your overcoat on if you are cold,' his advice. Even the use of electric lighting is restricted. So you'll be surprised to learn that my mother *is* allowed a television. It's an old television, nearly thirty years old. But we live in a remote part of the country where the reception is poor. A watchable picture can only be achieved for two channels, and one of those is in Welsh. By contrast my father has a modern widescreen television. And a subscription to Sky. He bought it originally to watch the sport, but I often catch him watching the shopping channels. How ironic that he is happy to rack up the electricity bill watching people trying to sell him things that he will never buy.

My mother had a dog. Taking him for a walk was her only escape from this life of misery. But when her faithful companion got ill, my father would not countenance the expense of veterinary bills. If the dog did not get better it would have to be put down, was his edict.

The dog did not get better, and father shot him. No more money would be wasted on dog food.

Winter Break

I have to content myself with a simple act of rebellion – flushing the toilet. This annoys him greatly. 'A waste of water.' It's only supposed to be flushed when someone has defecated. My father's aim is poor and he often misses the bowl. You can imagine the aroma. All it needs is for some homosexuals to start hanging around to complete our bathroom's resemblance to a Gent's Public Convenience.

What's stopping me from leaving this miserable existence? you are probably thinking. Yes, I should have walked away years ago. But you could say the accident put paid to that. That happened one December, too. I slipped on a patch of ice and fell awkwardly, breaking both my legs. Rather than call an ambulance, my father decided to operate himself. 'Look on the bright side,' was what he said, 'you won't need to buy a new pair of shoes ever again.'

Well, the general populace has got its wish for a white Christmas. But irony of ironies, my father has fallen on the ice and is hurt badly.

"Get an ambulance!" he cries.

Normally only *he* is allowed to make telephone calls.

I go to him, but naturally my approach is slow. His screams increase as I get closer.

The snow glistens whitely. The red gleams so brightly upon it. You should be proud, dad. I didn't waste a bullet. The axe you used on my legs was the cheaper, logical method of dispatch.

Rather than pay for a plot in the cemetery, he has always said that when his time is up, to bury him in the garden. But the ground is frozen hard, and being stuck in this wheelchair (found on a tip, of course), I'd find the digging difficult. Burial would be such a waste, too. So, Mother and I will eat well this Christmas. And it's time mum got another dog. That would make good use of the bones, too. 'Waste not, want not.'

I learned my lessons better than you thought, dad.

DE VERMIS INFESTIS

John Llewellyn Probert

Someone had attacked M. R. James during the night.

Not the much venerated writer himself you understand, but rather Tom Parsons' paperback copy of that particular author's *Collected Ghost Stories*, the one he had left on his bedside table overnight and which was now in a considerably different state to that in which he had left it.

Tom picked up the book from its resting place and examined it. On occasion things on his bedside table got knocked to the floor during the night but this was the first time he had woken to find a book of his looking as if it had been pulled to pieces.

Or even torn to pieces, he thought. As he prodded the desiccated board of the front cover to be rewarded with a flurry of cardboard dust motes, the word 'rotting' also sprang to mind, but Tom quickly dismissed it. Decay was far too unpleasant a topic for consideration on such a sunny Wednesday morning.

Downstairs he could hear his wife Sally clattering utensils in the kitchen, invigorated by the recent lovemaking they had enjoyed as the lemonade light of early morning had pierced the chink between the curtains only hung a couple of days ago. Tom heaved himself out of the bed, pulled on a thick towelling dressing gown and drew back the pale yellow drapes that Sally had made so that he could look out of the window.

The dressing gown was for warmth rather than modesty. The chances of there being someone around to view any naked display of exhibitionism he might choose to embark on were slight out here in the wilds of the Welsh countryside, but then the absence of nosy neighbours peering over into their property from each and every angle was the main reason they had moved here. The old cottage had been going for a song, and Sally had been determined that if they were to have children they not be brought up in the city. So, now that she

De Vermis Infestis

was six months gone and everything seemed to be well, here they were.

Tom stretched and leaned on the window sill as the unusually warm autumn sun did its best to convince him that they had done the right thing. For a second he thought he caught a glimpse of something scurrying across one of the fields in the far distance, but when he blinked again it was gone. Probably a stoat or a badger, he guessed – they had things like that out here in the country, didn't they?

He turned round and looked at the bedroom. They had only been here a week but already Sally had managed to make it look like their home. The dressing table had been polished and adorned with the trinkets he had bought her on birthdays and the two wedding anniversaries they had shared; the cupboard opposite the bed was filled with neatly stacked immaculately folded linen, and the carpet, while worn, was spotless, as was the rest of the room.

Except for the bedside table. Tom frowned again as he looked over at the book. Actually, he thought, *gnawed* was actually the most appropriate – and the most worrying – adjective he could apply to the way it looked. Did the cottage have rats? He was well aware that old places like this were prone to all kinds of infestations, but the idea of rats really bothered him. Especially rats that crept into the bedroom at night, climbed up onto the bedside table and sat there chewing on the book he had just been reading, their yellowed fangs only inches from his face. Or even worse, just inches from Sally's.

He went over to the table and brushed the grey particles of half-eaten book away before Sally could spot them and blame him for messing up her nice tidy bedroom, clapped his fingers clean, tucked the volume under his arm and made his way down the creaking spiral staircase to the lounge.

He had intended to replace the book on its shelf downstairs and forget all about it, but when Tom reached the ceiling-high bookcase he realised that poor old M. R. James had not been

De Vermis Infestis

the only casualty of whatever it was that had been creeping around their house last night. The thing that obviously had quite a taste for paper.

Some of the books in the lounge had been attacked as well.

Sally's copies of *Pride and Prejudice* and *Wuthering Heights* had been reduced to little more than their covers. Two volumes of the set of Dickens Sally's mother had given them because it would 'look good for visitors' had almost entirely disappeared. At the end of one shelf the only thing left entirely untouched was a copy of *The Da Vinci Code* which one of Tom's friends had loaned his wife and which she had found herself challenged to finish. Despite his horror at this literary carnage Tom couldn't help but suppress a smirk. Whatever it was that had invaded their home last night, at least it must have had some taste.

His ruminations as to What On Earth Might Be Going On were interrupted by a cry from his wife.

"Darling! The bloody cat's got worms again!"

Glad of the distraction, Tom padded through the hallway and into the kitchen.

Boggis the cat regarded him disdainfully from just outside the open back door as Sally picked something up, wrapped it in a tissue, and threw it into the dustbin.

"Why he can't eat the tinned stuff we buy for him I'll never know," she said, pushing strands of shoulder-length auburn hair away from her face. "But oh no, he has to go out into that garden and sniffle around in all sorts of crap. I wouldn't be surprised if he's picked up something really nasty, especially as we've barely had time to sort the house out, let alone the outside." She opened the cupboard under the sink and took out a shiny can that sloshed when she shook it. "There's still some of that anti-worming stuff left from last time," she said, thrusting the can at Tom, who grimaced, but nowhere near as much as the cat seemed to as the overfed tabby gave it a knowing look.

Ten minutes later saw Tom trudging towards the shed at the

De Vermis Infestis

end of the garden, Boggis under one arm and a large uncomfortable-looking brass syringe full of Webber's Worm Away under the other.

"I don't know why you can't just behave yourself and eat the Chunky Chunks we buy for you," he said to the animal, who was already looking very sorry for itself as it recognised the preparations for a ritual it had been through on countless occasions. "I mean what could be so interesting in this bloody garden that you should want to eat it?"

The secluded cottage had come with a two acre plot of land that neither of them had especially wanted, but the location had been ideal and the price more so. Besides, Sally had said, when the summer came it would probably be nice to have somewhere to have barbecues and the like. Now though, in late October, Tom thought the stretch of land behind their new home looked distinctly unattractive, and the small barn of grey mildew-encrusted wood which had come with the house, standing over to the far left, looked less like a rustic storage haven for clean golden straw and more like the sort of place a serial killer might keep his severed mementoes.

The land itself was a broad area of tallow grassland currently shrouded by dead leaves torn from trees that grew on the bordering estate, blown across by the unforgiving Welsh winds and left to slowly rot in the late Autumn sunshine.

A broad area of tallow grassland that now had a hole in the middle of it.

Tom approached the gaping depression and frowned. It was approximately two feet square and one foot deep, and its ragged sides were threatening to cave inwards.

It hadn't been there yesterday.

"That's rather strange, don't you think?" he said to Boggis who, sensing Tom's momentary distraction, used the opportunity to claw his way to freedom. The cat dashed off into the trees where he no doubt intended to remain until he realised that Chunky Chunks were rather more tasty, and considerably more nutritious, than anything he could hope to

De Vermis Infestis

find in a dying forest at winter time. Tom hardly noticed the cat had gone as he peered into the hole.

There was something at the bottom of it.

Or rather a broken something. As Tom crouched to get a better look he realised that he was staring at the remains of a battered wooden box, the chewed-looking muslin cloth it had contained stained with earth the colour of clotted blood.

Well Boggis my old friend, whatever it was that you dug up I hope you found it tasty, thought Tom as he straightened up to look for their pet. At the time it didn't occur to him that he might never see the cat again.

Not alive, anyway.

*

"What in God's name have you got there?"

Tom realised far too late that he had probably done the wrong thing in depositing his find on Sally's kitchen table. Which she had just cleaned. And which was now covered in a mixture of earth, broken wood, filthy cloth and something else, something that Tom was picking at to try and unfold without causing it any further damage.

"Whatever it is, I think it's very old," he said, engrossed in what he was doing.

"I don't care how old it is," she said. "In fact that should have been reason enough for you not to bring it inside. And oh God it stinks!"

"It might be worth something," said Tom, finally managing to tease apart the tightly compressed layers of the parchment he had found at the bottom of the cracked casing. He had intended to fill the hole in, not wanting to leave it so that grass could overgrow its edges and conceal it, making it a hazard either he or Sally might twist an ankle from. But as he had reached for the spade he had seen something moving at the bottom. Worried that an animal might be trapped he had pushed aside the crumbling splinters of wood, meaning to

De Vermis Infestis

rescue it before covering up the box.

Which is how he had found the parchment.

He presumed it was parchment because the top left hand corner of the thick material had become folded back on itself, revealing a glimpse of spidery black handwriting. Tom had tried to unfold it there and then but the cold and the muck had made it impossible.

And so, much to the wrath of his wife, he had brought it inside, forgetting all about the creature he had thought he had seen and which had vanished anyway once he had started ferreting around in the hole.

"I've nearly finished," he said, peeling apart another layer. He lifted a hand to stop Sally just as she was about to attack it with a bottle of air-freshener.

"You might damage it!" he cried.

She refused to be put off.

"It stinks, Tom and to be honest I don't care how old or how valuable it might be," Sally said, suddenly feeling a chill and going to close the still-open back door. "I don't want it in the house. It's filthy and it's horrible and whoever buried it must have wanted it out of the way for a very good reason."

"Or they needed to hide it because it was so incredibly valuable," said Tom, his eyes gleaming with the thrill of discovery. His enthusiastic expression quickly gave way to frustration as he tried to read the document.

"I have no idea what it says," he said.

His wife wrinkled her nose as she peered over his shoulder at the black scrawl.

"Is it Welsh?" she asked.

"I don't think so," said Tom, for whom languages had never been a strong point. "It looks more like Latin."

"As if you'd know," said his wife, fetching a cardboard box from beneath the kitchen sink and thrusting it at him. "But at least that's an end to it. You can put all that crap in here and then leave it for the dustman tomorrow."

Tom took another look at the tiny cramped letters on the

De Vermis Infestis

greasy stained parchment, noting how certain words had been underlined and the way the script became more illegible towards the end of the document, almost as if the person writing had been rushing to finish it.

"I can't throw it out," he said. "It might be important. It might even relate to this cottage."

Sally paused. Her husband had a point. Maybe he'd stumbled on some sort of ancient charter that granted them sole rights to the land without them ever having to pay the mortgage. Or more worryingly, perhaps it somehow confirmed that the land belonged to someone else and they would have to leave. Either way it was probably best for them to hang onto it. For now.

*

Boggis failed to return that evening, which was extremely unusual for a cat so domesticated Tom had often commented on how he really needed a valet service to do his licking for him.

"He's probably found some gorgeous lady cat who's showing him the joys of country life," said Sally with a grin as she finished her wine and regarded Tom with the hungry look he had come to know so well.

As she led him upstairs neither of them heard the weak mewing accompanied by the scraping noise that came from the fireplace.

*

The village boasted little in the way of shops other than a newsagents-cum-grocers run by Martin Walton, a burned out thirty-five-year-old investment banker who could barely manage a proper facial expression let alone a smile as Tom handed over money for his paper the next day.

"I don't suppose you know of anyone around here who

De Vermis Infestis

specialises in antiques, do you?" Tom asked as he scrutinised his change.

It took a little while for Martin to register that he had been asked a question, and even longer to formulate his reply, by which time an elderly lady with a small but angry dog was behind Tom waiting to pay for her copy of one of the more perniciously unpleasant national dailies.

"There's no antique shop around here as far as I know," Martin managed to drawl after much thought. "I've no idea who might know either."

Tom ignored what sounded suspiciously like a harrumph behind him and tried again.

"How about someone who might know a little local history? Perhaps a collector or someone who runs a local society for that sort of thing?"

Martin shook his head. Tom grimaced as he felt a tap on his shoulder.

"All right," he snapped, turning to face the old lady. "I'm sorry for holding you up."

"All I wanted to say to you, young man," she said as her dog attempted to endear itself to Tom's leg, "is that the person you would be best talking to would be Ralph Peterson. My husband sold him quite a few items of antique erotica some years ago and I believe he has an interest in local history as well."

Tom immediately apologised, smiled his most charming smile and asked where Mr Peterson might be found. He was rewarded with the address of the local pub and a worrying rubbing sensation against his foot. Eager to be on his way but feeling guilty that he had initially felt such animosity towards her he pointed at the newspaper headline and said:

"Terrible what some people can get up to isn't it?"

She glanced at the hysterical caption and smiled.

"Oh I dare say it's a load of old bollocks," she said. "I only buy the sodding thing to make sure they haven't made any more spurious allegations about *me*."

De Vermis Infestis

*

On first impression the Royal Oak shared, along with the same name as at least a hundred other country pubs, the kind of suspicious attitude towards strangers that would have had Tom turning on his heel the moment he walked inside if he hadn't wanted something. The presumed landlord barked something at him in Welsh and when Tom shrugged his shoulders the man shifted his tone from confrontational to patronising.

"And what can I get for you, sir?"

Tom ordered a pint of bitter. When he was offered a choice he obviously picked the wrong one, judging by the grimace it produced, one that might quite conceivably have taken more effort to achieve than the drawing of the thick creamy ale that followed.

"I wonder if you can help me?"

Tom already had a good idea of what the man's response would be but he still had to try, and when he mentioned Peterson's name he was met by a stony silence as the man took his money, opened the till, brought him his change, and continued to say nothing.

Right, thought Tom. I've got to try and earn this bloke's respect, and there's only one way I know that I might be able to do that.

He picked up his glass, and with the measured practice of many evenings spent in University bars when he should have been revising for exams, downed the beer in three seconds. He stifled a hiccup, congratulated himself on still being able to maintain his record, and then with as straight a face as possible said:

"A little woody and with a decent aftertaste. Not as smooth as Old Peculiar but a damned sight better than McRumbly's Bowel Basher."

Now, for the first time, there was a trace of a grin on the landlord's face.

De Vermis Infestis

"Can't say I've heard of that one, sir," he said.

"That's because I just made it up," said Tom with a smile. "After all if I'm going to be a regular here I need to be assured that you know your stuff as well." He pointed to the next tap along. "I'll try that one next if that's okay."

"Certainly," said the landlord, reaching for a fresh glass after introducing himself with a friendly handshake as Dan Lewis. As he pulled the second pint he said that by way of an apology and as a gesture of goodwill he would be happy to sell Tom a barrel at a discount price, to which Tom thought he had better readily agree as Dan handed the beer over. "And that should keep you going until Ralph arrives," said the publican. "He's usually here around lunchtime."

Tom sipped at his second pint.

"Could you point him out to me when he comes in?"

The landlord leaned forward.

"He buys and sells old porn and he's into local history. You won't be able to miss him."

Sure enough Ralph Peterson wore a bright yellow cravat, a magenta velvet jacket and sported a carnation of a colour undreamed of by mother nature. He ordered a large Campari and soda, sat in the corner near the fireplace, and was perusing the lunch menu when Tom approached him.

"Can I help you, dear boy?" said the elderly man, radiating mixed messages.

"I hope so," said Tom, sitting next to him but not too close. "I was told you deal in antiques?"

Peterson put down the menu.

"Dan always knows I order the same thing anyway," he said with a grin at the landlord, who had already instructed his wife to heat up one of their steak and kidney pies. "I suppose it would be more accurate to say I deal in esoterica. Why, do you have something that might be of interest to me?"

Tom looked apologetic as he produced the cardboard carton he had been dragging around with him all morning.

"I really don't know," he said. "My cat dug this up in the

De Vermis Infestis

back garden yesterday. It could be something interesting, on the other hand it could just be the result of some mad old woman hiding something she thought was important. That parchment was lying at the bottom."

Peterson took a sip of his Campari, looked into the carton and regarded the grimy splinters and the filthy muslin bag with a grimace.

"My dear boy whatever it is it's hardly something to be discussed at lunchtime," he said, before giving Tom a lugubrious wink. "But seeing as you seem such a nice chap let's see what the parchment says."

They moved their drinks onto another table and spread the sheet out. Peterson's face fell.

"Oh dear," he said. "Latin."

"You can't translate it then?" said Tom.

The other man shook his head.

"Used to be able to, and a bit of Greek as well – New Testament stuff rather than classical – but it's been so long that any vestiges of what Mr Hardacre beat into me at school vanished around the time we entered the Common Market. It's rather odd, though – such a modern document being written in the language."

"Modern?" said Tom. "You mean this hasn't been in the ground very long?"

That caused Peterson to laugh uproariously.

"That depends on what you consider to be long my dear chap. The date's written at the bottom – see?" He pointed to the last line, below the scrawled signature. "Eighteen hundred and twenty three. Modern by my standards, but still long enough ago to make this worth looking at."

All pretence at disinterest had now vanished and Peterson ignored the plate of steaming food that had been brought over to him as he gently lifted out the pieces of wood.

"Yew," he said, using what looked like his front door key to scratch the muck from the piece he was holding. "Known for its magical properties. And when you combine it with this," he

De Vermis Infestis

held up the stained muslin bag, its torn holes now all the more obvious, "which if you tested it would probably be shown to contain a mixture of linen and hemp, then we could indeed have something quite fascinating here. Where did you find it?"

Tom told him and Peterson clapped his pale hands in excitement.

"My dear boy, how odd that you should mention the phrase: 'mad old woman'!" he said, his face far more animated now than it had been when Tom had introduced himself. "Because there really was someone of that sort who lived there around the turn of the nineteenth century. The only reason I know is because it's such a good story. You see – anyone who dared challenge her tended to meet with a ghastly fate."

Tom wasn't sure he wanted to know but he asked anyway.

"Accidents you mean?"

"Not exactly. The person in question would be found in their bed, dead, dried blood running from their eyes and ears. And when they moved them…"

Tom leaned forward as Peterson took another sip of his Campari.

"What?"

The old man paused, obviously preparing to relish what he was about to say.

"When they moved them, in every case they found that the back of their skull had been eaten away. Their empty skull."

Tom coughed a mouthful of beer back into his pint glass.

"You mean something had eaten their brain?" he said.

"Or torn it out, yes," said Peterson, selecting a particularly chunky piece of beef and chewing on it thoughtfully. He tapped on the parchment. "You had better keep this safe somewhere, just in case anything odd happens around your house."

Tom's expression made it obvious that it already had.

"Go on then," said Peterson, "tell me."

As Tom explained about the carnage rent on his library Peterson began to look worried.

De Vermis Infestis

"To be honest I'm not sure what to suggest," he said. "The most likely explanation is that you've got an infestation of something that has a taste for paper, and what you've dug up probably has nothing to do with it. For all I know this parchment here could just be a list of recipes that have been buried for posterity. But I'd suggest you get it translated. Just in case."

"Just in case what?" said Tom

Peterson leaned closer.

"I am an old man with a penchant for the weird and the macabre, and an overactive imagination that has got me into trouble in the past so please take what I say with a pinch or even a pillar of salt. But I would get that translated just in case that old woman created things to serve her that had a desperate appetite for knowledge. Things that she turned on her enemies and which consumed their brains in their hunger for something filled with learning. And perhaps they got out of control, or perhaps she ran out of enemies and had no further use for them. And what if the only way she could safely get rid of these things was to bury them in the garden, wrapped in something that could provide mystic protection, perhaps even with some handy instructions in case they got out again. I would get that translated just in case those things have now escaped and for the moment are contenting themselves with receptacles of learning that probably weren't that common in a Welsh village over two hundred years ago. Because sooner or later your house is going to run out of books. And then what are they going to do?"

Tom downed the rest of his second pint. The fact that this strange old man had probably just fed him a load of nonsense did little to change the fact that he still felt unreassuringly sober.

"Do you know anyone who could translate it?"

"I got very very drunk with that young Dr Rawlings once," said Peterson. "And we ended up throwing Latin quotes at each other that we could occasionally half remember the

De Vermis Infestis

meaning of. He's the only person I know of around here who might be able to help you."

It also helped that Sally was due a check-up with Rawlings the day after tomorrow.

*

"Well everything seems to be fine."

Harry Rawlings looked about the same age as Tom and effused the kind of quiet confidence that had made both Tom and Sally glad that he was their GP, especially now that Sally was pregnant and the nearest hospital was far enough away that if a local doctor should be needed to attend an urgent birth it would be Harry doing the honours. At the end of the consultation Sally left but Tom hung back. He had explained to his wife last night what Peterson had said and that, combined with the fact that when they had woken up this morning many of Sally's cookery books had been reduced to tatters had convinced her that translating the parchment might be a good idea. But only, she had emphasised, if Tom also agreed to call in a good exterminator to deal with the far more likely cause of the problem.

"Something bothering you, Tom?" said the doctor, closing Sally's file and returning it to his 'Out' tray.

Tom looked uneasy, which prompted Harry to reassure him that it was unlikely to be anything he hadn't had to deal with before.

Before, that was, he heard what Tom had to say.

"I'm sure you won't be surprised to learn that I've never had anyone try to avail me of my translating abilities before!" Harry said, scratching his head and grinning in bemusement at Toms' request. "To be honest my Latin's probably as bad as Peterson's. I think I've still got a Latin dictionary somewhere but you'd probably be better off taking that parchment down to Cardiff."

Tom explained that he had tried ringing the university, but

De Vermis Infestis

because it was term time anyone sufficiently qualified was either too busy teaching or setting exams. He had however been assured that someone would be happy to take a look at it for him once term was over.

Which was in six weeks' time.

"If you could just give us an idea of what it says," said Tom, trying hard not to sound as if he was pleading. "I'd hate for there to have been anything in that box that could be a threat to Sally."

"Well at the risk of sounding a little less than sympathetic do you realise how completely daft that sounds?" said Harry, realising even as he uttered the words that they were unlikely to have much effect on his patient's husband. "But if it makes you feel any better I'll come and have a look at it this evening. Just as long as you understand that I'm not promising anything."

Tom nodded and made a mental note to have a case of something nice delivered to Harry's home for Christmas this year.

If he and Sally were still here then.

*

"It feels horrible," said Harry, wrinkling his nose. "And it smells a bit."

"Well it's been in your lovely Welsh earth for who knows how long so don't blame me," said Tom with a forced smile.

Rawlings pinched a tiny corner of the parchment and carefully teased it apart before frowning at the cramped, smeared inky black handwriting. It started off neat and well-spaced, but towards the bottom of the page the words became cramped, the letters running into each other and becoming far less legible.

"Looks like they got bored towards the end," said Tom.

"Either that or they were in an awful hurry," said Harry, pointing at the last few squiggles. "These are barely the

De Vermis Infestis

beginnings of words, I'm afraid. I'm not going to be of much help with those."

"Can you read any of it?" asked Sally who had been feigning disinterest since Tom had sat Harry down at the kitchen table but had now come over to stand behind him.

Harry frowned

"I might be able to, but don't forget my Latin's pretty rusty, and for all we know the person who wrote this might not have exactly had an 'A' Level in it so some of the original meaning might get rather lost in my very poor translation."

"Would you mind having a go anyway?" said Tom, sensing the doctor's reluctance.

Harry reached for the dictionary he had brought with him.

"Okay," he said. "Let's take a look at the title."

He pointed at the spidery script at the top of the page beneath which a line had been drawn.

"'*De Vermis Sapientis*'" he read aloud. "That probably means 'Concerning the Worms of Wisdom', or something like that."

Sally muffled a giggle. "Clever worms?" she said

"No, not exactly," said Rawlings, his expression darkening as he read further down the page. "There's a passage here that translates as something like 'By day they sleep in the warmth of the soul, by night they forage for the food of the mind.'"

"What's that supposed to mean?"

Rawlings looked at Tom.

"Well I suspect there's a lot of poetic licence involved. How old did Mr Peterson say this box was?"

"He wasn't sure either," said Tom. "But the parchment has the date 1823 at the bottom."

"Well that makes it Victorian," said Harry, "and of course the Victorians used all sorts of euphemisms to try and get across what they were actually trying to say."

As Sally leaned over Harry's shoulder to take a closer look at the manuscript the grating damp odour Harry had been trying to ignore caught in the back of her throat.

De Vermis Infestis

"Why?" she coughed.

"Lots of reasons. To make it sound more important, to keep secrets from the uneducated lower classes, and, of course, if the subject matter was extremely distasteful. Such unsavoury matters could only be mentioned using the subtlest of implications by a gentleman of breeding."

"Or a lady," said Sally, still wrinkling her nose.

Harry winked at her. "I don't think such matters would have been considered the province of lady gentlefolk," he said.

"Well this one was," she replied, braving the stink of the document to lean over his shoulder and point at the painfully inscribed signature.

Tom peered at it as well.

"Leonora... something," said Harry. "Unless it was a Leonard with supremely bad handwriting."

"Or gender issues," said Tom, ignoring Sally's 'don't be so stupid' expression.

"Okay, so we've got clever worms that come out at night," she said, doing her best not to sound as disturbed as she was feeling. "Anything else?"

"It's a real mess I'm afraid," said Rawlings. "The handwriting is either terrible or those words that would otherwise be legible have been smeared by the damp. There's something about if the worms escape then there's a way to get them back into the box, but my Latin must be worse than I thought."

"Why?" said Sally, pulling at the fingernail she realised she had been unconsciously biting.

"Because the method for getting them to return is so disgusting that I'm either horribly wrong or whoever wrote this must have been raving mad."

"Hang on," said Sally. "Are you saying that worms that must be over two hundred years old have got out of that box, been crawling around our house at night, eating our books, and then going somewhere to hide in the daytime?"

"*I'm* not saying it," said Harry, holding up the parchment by the tips of his fingers. "Whoever wrote *this* is saying it."

"Never mind that," said Tom, scowling at his wife. "What else does it say?"

"You don't want to know," said Rawlings with an exaggerated grimace as he got up to leave. "Or at least you don't want my piss-poor attempts at translation scaring you unnecessarily. Look, I have to get going. If I were you I'd bury that nonsense back where you found it."

"Really?"

Rawlings gave a wistful smile.

"Actually no – I'd probably try to translate it, wasting hours and hours when I could be doing something far more worthwhile."

"Would you mind?" said Sally, giving him one of her best imploring looks.

The doctor shook his head.

"I'll already be in the doghouse with my wife for being here so late, so I'd better leave you to follow this one up on your own."

*

The exterminator arrived the next day. The tall scrawny man wore a white overall with a badge over the left breast that said his name was Dave Tipton and that he worked for the charmingly named BUG GerOff! Exterminating Company. He took one look at the Parsons' lounge, whistled, and explained that he would be 'all day on this one'.

Which allowed Tom and his wife the opportunity to spend the day together getting to know the area a little better. They visited two castles and a museum dedicated to Welsh cuisine, and by the middle of the afternoon found themselves in a small teashop after Sally had expressed a craving for scones. Pots of jam and a mountain of clotted cream were being delivered to the table when she frowned and clutched at her belly.

"Are you all right?" Tom asked.

De Vermis Infestis

"Just a bit of indigestion I think," said his wife with a pained smile.

"Well it wouldn't surprise me," he said. After all they'd had the most enormous lunch, again at Sally's insistence, only a couple of hours ago. "That second helping of ginger cheesecake you had was huge."

"It was also delicious," said Sally, just starting to relax as another cramp hit her and she almost doubled over.

"That's not good," said Tom getting to his feet. "I'm taking you to the hospital."

"Oh no you're bloody well not," his wife gasped, leaning on the table for support as she stood up. "I'm not hanging around in casualty for hours just because of a bit of wind. It's the food and those bloody winding roads. All I need is a lie down."

"All right," said Tom, not at all convinced. "We'll forget the cream teas and get you back home. Mr Tipton ought to have finished by now."

He had, but as they came through the door it was obvious the exterminator wanted to tell Tom something on his own, so when Sally went up to the bedroom Tom followed the man into the lounge.

"Have you got a cat?" Tipton asked.

Tom nodded.

"Or at least we did have," he said. "We haven't seen him for a couple of days."

"Thought as much," said the exterminator, pointing at something he had draped with one of his protective white sheets. "Big tabby by any chance?"

Tom felt a chill at the base of his spine.

"Yes."

"Figured that might be the case," said Mr Tipton, raising the sheet "Found him stuck near the bottom of the chimney. That's why I covered him up. Not nice for you to both to walk in here and come face to face with something like this, especially not with your missus being in the state she is."

Tom said nothing as he stared open mouthed at the

De Vermis Infestis

desiccated corpse of Boggis. Poor old Boggis, who in a last resort to warm himself must have climbed up onto the roof of the cottage and fallen down the chimney where his plaintive wails had gone unheard until such a time as he was too weak to cry any more. He must have died shortly afterwards and then his body had stayed there until it had been retrieved unceremoniously by Mr Tipton. And that gaping rent in his belly must have been caused by his fall down the chimney.

Mustn't it?

Tom frowned.

They need something warm to hide inside, to allow them to digest their food.

Tom shook his head. The idea was too horrible, too impossible to contemplate. And yet it was most likely Boggis who had somehow unearthed that box in the first place, probably by breaking the thin surface of earth covering it with his considerable weight than by any actual effort on his part.

But if Boggis had been dead for some time, then how had the worms managed to survive? The only other living things in the house were him and Sally.

Sally.

Oh God.

Sally had touched one of them. When he had come into the kitchen that afternoon he had seen her putting it into the dustbin.

He snorted at the absurdity of the thought that had just entered his head. Sally was fit and well. Heavily pregnant, yes. but that was hardly cause for concern. They couldn't exactly be hiding inside her, could they?

Could they?

They need somewhere warm to live during the day.

And the cat was dead.

And Tom felt fine.

Which only left—

He hurried Mr Tipton out, signing the cheque and not quibbling over the fee. The man was scarcely in his BUG

De Vermis Infestis

GerOff! van before Tom was running up the stairs to the bedroom.

Sally was asleep, her belly seeming to swell with every breath she was taking.

Tom jammed a knuckle in his mouth. He felt close to panic, even though the rational part of him was still convinced that the whole thing was ridiculous, that there was a logical explanation for all that had happened. Even for the bloody cat ending up dead in the fireplace.

But then he saw something move. Or rather several somethings.

Just beneath the surface of her skin.

Tom stood and watched in horror as his sleeping wife's belly rippled and undulated, and it was only when the squirming unnatural movements had settled down again that he was able to prise himself away from her.

With a terrifying task ahead of him.

*

"Hi Harry. I'm sorry about ringing you when you're in surgery."

"That's all right," said the voice on the other end of the phone. "Is everything all right with Sally?"

Tom gripped the receiver so tightly he heard the plastic crack.

"She's... fine." Or at least she would be, if he could work out what to do.

"You don't sound sure," said Rawlings, sounding concerned. "I can come over if you like – I really don't mind."

Tom thought of her swollen figure on the bed upstairs.

"No Harry – that's fine. I was actually ringing about something else completely unrelated." Did that sound convincing? Tom hoped so.

"Completely unrelated, eh?" said the voice, lightening considerably. "Well if it's about investing in fine wine I'm

De Vermis Infestis

your man. Just don't expect me to know anything about gardening or how to fix the car."

"Actually it's sort of about the garden," said Tom, grateful for having been given a way of steering the conversation round. "Do you remember that thing I dug up? That parchment I asked you to take a look at for me?"

There was a pause.

"Yes," said Rawlings. "Although I must admit I thought by now you would have got rid of that."

"It's just that I remember you saying there was something on it about how to get the worms back in the box."

This time there was a longer pause before Tom eventually heard Harry's voice again.

"Tom, what are you up to? Are you sure you're okay?"

"Fine," said Tom, feeling anything but. "It's just I've found someone who might be interested in buying it but they want more of an idea of what the words might mean. I haven't got the time to go down to Cardiff and talk to anyone there but I wondered if you might be able to give me an idea of what the rest of it said."

"It's probably best if I don't," said Harry. "I very much suspect I didn't translate it properly anyway – that's why I didn't tell you."

"If you could just give me a vague idea I'm sure that would be enough," said Tom, adding a mental *please* to the statement.

"Well – if it'll help you get rid of the bloody thing I suppose it can't hurt," said Harry, not sounding at all happy. "The last bit of writing said something about how the box needed to be filled with 'the knowledge and learning a man might glean during his lifetime'."

"What," said Tom. "Do you mean you have to fill the box with encyclopaedias?"

"No. But I'm sure that should be enough for your buyer," said Harry, sounding as if he was about to put the phone down.

"But it doesn't make sense!" said Tom, trying to stop

De Vermis Infestis

himself from shouting into the mouthpiece. "He won't buy it if it doesn't make sense!"

He could hear Harry taking a deep breath.

"Think about it, Tom," he said. "What contains a man's 'lifetime of knowledge and learning'?"

It took a while for Tom to realise what Harry meant, and when he did his mouth went so dry he could barely croak the words.

"You mean whoever buried that box in the garden must have smeared the insides of it with... with..."

"Yes. I trust you're not going to blame me for putting you off your tea?"

Tom thought it unlikely that he could feel any sicker than he did right at that moment.

"No. Thanks, Harry. That's been very helpful."

Tom dropped the receiver onto the cradle, gripped the edge of the table, and fought back waves of nausea.

There was a scream from upstairs.

And a knock on the door.

Tom raced up the wooden steps, tripping at the top and nearly sending himself sprawling. He looked at Sally and realised with relief that she must have cried out in her sleep. Her hands were clasped over her swollen belly and Tom had to try hard not to imagine that he could see things moving beneath the blankets. Things writhing, things wriggling, things desperate to be outside in the open air again and foraging, foraging before they once again returned to—

There was another knock. Harder this time.

Satisfied that for the moment his wife was unharmed, Tom did his best to stop himself shaking as he made his way back down the stairs to answer the front door.

Where he found Dan Lewis waiting for him.

"Well I did say I'd bring that barrel over!" the publican said, stepping back to reveal the shiny container he must have rolled up the garden path. "Now where do you want me to put it?"

Well it wouldn't fit in the house, thank God, thought Tom.

De Vermis Infestis

So the best place for it would be...

"The barn," he said, again giving thanks that his keys were in his pocket so he didn't have to go back inside and risk Lewis hearing Sally scream again. "Come on – I'll give you a hand."

In the early evening darkness they rolled the barrel around the corner of the house. Tom fumbled with his keys and hoped Lewis wouldn't see how much he was shaking as he pulled the door open and switched on the light. The landlord rolled the barrel over to the far wall as Tom closed the door behind him.

"Keeping it for a rainy day, eh?" said Lewis, giving the steel a friendly pat and turning round to see Tom coming straight at him with a pitchfork. The publican barely had time to scream as the rusty spikes punctured his throat and reduced his scream to a throaty gurgle. He fell forward and flopped to the earthen floor as the pitchfork was pulled out. Tom had no idea what he was going to do with the body yet, his impulsiveness having been fuelled by the darkness, the location, and the thought that he might not get another opportunity.

He stood there, thinking for a moment. Then he went back into the house to fetch the box.

And a hacksaw.

*

The whole job took a lot less time that Tom expected and about an hour later, having showered and changed into fresh clothes so that he could burn the others he found himself climbing the stairs to their bedroom. The box, the insides of its wooden walls smeared with what he hoped would be enough of what the worms needed, was tucked under his arm and wrapped in greaseproof paper to stop any fluids from trickling through the gaps and staining his shirt.

He pushed open the door, and was relieved to see that Sally hadn't changed her position from when he had last checked on her. He put down the box, bent over and kissed her forehead

De Vermis Infestis

before peeling back the blankets and lifting up her nightgown. Then he picked up the wooden case again, stood at the foot of the bed, and lifted the lid.

"Come on!" he hissed when nothing happened. "What are you waiting for?"

He waved the box up and down, hoping that the odour of the publican's brain that was already beginning to become too much for him would soon reach the creatures inside his wife's body and cause them to leave her.

Nothing.

Tears filled his eyes as he realised his efforts had been in vain. The brain of a Welsh pub landlord obviously wasn't as attractive to them as his educated girlfriend's womb. He staggered back downstairs, the box once again beneath his arm, wondering what the hell he was going to do now.

Which was when the phone rang.

He was tempted to ignore it, but something told him that if he didn't answer then whoever was phoning might come over and he couldn't risk that, so he picked up the receiver.

It was Harry Rawlings.

"I'm sorry to be the one bothering you this time, Tom," said the doctor. "But you sounded so shaken up and so entirely unlike your usual self I had to ring before I turned in just to make sure there wasn't anything seriously wrong."

Tom looked at the box he had put to rest on the chair next to the telephone table, the box that even now was seeping pale brown bloodstained matter onto its greaseproof covering.

The box that needed to be smeared in more than the brain of one of the locals to satisfy the creatures inhabiting his wife.

"Actually I am a bit worried about Sally," he said. Which was true.

"In what way?"

"Well," and here Tom didn't have to fake the tears, "she's upstairs now, but she really doesn't look well at all, and I can't get her to wake up. I really don't know what to do."

"If she's that bad your best bet is to ring for an ambulance,"

De Vermis Infestis

said Harry.

Oh God no that wouldn't do! Tom did his best to keep his voice steady. "She hates hospitals," he said, still saying nothing but the truth. "I'd hate for her to come to and find herself in one. Couldn't you come and look at her? If it's bad enough then I can take her to the hospital myself."

"You don't sound fit to drive to be honest, Tom, but if it makes you feel any better I'll come out."

Tom put down the receiver and began clearing the furniture from the hallway to make a space for the body to fall.

*

Harry Rawlings was more difficult to take care of than the landlord, but that was because Tom was in such a hurry he didn't check to make sure Harry was dead before he started to saw open his skull. Scarcely had he drawn the serrated edge of the hacksaw across the doctor's scalp when Rawlings began to struggle. Panicking, Tom dragged the blade across the doctor's throat and held him down until he stopped writhing on the floor before going back to what he had been doing.

He was halfway up the stairs when a scream that could wake the dead came from the bedroom. He pulled open the door and almost skidded on the blood that had been caused by his wife's injuries, and as he regarded the scarlet writhing forms on the bed Tom realised three things:

That there was no hope for his wife.

That the box was far too small.

And, as the squirming horde of wriggling things dropped to the floor and began to make their way with frightening speed towards him, he realised that he was by far the cleverest living thing in the house at that moment.

NO SUCH THING AS A FRIENDLY

Richard Staines

The heat was rotten. The flies were everywhere. And it was pissing down with rain. When I had been called into the England B team it wasn't what I'd expected. I'd never even heard of Goboya, and when I found out it was some island off the coast of South America, I imagined sun-kissed beaches and dusky-skinned birds in bikinis. Instead the team had got off the plane and straight onto a clapped-out motor coach driven by some chattering old darkie. Goboya had recently been a British colony, and, before independence in 1965, had been called Prince Albert Island. But it didn't look anything like home.

Five miles along a rutted road, crawling through a steaming jungle, it had started to rain. Not cold rain like in England, this was tropical. It was like pissing in a sauna. The motor coach got jammed in potholes, and we were crying out for cold beer. We could only puff on our smokes and look at each other with disbelief.

It was the 14th of June 1970, and while the England A team were defending the World Cup in sunny Mexico, having already made the quarter-finals by the time we arrived in Goboya, we were given the shitty end of the stick. What was the point of a friendly match against Goboya? No one had even heard of the country. Sir Alf Bloody Ramsey thought it was a good idea that's why. And having won us the World Cup last time around, no one at the FA dared questioned his decisions. The England A team sung 'back home, they'll be thinking about us while we are far away'. Alf's boys were up there in the pop hit parade. We'd be lucky to get one line in the back pages of a Sunday tabloid newspaper. Our song should have been 'back home, no one gives a toss.'

Half the players the FA had called up had cried off the South American friendly tour. It was only against the countries that hadn't qualified for Mexico 1970 anyway. All the players from

No Such Thing as a Friendly

the glamour clubs, Chelsea, both Manc clubs, both Scouse clubs, Derby and Leeds: none of them wanted to know. So we'd wound up with a bunch of Second Division kids, except for me, the odd man out. The veteran. First up Goboya, then Suriname, and finally Paraguay. Alf had said we weren't to play the Argentines because they were animals, and he still hated them, and that business with Bobby Moore and the nicked bracelet in Bogota meant that Colombia had been taken off the list of opponents too.

So they'd made me captain. Me, Vince Kemble of Crystal Palace F.C. Aged 34, and almost past it in football years! The club had finished twentieth in the First Division, avoiding relegation by one point. I was stupid enough to accept, not old enough to know better.

Had I been told that they'd also chosen Mad Mickey Clinch as our coach, there's no way I'd have agreed to go. The bloke was a nutcase. Mad Clinch with his glass eye. He was not the *manager* on paper of course, no, that was Sir Alf himself, and he had his hands full right now up in Mexico, what with the World Cup and all. But it was Mad Clinch in charge of us in practice. He was between clubs at the moment. And everyone knew why. He played football as a game of war, not of skill. Mad Mickey Clinch. One-Eyed Clinch. Lost the other one fighting the Japs in Burma. He'd lost his marbles there too.

I remember him saying on the motor coach, looking at our sullen faces as it pissed down outside:

"Oi, Lads! Get those fucking frowns off your faces! You're representing England now. We're the World Champions!"

You know, he looked like the Sergeant Major from that film *Zulu*. He really did. Right down to the mutton-chops.

"Oi, Lads! Remember one thing: put the boot in." That was his philosophy. If you come across some coon or dago who's too skilful and mucks you about:

Put the boot in.

And he meant it too. Either you put the boot into their players as instructed, or he'd put the boot into you when he got

No Such Thing as a Friendly

you back in the changing room.

After a couple of hours, the motor coach arrived at Victoria Town, which seemed to me less like a capital city and more like a collection of wooden shacks nailed together and dropped down the side of a mountain. Clinch was first off the coach, and started doing ridiculous star-jumps outside in the warm rain. A couple of the players were looking at him like he'd escaped from Colney Hatch. I wouldn't argue about that, myself. It seemed likely.

Come on lads, he said, keep yourselves supple! The match kicks off in three hours! He was so preoccupied, he didn't notice us laughing.

Then we sloped off towards the hotel, a grotty little place where the FA had decided we'd stay. We dumped our bags and immediately the team went to the bar, while Clinch sorted out our reservations with the receptionist. Most of us liked to play with a couple of stiff drinks inside us: it helped calm the nerves. Common practice at certain clubs. But Mad Clinch was having none of it. As soon as he found us there in the bar, he went mental. He kicked over a couple of tables, smashed glasses, and got Derek Phelps, our seventeen-year-old goalie from third division champions Orient, in a headlock.

Clinch made us play dominoes instead. Something about building team spirit. He'd slam those dominoes on the table like he was nailing them down.

An hour before kick-off it had stopped raining and we got back on the coach and were driven to the ground, which was about 10 minutes away. We passed crowds of people on the streets, all darkies carrying yellow and blue Goboya flags. They banged and spat on the sides of the coach as we crawled through the narrow streets. When we saw the ground we were shocked. For a national stadium it was a joke. I reckon it had a 3,000 capacity. There was a big sign outside saying:

THE GOBOYA NATIONAL STADIUM.

Well, it should have said that. Trouble is, it actually said:

THE GOB YA NATION L TADIUM.

No Such Thing as a Friendly

Some of the letters had fallen off.

Mad Clinch had started whistling the theme tune from *Zulu*, and kept trying to encourage us all to join in, but only Phelps did, and he hadn't seen the film. The poor kid was probably terrified of being the victim of another headlock.

We got inside the stadium sharpish. The away team changing rooms stank to high heaven. At least there was a bathroom, if you call a closet with a shit hole in a floor and overhead cold-water tap a bathroom.

Mad Clinch went over his tactics for the match, smashing his fist against the door when he thought we weren't paying enough attention. We were playing some bloody fool formation that required me to run around man marking as if I was ten years younger. Still, it was no surprise that his main instruction was to kick the Goboyans off the park if we found ourselves in trouble early on.

Well, when we finally got out on the pitch, it was a shock. There were three thousand screaming darkies in the stands, and not a single white face amongst them. A chorus of boos and whistles greeted us as we warmed up. Then the ref and linesmen came on, and they were all as black as the ace of spades too. It didn't look good. They even had armed police out there!

And then the Goboyan team came out. And things looked worse. A deafening roar went up from the crowd, and I swear, rather than 3,000 they sounded like 30,000. They began to sing:

GO BO YAH! GO BO YAH! GO BO YAH!

I watched the Goboyans warming up and couldn't see anything special about them, except for this one kid. He didn't look more than fifteen to me, but he did keepy-uppy like nothing I'd seen before. Knees, both feet, heels, back of his calves, head, the lot, the whole bag of tricks. And from the number on the back of his shirt, 10, I realised I was supposed to be marking him.

Just my luck.

No Such Thing as a Friendly

The ref blew for kick off and we were underway. The crowd were on our backs right from the start.

I heard a few shouts of: *Hey whitey!* A couple of times a coin whistled past my head, but I ignored the provocation. I had my hands full keeping up with that number 10. He was more slippery than a tart's gusset.

The Goboyans weren't as good a team as us, no doubt about it. They had no proper organisation, and ran around the pitch like a bunch of headless chickens. Still, they were fitter than we were, and not afraid of us.

Well, the first time that number 10 got the ball, one of those new black and white Telstar ones, he nutmegged me and raced off straight towards goal. I panted and puffed after him, but all I saw was the back of his yellow and blue shirt in the distance. He did a body swerve around one of our centre backs, left another one flat on his arse after a mistimed sliding tackle, and the next thing I knew our goalie Phelps was picking up the ball from the back of our net.

Goboya (1) England B (0)

As the two teams made their way back to their halves of the pitch for the restart, I asked one of the Goboyans who their number 10 was.

"His name's Winston Pietas Les Saintes, we call him Genio for short, and he's going to win us the match," the Goboyan said, flashing me a big white smile.

I looked over at the bench and saw Mad Clinch sat there. He had a fag burning away, hanging lifelessly from his bottom lip. His arms were crossed and his expression was furious. His face was redder than a smacked arse. Unless I could stop this Genio kid, Clinch would be banging my head against the door at half time, and not his fist.

From the restart, it was obvious that the Goboyans were trying to get the ball to Genio as much as possible. He was their secret weapon. The crowd started chanting his name.

GENIO! GENIO! GENIO! GO FOR GOAL, GENIO!

The next time he got the ball, I dived in with a hard tackle. I caught him with my studs on the ankle and he went down. The thing is, he didn't make a meal of it. Didn't roll around on the pitch, screaming for the ref. He just lay there for a while as the ref blew for a foul and then booked me. When Genio got up he looked me straight in the eyes. There wasn't any malice in his stare. Only pity. I swear he felt sorry for me.

Well, after that I lost the desire to try and chop him down. I tried to play him fairly, but I had no chance. He was faster than me, more skilful and with damn sight more of a future ahead of him.

Next thing I knew he'd lost me again and had gone and cracked a stunning thirty-yard volley into the back of the net. I stood there and admired the goal he'd scored. Bloody hell. I nearly even clapped too. That picaninny should be up there in Mexico playing in the World Cup, not down here, I thought.

Goboya (2) England B (0)

Mad Clinch was off the bench and jumping up and down in the technical area like he was having a fit.

"Take him down, someone! For fuck's sake!" he was shouting.

But now no one could get near Genio. He jumped tackles, skipped tackles and weaved round them like they weren't there. The only way to get him now was to dive in from behind, hard and fast, straight through his legs. If he didn't see you coming there was a chance of stopping him. But that could mean a red card and doing Genio a serious injury. No one in our team had the heart to resort to outright thuggery.

No one out on the field, that is. We hadn't counted on Mad Clinch.

One second Genio was racing along the touchline, right in front of the dugouts, and the next second the kid was a flattened wreck on the turf. Clinch had waited for him to get within range and had then given him a hefty right hook. They turned him over, and the kid's nose had been smeared across his face. His mouth was a bloody mess and his teeth were all smashed up. Most of them were now just litter on the pitch.

No Such Thing as a Friendly

The crowd went crazy. I thought there was going to be a riot. If it hadn't been for the armed police presence pitchside, it would have all kicked off.

But the ref quickly blew for half time and we tramped back to our dressing rooms, heads down.

At that time I didn't know what had happened to Mad Clinch. I assumed the ref had sent him to the stands, but Phelps said he saw him being dragged off by the Goboyan coach and substitutes into the tunnel. In any case, he wasn't in our dressing room. And who cared? Fuck him. He'd never be able to coach again. I'd always known he was a nutcase. So, as captain, it was up to me to give the team talk as we each ate our oranges. It wasn't much of a talk. What was there to say?

But we had to finish the match. That was clear. The ref came in and said so. There really would be a riot if we didn't do that, armed police or not. The Goboyans were two nil up, remember. They didn't want the match abandoned, even if their star player had left the ground in an ambulance.

When we came out for the second half, the crowd had gone back to chanting:

GO BO YAH! GO BO YAH! GO BO YAH!

Genio had been taken off to hospital and they'd replaced him with some rubbish centre forward who was useless in the air, and even more useless with his feet. There was another change too. The new Telstar ball had been replaced with an old leather one. It was much heavier than the Telstar, heavier than any ball I'd played with, and it hardly bounced at all, but we had no complaints. We felt we had no right to complain about anything.

Well, without Genio in their side, the Goboyans were a pushover. They had no one to hold their play upfield. They kept trying to hoof the ball as far forward as possible to the new striker, but our centre backs had him in their pocket. Halfway through the second half we'd levelled the score at 2–2, both scrappy goals, one from a corner and the other from a free kick just outside the box. We even had a couple of good

No Such Thing as a Friendly

penalty shouts waved away by the ref, though it seemed to me he was paying us back for what Clinch had done.

And then in the 90th minute, our striker was pulled back in front of goal. His shirt had been practically torn off his back. No ref could fail to award us a penalty kick.

The team wanted me to take it, and as captain I decided I bloody well would. Now, I did seriously think about deliberately scuffing the kick wide of the upright. There was a part of me that knew we didn't deserve to win. There was also a chance we wouldn't get out of the stadium alive if we did beat the Goboyans. But that's not how Englishmen play football. For all I knew, this might be my last chance to represent my country, even if it was a shitty B match and a friendly. I knew that after what had happened here, the whole South American tour would be cancelled. What I didn't know at the time was that that poor picaninny Genio had died on the way to hospital. He suffered a clot in his brain because of Clinch's punch. Maybe if I had known then… maybe…

But I didn't know.

So I walked to the penalty spot and picked up the ball. The crowd were almost silent and muttering amongst themselves. I looked around me at the sea of hostile black faces, at the armed police, at the Goboyan players and then I looked at the ball in my hands.

It had taken quite a beating. The Goboyans had been kicking it upfield all through the second half. Crazy tactics. Booting it as hard as they could. They'd damaged the ball. There was a strip of its outer leather coating hanging loose. I lifted up the loose flap and underneath saw shrivelled white skin and a staring glass eye.

I put that ball back down on the penalty spot as if I'd noticed nothing, backed away, took my run up, and then belted it as hard as I could towards the top right hand corner of the goal.

Final score: Goboya (2) England B (3)

Believe me, I hated Mad Clinch almost as much as the Goboyans did. He deserved what he got. He'd lost his head all

No Such Thing as a Friendly

right.

The tour was cancelled and the whole thing hushed up.

But on that day, 14th June 1970, at least we got a better result than Sir Alf and his bloody England A Team in sunny Mexico.

SCHRÖDINGER'S HUMAN

Anna Taborska

The cat had the uncanny ability of seeming to be in two places at once, and it appeared logical to the man that he should name it Schrödinger. The cat evidently approved the name, purring as the man tried it out.

"Well, Schrödinger, I expect you *must* want some dinner *today?*" the man asked, backing away from the plate of cat food to allow the animal a chance to feed. But the cat stayed where it was, high up on the kitchen cupboard, and refused to give the cat food the time of day, just as it had refused milk and water, and even ham.

The man had first come across the cat on his return from work the previous day. It was thin and dirty, a mud-smeared black, with cold green eyes and a tattered left ear. The pitiful-looking thing was stretched out on his doorstep and refused to budge, even as the man approached. Instead it fixed him with an expectant stare and weaved its tail from side to side. The man studied the cat, and a long-forgotten joy stirred within him.

Ever since he was a child, the man had enjoyed torturing animals. His grandfather had bought him a butterfly net, and the boy quickly worked out that if you rubbed too much of the colourful dust off a butterfly's wings, it had trouble flying. And things got even more interesting if you pulled off its wings altogether and put it on an anthill. You could watch the black specks of the ants swarm all over the wounded intruder; watch the butterfly that was no longer a butterfly, but a fascinating broken thing, try to lift itself out of the writhing mass of small stinging creatures, helplessly flailing its long thin legs, its proboscis furling and unfurling in some strange insect rhythm of pain.

Butterflies continued to fascinate for a long time, but

Schrödinger's Human

eventually the allure of real animals – ones which screamed and bled – took over from those that merely twitched pathetically. After much begging and family debate, he was finally given an air rifle for his birthday, but sadly this was confiscated when he moved up from shooting crows and squirrels to shooting the neighbours' pets.

If necessity is the mother of invention, then a twisted imagination is its father, aunt and uncle. The boy came to understand that the air rifle which he had so mourned wasn't even a drop in the endless ocean of possibilities when it came to inflicting suffering on anything small and fluffy that had a heartbeat. And the smaller and fluffier it was, the easier it could be lured with a warm tone of voice, a friendly smile, a tickle behind the ear and, if all else failed, a piece of ham.

The boy tried a variety of techniques on his victims: dismemberment, disembowelment, decapitation, throwing off the roof or out of a window, the breaking of individual bones with a blunt instrument, blood-letting, crucifixion, and even electrocution – he was particularly good at this, as he had an excellent science teacher at school and displayed a definite propensity for the subject. But his favourite was luring a cat with the promise of food or affection, trapping it in a cage and carrying it to his parents' roof, where he would douse its tail with petrol and set it alight before pushing it headfirst down the drainpipe. The trapped animal, its tail ablaze, would scream all the way down the drainpipe until it got trapped in a bend, where it would burn to charred bones and then fall out the bottom. This method only worked on small cats and kittens, but could also be applied to some breeds of puppy. The boy's attempts to involve the little girl next door in his pastime resulted in his being sent to a boarding school run by monks, where his sadistic horizons expanded to the use of canes, whips and rulers.

The boy left school with top results in science and went on to university, where his interest in animals waned somewhat, as his physics studies and unreciprocated fascination with girls

Schrödinger's Human

led him to attain a First Class degree, despite almost being sent down for peeping through a female student's bedroom window. He stayed on in academia, eventually becoming a lecturer at a good university, where he could continue to indulge in physics and his unreciprocated fascination with girls.

And now here he was, trying to get home after a tiring day of lectures, and this scruffy, ugly cat was lying on his doorstep, as if daring him to gouge out its eyes and cut off its paws. Old passions awoke within the man, but he was too tired to act on them. He picked up a piece of brick that was lying in the roadside and aimed it between the cat's eyes. Just then a piercing pain shot through the man's temple. He dropped the brick and put his hands up to his head. As quickly as it had come, the pain was gone, but the man was left feeling bewildered and a little dizzy. As he rubbed his eyes to clear his head, he heard a voice close by his ear.

"Let me in," it said.

The man span round, but there was nobody nearby – only the cat sprawled on his doorstep, eyeing him like a scientist eyes a mildly interesting specimen before dissection.

"Let me in," the voice continued, "and I'll show you things you've never seen... I'll take you to places you can't begin to imagine."

The man closed his eyes for a moment. When he opened them, the voice was gone and he felt his normal self again. He looked at his front door; the cat was no longer reclining, but sat alertly a couple of feet away from the door, as if waiting for the man to open it.

What the hell, thought the man. If the cat wanted to come in, then let it. He was tired now, but he would amuse himself with the animal later. He opened the door and stood back to let the cat in. It eyed him suspiciously for a moment, then darted past, leaping over the threshold and heading straight for the kitchen.

The man followed it, locking the door behind him. He put

Schrödinger's Human

his briefcase down in the hallway and went to see what the cat was doing. The kitchen was bathed in darkness and before the man switched on the light, he caught sight of the cat's eyes glowing in the shadows by the sink. But as the light from the overhead lamp illuminated the room, the man saw that the cat was not by the sink. Surprised, he looked around and spotted the creature sitting high on a kitchen cupboard, peering down at him with some curiosity and possibly a hint of malevolence.

"Well I'll be damned," he told the cat. "The rough and tumble world of quantum physics would have a field day with you." The man laughed at his own wit and went to the fridge to get some milk. If he was to get any use out of the cat, he'd have to start by getting it down from the kitchen cupboard.

But no end of coaxing would bring the cat down from its vantage point – not even a slice of premium ham. The man contemplated standing on a chair and dislodging the cat or throwing something at it, but he really couldn't be bothered. Besides, it would be much more fun to get the cat to trust him and then see the surprise in its furry little face when he took his penknife to it. The man made his own dinner, ate it and went through to the sitting-room to mark first-year physics assignments, leaving a plate of ham out to see if the cat would come down in his absence.

That night the man dreamt that he was walking through an unfamiliar landscape of red and black. The landscape was constantly shifting and changing. One moment he was walking along a mountain path, looking down into a valley of houses and fields, next he was in a labyrinth of tunnels, the walls made of human bones and skulls arranged in intricate patterns, one on top of the other. Somewhere ahead of the man a fire burned, and light from it bounced around the bone walls, bathing them in a warm glow and sending shadows flitting around the man. Beside him walked Schrödinger the cat, watching him with a modicum of curiosity, as if all this were familiar to the animal and it was merely interested in what the man made of it all – interested, but not that interested.

As the man approached the source of the flames, he became aware of the crackling sound they made. The crackling became a scratching, and the scratching grew louder until the man awoke. The scratching continued and the man realised that it was coming from his wardrobe. The damned cat had somehow gotten into it and was probably ruining his suits. He reached over to switch on his bedside lamp and jumped as his fingers touched fur. The man sat upright and the cat leapt off the bedside table on which it had been sitting.

"Goddamn you, Schrödinger!" The man switched on the lamp and glared at the creature now sitting in the doorway. He swung his legs out of bed, but the cat had already gone. The man closed his bedroom door and went back to sleep.

In the morning the cat was back on the kitchen cupboard, and the ham was untouched on the plate where the man had left it the night before. The creature obviously hadn't eaten for a while and it had to be hungry. Either it was sick or it had been trained not to eat anything other than cat food. The man determined to buy some Whiskas on his way home from work.

But the cat wouldn't eat Whiskas, or Sheba or Felix. It wouldn't drink milk or water and it wouldn't eat cat biscuits. In fact, it was a miracle that it was still alive. It was growing more emaciated by the day, and its protruding ribs only served to make it look scruffier and uglier. For a moment the man astonished himself by contemplating taking it to a vet, but quickly shrugged off such an insane idea and decided to kill it. He placed a kitchen chair next to the cupboard on which Schrödinger was perched, and went to get the meat cleaver. Then the doorbell rang.

The man put the cleaver down and went to answer the door. It was the teenage girl from the house next door.

"I'm sorry to bother you," she said, "but I'm locked out of the house. I forgot to take my keys this morning and my mum isn't back till seven. A couple of workmen followed me home

Schrödinger's Human

from the high street and I don't want to wait outside. Can I hang out at yours until my mum gets back?"

The man studied the girl's short skirt and the way her blonde hair was pulled back in a ponytail, revealing the curve where her neck met her shoulder.

"Sure," he told the girl and stood aside to let her in. He cast a quick glance around the street. Sure enough, he saw two workmen loitering across the road, but they quickly turned on their heels and disappeared. There was no one else around.

"Would you like a cup of tea?" the man asked, leading the way to the kitchen.

"No thanks. Have you got any coke?"

"Yes." The man got a coke from the fridge and handed it to the girl. "Would you like a glass?"

"No thanks." The man indicated for the girl to take a seat. That was when they both saw Schrödinger. It was standing on the kitchen table, tail twitching, staring at the girl.

"Oh, what a cute kitty!" cried the girl and moved towards the animal.

"Schrödinger, what the hell are you doing?"

The tone in the man's voice stopped the girl in her tracks. The man moved forward, ready to swipe the cat off the table, but as he did so, the sharp pain in his head came, then went, and a voice near his ear said, "Kill her!"

"What?" exclaimed the man.

"What?" asked the girl, staring at the man uncomprehendingly.

"Nothing, honey, nothing."

But the voice came again, more persistent this time: "Kill her... now!"

The man felt confused. He looked at the girl. Her tanned arms and legs looked so inviting. A small artery in her neck was throbbing. The man found himself wondering how far the blood from that artery would spurt and whether it would reach the ceiling or just spatter the walls. He wondered whether the look of surprise in her eyes would be like that of the kittens and puppies he had dispatched to kitten and puppy heaven as a boy. He suspected that it would be better – much better – than anything he had experienced before. His cock was throbbing and he realised that the cat was staring at him, green eyes blazing, its customary disdain replaced by a feral excitement.

The artery in the girl's neck was still throbbing. Her lips were cherry red and a look of alarm was creeping over her face. She raised her hand to cover her mouth and, as she did so, her top rode up a little and the man could see the silver ring in her pierced belly-button. As time seemed to stop then stretch around the man, he noticed that the blue of the small gemstone on the ring matched the colour of the girl's eyes.

The artery in the girl's neck was throbbing, the man's cock was throbbing, and now a blood vessel in his head started to throb. The light in the kitchen seemed to throb and then the whole world was throbbing – a glorious red throbbing, pulsating, pounding. Then the meat cleaver was in the man's hand and the look of surprise in the girl's eyes was better than the puppies and the kittens – it was better than anything the man had experienced before, and the girl's blood was on the walls and on the ceiling and on the floor.

When the throbbing subsided, the man was sitting on the floor, his hands and clothes covered in blood. He felt calm and he felt good. The cat was standing beside him, face and whiskers stained red, frenziedly lapping up the girl's blood from the floor. The man stared at the animal in disbelief, but made no move to stop it. Despite the blood on its snout, the cat seemed less dirty than before: its fur seemed sleeker, it seemed somehow fatter and healthier, even its tattered ear seemed to have grown back together.

"Goddamn you, Schrödinger," the man said quietly, but the cat didn't even acknowledge his presence. It had licked the vast amount of blood off the floor and was now licking the girl's fingers. The man crawled around the girl's body to the hand that wasn't being worked on by the cat. He lifted the

Schrödinger's Human

hand and sucked the blood from the index finger. It had a sickly taste, sweet and metallic. The man sucked on the girl's thumb and found that the taste was no longer sickly; it was, in fact, rather good.

A feeling of contented tiredness overcame the man, and he dozed off right there, on the kitchen floor, next to the girl's lacerated body. When he woke up it was dark and Schrödinger was nowhere to be seen. The man chopped up the girl's body with the meat cleaver, removing clothes, hair, bones and anything else that was inedible – this he would take to the municipal dump on his way to work tomorrow, along with the girl's faceless head. Everything else he washed and divided between his fridge and the freezer. He cleaned the walls as best he could, then dragged the kitchen table across and made an attempt to clean the ceiling. He would have to buy a large tin of paint and paint over the stains that wouldn't wash off.

That night the man dreamt that he was standing over a precipice, looking down into a vast pit. The pit was filled with fire. The man noticed movement in the flames and realised that the pit was full of people – thousands of people – burning. He found that if he concentrated, he could hone in on individuals. He could clearly see the expressions of torment on their faces, the pain in their eyes. Their bodies were writhing and their limbs flailing about helplessly. The man remembered the wingless butterflies flailing around on the anthill in his parents' garden, and smiled. He looked down and saw Schrödinger gazing up at him, reflections of the flames dancing in the animal's eyes.

Next morning the man awoke to purring by the side of his bed, but wasn't all that surprised to find that Schrödinger was not by his bed at all, but was waiting expectantly in the kitchen, sitting by the spot where the man had previously left its unwanted plate of cat food.

"Oh, so now you want to eat?"

Schrödinger's Human

The man knew what the cat wanted, but decided to tease it and put out a bowl of milk. But the joke was on him, as Schrödinger gave him such a look of malevolent contempt that the man's blood seemed to freeze in his veins and a nasty shiver went down his spine.

"Sorry," he said, and poured the milk down the sink. He got out a mincing machine and took some of the girl's flesh out of the fridge. He pushed it into the mincer and watched the pink worms come out the bottom. A sharp meow distracted him, and he glanced down to see Schrödinger dancing around on its hind paws, teeth bared. He put the mince on a clean plate, and hardly had time to place the plate on the floor before Schrödinger was upon it, wolfing down the meat like it hadn't eaten in days – which, after all, it hadn't. The man couldn't help thinking that if he hadn't withdrawn his hand in time, the animal might have devoured that too.

As he watched the cat feed, the man noticed how healthy it was looking. He thought he might have imagined it last night – in all the excitement, but in the cold light of day he could see that the cat's fur was a sleek, clean, shiny black, its protruding ribs had disappeared – concealed by a respectable plumpness – and its left ear looked like it had never encountered the Mike Tyson of the feline world.

The man cut a few thin slices of meat, and treated himself to a full English breakfast.

Over the next couple of weeks the cat and the man ate what was left of the teenager. The police came round and asked questions, but only the two workmen had seen the girl enter the man's house, and the police knew nothing of their existence. Officer Jones commented on the man's cute cat and Schrödinger purred obligingly, and that was that. Or would have been, except that the man couldn't stop thinking about the girl. Sometimes he worried about getting found out, but mostly he reminisced about the unbearably sweet sensation of plunging the meat cleaver into her soft flesh. His craving for

Schrödinger's Human

more flesh and more blood wouldn't let him rest or concentrate on his work. Despite their shared diet, as the cat got fatter and silkier, the man lost weight, grew pale and haggard. When he slept, he dreamt of the burning pit and the bodies in it, writhing in perpetual torment. But mostly he just tossed and turned in bed, listened to Schrödinger scratching in the wardrobe and watched its eyes glow by the side of his bed.

About the time that the girl meat ran out, the man's cravings reached an unbearable pitch. He was horny and hungry and confused all at the same time. He was distracted in his tutorials and it was just a matter of time before one of the students complained. Schrödinger was refusing to eat anything that wasn't human, and its body was atrophying. Its left ear was hanging in tatters by the side of its head, and its teeth started falling out, so that its tongue protruded, giving it a rather unsavoury and slightly demented expression. It eyed the man with barely disguised contempt, and the man found himself feeling increasingly uncomfortable around it.

The student was only in her first term, but she was already behind in her work. She had been good at physics at school, but university was different. The professor was bombarding them with new information every day, and they were expected to come up with their own ideas and solutions to problems. When the professor asked to see her, she was terrified that she was in trouble. She was relieved when he spoke kindly to her and offered to spend some time with her, going over problems they had tackled in class, to help her catch up with the others. The professor explained that he had a variety of textbooks at home and it would be easier if she dropped by his house, where they would have all the books at hand.

"I realise that young ladies sometimes feel uncomfortable being alone with a man," he told her, "and you are very welcome to bring a friend with you, as long as your friend won't mind keeping my cat company while we're studying."

"You have a cat?" The girl smiled.

Schrödinger's Human

"His name's Schrödinger. He's very friendly and he's especially fond of young ladies."

The girl smiled again and lowered her eyes.

"Do you have a friend you would like to bring?"

The man knew full well that the girl had no friends. Shy and from a state school, unlike the privileged majority of the students, he often saw her sitting alone in the lecture hall and leaving alone when the lectures were over.

"Oh, that's okay," the girl replied. "I don't feel uncomfortable."

"Well, that's just fine. My cat would love to meet you. He's been feeling a little under the weather lately."

The plan seemed foolproof, but when the student arrived at his house, the man found himself having second thoughts. This was not something he'd envisaged – he'd wanted another girl desperately for weeks. But when he saw her standing on his doorstep in her knee high socks and pink sweater, physics notes in a file under her arm, his palms suddenly felt clammy and a nerve under his eye started to twitch. She was his student, after all, and maybe that meant that he was crossing some kind of line – a line between fair game and… well… not.

"Come in," he told the girl, seriously considering actually giving her a physics lesson. But as soon as he shut the door behind her and ushered her into the kitchen, Schrödinger was there in front of them, meowing and twitching its tail.

"Oh," exclaimed the girl, "he doesn't look too well."

"He hasn't been eating properly," the man explained. "In fact, he's been feeling rather sorry for himself, but I'm sure he'll cheer up now that you're here."

The girl stooped down to stroke the cat, but something in its unappetising appearance and intent stare put her off. She straightened up and smiled at the professor, who offered her a cup of tea and put the kettle on.

The cat meowed loudly and the man tried to swipe at it behind the girl's back. But the pain in his head was back. The man winced and clapped his hands to his temples.

"Are you okay, professor?" There was concern in the girl's brown eyes.

But the pain in his head was gone, and the dizzy feeling was back, and the voice was telling him to kill.

"Professor? Are you feeling alright?"

But the kettle was in his hand and, before he knew it, he was pouring boiling water over the girl's face and she was too shocked to make a sound as her face started to blister. And then he was bashing the girl over the head with the kettle, bashing her face and bashing her chest and bashing the base of her skull. The girl slid to the floor, but still he kept hitting her. He could feel his skin burning as some of the boiling liquid splashed on his hands, but still he kept smashing the girl with the kettle until her head was a bloody pulp and her legs ceased twitching. Then he stopped. He put the kettle down and went to the sink, soaking his hands under the cold water tap until he was fairly confident that they wouldn't blister. He glanced occasionally over his shoulder at the cat, which was greedily lapping up the puddle of blood beneath the dead girl's head.

The cleaning and carving took a long time and the man went to bed exhausted. He fell asleep quickly and dreamt that he was falling into the burning pit. He fell slowly, and had ample opportunity to watch and feel the flames getting closer. The rising heat overtook him on his way down and, by the time he reached the bottom of the pit, his flesh was already blistering and smoking. His skin caught fire and was burnt away, and, as the flames reached the fat beneath, the man went up like a torch. He tried to scream, but his throat was burning on the inside. He looked up and saw Schrödinger looking down at him from the edge of the pit. The cat's expression was one of mild amusement.

The following day the man determined to kill Schrödinger. He minced some meat, laid it out on a clean plate and put it down in front of the waiting cat. While the creature was preoccupied, the man opened the drawer and took hold of the meat cleaver. The pain hit his head like a spear and he dropped the cleaver back in the drawer. He looked over at Schrödinger, but the cat didn't even interrupt its meal long enough to cast him an evil glance.

It was a while before anyone reported the student missing. The police came to the campus and interviewed everyone who knew her. The interviews didn't last long, as even those students who recognised her picture weren't able to provide any information about the girl. But Officer Jones recognised the physics professor as the next door neighbour he had interviewed in his previous unsolved missing girl case, and decided to pay him a home visit, complete with warrant.

Officer Jones arrived at the house with two other policemen. If the man was shocked to see three police officers on his doorstep, he didn't show it. He invited them in politely and stood back as they ransacked his home.

Officer Jones spotted a pair of green eyes in the shadows under the coffee table in the sitting-room, and remembered the man's cat. He had a soft spot for cats and bent down to the animal, but saw to his surprise that the space under the coffee table was empty. As he straightened up, he noticed the cat sitting on an armchair at the far side of the room, watching him. Before he had a chance to approach the animal, one of the other officers summoned him from the bedroom. He hurried over to his colleague.

Officer Trevayne was standing by the open drawer of the man's bedside cabinet, holding a silver belly-button ring with a small blue gemstone in his latex-gloved hand. Officer Jones recognised it immediately from a photograph given to him by the parents of the missing girl from the house next door. He moved rapidly out into the hallway, where Officer Green was waiting with the man.

Schrödinger's Human

"Sir, we need you to come with us to the station, to answer some questions," Officer Jones told the man. For the briefest moment the man looked shaken, but regained his composure almost instantly.

"Of course," he said. "Anything I can do to help... I'll just grab my coat." The man went over to the coat stand and reached for his coat, but just then he felt the familiar stabbing pain in his head. It came and went, leaving him confused as to how it was that he'd lifted the heavy coat stand and why it was that he brought the full weight of it down on Officer Green – brought the large wooden object down again and again on the policeman, until he felt a stinging pain rip through his shoulder, and the whole world went red, then black.

Officer Jones put his gun away and radioed for an ambulance. He moved swiftly over to the man and checked his pulse; the bullet had passed straight through his heart and the man was dead within seconds. It was a bad situation, but the man would have killed Officer Green – if he hadn't already done so. Officer Jones knelt beside Officer Trevayne, who was tending to their badly wounded colleague.

"He's alive," said Officer Trevayne, "but he needs to get to a hospital ASAP."

"I'll go outside and flag the ambulance down."

But as Officer Jones moved towards the front door, he felt a sharp pain in his temple. He winced and put his hand up to his head, but the pain was gone, replaced by a slight feeling of nausea and bewilderment. This in turned passed, and a voice spoke in the policeman's ear.

"Take me with you," it said. "I'll show you things you've never seen."

Officer Jones looked round and saw the black cat eyeing him dispassionately.

THE CHAMELEON MAN

David Williamson

The ugly buboes nestling in his armpits were swollen to the size of a hen's egg. They were bloated and angry looking and burst suddenly with an audible popping sound, sending a trickle of red-grey viscous pus streaming down the man's rib cage.

The rest of his skin was covered in small bleeding spots that quickly turned almost black, giving the disease its terrible name: The *Black Death* otherwise known as *Bubonic Plague*.

The audience oohed and aahed and erupted into spontaneous applause as Charlie Benton completed his remarkable display. Within seconds, the buboes, horrible black spots and open running sores had completely vanished and his body was once more clear of blemishes and healthy looking.

Professor James Watson stepped forward on the small stage and congratulated Charlie, slapping him heartily on the back with undisguised affection and respect.

"Magnificent, Charlie. Absolutely magnificent! You truly are a wonder to behold!" he shouted above the general uproar in the exhibition chamber. All around the packed circular amphitheatre, more usually employed for demonstrations of surgical procedures, the assembled medical students, doctors, surgeons and dignitaries cheered and applauded as Charlie Benton smiled wanly. He'd given similar displays of his talents at other venues across Europe and America, but never before to such a large and celebrated audience as this one.

The Professor rapped his gavel on the oak podium in an attempt to bring the hall to order. After several attempts, the rapturous applause died to a trickle and finally to a single overexcited medical student that Watson silenced with a withering stare.

"And now... Mr Benton will demonstrate the next part of his performance... LEPROSY!" yelled the professor, not

The Chameleon Man

unlike a fairground barker at a dubious side show.

Charlie Benton really was an incredible man. Ever since his childhood, when he had discovered that he could mimic illnesses such as Chickenpox, Measles and the like simply by reading about the symptoms and then concentrating hard with their description in mind. It had started as a prank – a way of getting out of the classroom, but he had soon become a legend amongst his peers and word quickly spread. In earlier days, he would surely have been burnt as a witch but even in these enlightened times, he was shunned and feared by many and hated by a few.

Charlie was seventeen when word of the remarkable young man reached the ears of Professor Watson the world renowned expert in Tropical Diseases who was based at the London Institute. Once the Professor had 'discovered' him, Charlie rapidly became the toast of medical science, written about in every medical journal and newspaper across the globe, adored and feared now in equal proportions, condemned by the church as a demon at the same time praised by medical men for his amazing insight into illness and diseases.

But today was something very special for Charlie Benton.

The greatest medical brains from around the entire globe, together with all the top research scientists plus a handful of brilliant medical students were all gathered under one roof for an extra special display of his unique talents.

He would produce, before their very eyes, thirty-seven different diseases and severe disfigurements in one three hour session and then take questions at the end of the exhibition.

Imagine being able to see the Black Death from start to finish, right there in front of you. With no risk of contagion *and* all over and done with in less than four minutes. Incredible! Or witnessing deadly epidemic Cholera or Typhoid. The list of normally fatal diseases went on and on all in plain view from start to finish, each one bringing a further gasp of amazement from the assembled medical men.

It was this incredible ability to mimic these normally

The Chameleon Man

murderous afflictions that had given Charlie his stage name: the 'Chameleon Man', for it was the strange Chameleon-like properties within his body which created these fantastic phenomena with absolutely no actual bacterial infections present. Even though the display was one hundred percent safe, this hadn't stopped the occasional medical student from fleeing for his very life as Charlie began his incredible transformations.

Tonight was the culmination of six years of being prodded and poked, jabbed and examined and a thousand other medical tortures devised to get to the bottom of Charlie's unique talent. Tonight was the big one; he had been offered a great deal of money for this evening's display and he intended to give full value as the cash would keep him in grand style well into his old age.

He was a self-made man, celebrated around the world – the likes of whom had never been seen before and he had done it all himself. *Now* his father would laugh on the other side of his drunken face; or he would if he were still alive.

'Useless talent' indeed!

As Charlie completed his thirty-sixth disease, the applause in the auditorium was deafening. He had decided before the evening had started that he would have to end on a 'big one', something very special that he had been practising in the peace and quiet of Professor Watson's country house which had never been witnessed by a living soul.

The Professor stepped forward on the dais and tried to still the uproar in the hall.

"Please... gentlemen... PLEASE!" he implored. After several more minutes, silence finally fell upon the crowd.

"Mr Benton, Charlie... will now perform something that nobody... not even myself, has ever been privileged to see before this day. It is something so... so *remarkable*... so... *impossible*... that you will without doubt disbelieve your own eyes!"

The Professor took a step back as Charlie, now wearing a

The Chameleon Man

long cape about his shoulders, not so much for theatrical effect as to combat the chill in the old amphitheatre, took his place at the lectern. The room was so still, you truly could have heard the proverbial pin drop as Charlie prepared to speak.

"Gentlemen... the things that you have witnessed here this evening have been, I hope you will agree, incredible?" A murmur of agreement swept through the audience together with several hearty cries of: "Hear, hear!"

"But," continued the Chameleon Man, "all that is nothing... *nothing* to what I will now provide for your entertainment!" Gasps could be heard from the stunned audience and Charlie had to wave them silent once more before he could continue.

"All the diseases you have seen so far, are but mere... shall we say 'surface alterations' to my outer fleshy layer. But I have been working on something that I hope will be the greatest transformation ever performed in any public place."

Somewhere from the left of the small stage, there was a theatrical drum roll as Charlie threw off his cape. All the lights in the auditorium were dimmed save for the bright stage light.

"And now... for the first time ever anywhere in the world... I give you... curvature of the spine... otherwise known as... *HUNCHBACK!*"

The applause was totally deafening. *No one*, not even the Professor had expected anything like this. It was the greatest possible finale to a wonderful evening of medical surprises and chronic illnesses. The man was a true showman *and* a genius of the highest order.

Slowly, the room fell into hushed and expectant silence. Every eye was transfixed on Charlie Benton as he prepared himself for his latest wonderful transformation.

The flesh on his back started to stretch and ripple in an alarming manner. The spinal column under the skin began buckling and bending outwards, completely distorting his stance and the entire shape of his rib cage and upper body.

Within the space of two minutes and with what was clearly an incredibly strenuous effort, Charlie stood before the

The Chameleon Man

assembled medical brains of the entire world – a *hunchback*.

The other transformations had been miraculous, but this was on a whole new level. Was there nothing in terms of bodily disfigurement this man could not achieve? He truly was the Chameleon Man!

The applause and cheering was so loud, that the Professor feared that the glass roof high above them would shatter with the noise. He placed both hands over his ears, not daring to try and stop the crowd's appreciation of what they had just witnessed. It was nothing short of a miracle and everyone there knew it.

It took Charlie somewhat longer to revert back to normal than usual. The strain was clearly evident on his face as the Professor guided the younger man towards a chair at the side of the stage. Sweat ran down Charlie's face in tiny rivers and he trembled uncontrollably as he fought to regain his composure.

Watson placed an arm around Charlie's shoulder, his face a mask of concern. "Are you all right, dear boy? You look so pale?" he asked.

The young man nodded weakly.

After what seemed like hours but in truth no more that a few minutes, the applause still echoing around the hall, Charlie smiled hesitantly at his mentor and hoisted himself from the chair. His public were calling and he could not disappoint them. He walked unsteadily over to the lectern, held on tight and then took a deep bow.

"Encore! Encore! Encore!" the word coming from almost every voice in the auditorium. Charlie held up a trembling hand to try and quell the uproar and slowly, row by row, they fell silent. The great man was about to speak and they didn't want to miss a single word of what he had to say.

"Thank you. Thank you so much," he began shakily. His mentor stepped forward with a glass of water and Charlie took a sip before continuing.

"I hope that you have enjoyed my little exhibition here this

The Chameleon Man

evening. As you will no doubt be aware, this was my last public appearance. I am now going to study medicine myself in Vienna. I have had enough of being poked and prodded and feel it is now *my* turn to be the prodder."

Laughter briefly swept through the hall.

There were tears brimming in Charlie's eyes; tears of sadness but also of relief. These displays were starting to take their toll on the young man and it was time to stop them before they killed him.

The Professor stepped forward and draped Charlie's discarded cape around the younger man's shoulders and smiled warmly at the person he had come to think of as his son. Charlie returned the smile and turned to face the audience once more.

"I must thank you, every one – all of you who have supported me over the years. But especially my friend and saviour, Professor Watson. Without whom, I would surely have ended up as a freak in a carnival sideshow..." The young man choked by emotion and with tears streaming down his cheeks turned and was led away by his friend and mentor to the rapturous cheers of the audience.

Somehow, through all the bedlam, one voice seemed to stand out above all others and Charlie stopped to see who was shouting at him. He could see that it was a young man – a medical student no doubt, but he couldn't hear what was being said. Sensing that something was going on, the audience slowly fell silent as Charlie faced the young man seated below the stage.

"I'm sorry... what did you say?" asked the star of the show.

The student grinned widely. It looked for all the world as though he had been put up to this and Charlie had perhaps foolishly taken the bait.

"I said: 'do you feel that there is no illness or state of health that you cannot recreate?'" The student sat waiting; he had set the trap and it was now up to Charlie to avoid it or fall in feet first.

The Chameleon Man

The Chameleon Man was both puzzled and annoyed by this upstart's pointless question.

"Excuse me; have you just arrived? Or have you been asleep for the last three hours?" he asked, barely able to disguise the contempt in his voice.

"Did you not witness thirty-six diseases *plus* a severe curvature of the spine displayed here, on this very stage?" Charlie was clearly furious and this was made all the worse by the cool way the medical student sat staring and smiling in the seat below him.

A nervous titter ran around the auditorium as Charlie attempted to put the would be doctor in his place.

"So," continued the student, "there is no medical or physical state that you cannot recreate. That is what you maintain, is it?" sneered the younger man.

Charlie looked at the Professor who shrugged his shoulders hopelessly. The showman slammed his fist down hard on the lectern, knocking over the glass half full of water, which in turn shattered on the stage floor.

"Of *course* there isn't, you *idiot!*" he bellowed at the student. Another nervous laugh travelled around the hall. The audience was starting to sense there was something in the air and silence fell.

The cocky young student rose from his chair and stood right next to the stage where he could clearly be seen and heard by all.

"Right then, *Mister* Benton..." The boy paused for effect, "Have you ever tried to mimic the medical state of... DEATH?" he yelled loud enough for the whole hall to hear.

Charlie looked stunned, the Professor looked stunned, in fact everyone in the whole auditorium except the student looked stunned by the idea and the place was alive with speculation and chatter.

Charlie looked to his mentor for support and advice and the Professor was shaking his head violently. "*NO* Charlie! It cannot be done. Not even by you." The older man tugged at his

The Chameleon Man

ward trying to usher him away from the edge of the stage, but suddenly another voice called out "Do it!" Then another, and another, until the whole audience were demanding to know the answer to the young student's question.

For one of the very few times in Charlie's life, he felt scared.

He was scared that he had been challenged to attempt something that couldn't be done. He was scared that he'd look foolish in front of all these respected people and he was scared that if he didn't at least *try* to do it, he would lose every scrap of esteem and appreciation that he'd worked so long and hard for over the years.

He struggled free from the Professor's grip and strode back to the edge of the stage.

"I repeat for the benefit of the deaf and the dense amongst you; there is *no* medical state that I cannot mimic... given the time and practice... not even *death!*" He spat the last word and glared at the student as if daring him to continue. The younger man merely sat down and crossed his arms, an unpleasant grin spreading across his thin face.

"Then show us, Mister Benton. *Show us!*" he demanded.

"Please Charlie. This is *madness!*" begged the Professor "You *know* it can't be done. You'll *kill* yourself!"

Charlie brushed off his appeals and ripped off the cloak, tossing it into the audience.

"Don't you *see?* It will be the *ultimate* display in my career. The man who could feign death. The greatest trick since Jesus raised Lazarus from the grave! Just *imagine...*"

Watson realised it was too late. All because of some childish imbecile in the audience, the most amazing man who had ever lived was about to risk his very life. And there was nothing he could do to stop it happening. He sat down, a beaten man and waited for the inevitable, determined to take no part in what was about to occur.

The next few minutes were spent with Charlie Benton directing the stewards in erecting a high table on the stage so that the whole audience could witness the impossible. At last,

The Chameleon Man

everything was ready and the Chameleon Man signalled for the room to be silent. All chatter stopped as he clambered onto the improvised death bed. He glared at the young student in the front row and said:

"And now... for the benefit of those amongst you who disbelieve me... I will mimic the medical state... Of DEATH!" Once more the theatrical sounding drum roll rang out as Charlie Benton lay back on the bed, arms folded across his chest like an Egyptian mummy, utter silence pervaded the auditorium.

At first, his breathing increased and the blood hammered through his veins and arteries as he struggled to imagine what death must feel like. Every other illness he had mimicked over the years was well documented, but aside from knowing what a dead person *looked* like, there was of course no written description – no second-hand evidence for him to know what it would *feel* like.

He began to wish that he had kept his mouth shut and curbed his temper. That blasted student had this trap in mind all evening and he had blundered into it with eyes wide open. Fool!

There were the odd murmurs in the hall as he tried to concentrate. First one, then another until there was a general buzz throughout the auditorium.

"Concentrate Charlie... *concentrate!* You can do it... you can do it!" he told himself over and over again.

Gradually... very gradually, his heart rate began to slow and his breathing even out. It felt as though he was drifting into a heavy sleep. The noises in the hall faded into the background until he could no longer hear them and the bright lights were extinguished from his sight... just the slow and steady thud of his heart and the barely noticeable movement of his lungs. He was drifting... drifting on a sea with no horizons... There was no movement... he was just... *floating* it seemed. Then *nothing*.

The buzz of chatter grew into a roar as the Professor moved

The Chameleon Man

quickly to Charlie's side. He felt for a pulse. There was none. He desperately listened for a heart beat. Nothing. He placed a small mirror over Charlie's mouth to capture signs of breath escaping. There were none!

Finally, he took a large steel pin from behind his jacket lapel and jabbed it hard into the muscle of Charlie's right thigh. Not a flicker of movement.

For all intents and purposes, Charlie Benton was dead. Well and truly dead! The Professor faced the audience and shook his head sadly. Even the mouthy student had the good grace to go ashen and hang his head in shame.

There would be more tests, naturally. After all, the room was filled to the rafters with the best medical brains in the world. If there was any chance of finding life in the body of the Chameleon Man, these were surely the men to do so. Charlie had simply pressed his luck too far this time.

After an hour had passed, not a single person had left the hall. Some were weeping openly; the place was unnaturally quiet otherwise.

When three hours had elapsed and after every possible procedure had been employed to resuscitate Charlie Benton, he was declared dead and given the nature of the audience, talk naturally turned to carrying out an autopsy on the body of the most amazing man who had ever lived. Even though Watson was appalled at the notion, he was after all, a medical man and offered only a token argument against the idea.

Within the fourth hour, all was prepared for the investigation into the incredible body of the Chameleon Man and distinguished medical men jostled one another for the best view of proceedings like children at a playground brawl.

Charlie Benton lay naked and spread-eagled on the autopsy table, like a giant moth on a mount. Professor Watson had been elected as the person to carry out the examination of the strangest case in medical history and as he stepped forward scalpel at the ready, his hands were trembling slightly with anticipation.

The Chameleon Man

After hovering briefly above Charlie's abdomen, he vigorously jabbed with the scalpel, drawing it swiftly and evenly upwards and then across so that all the vital organs were exposed at a stroke.

Nothing unusual so far, he declared to the expectant audience. The examination continued.

Normal procedure was to remove all organs so that they could be examined and weighed, checked for growths, damage, et cetera.

The Professor always started with the heart in these cases and after all, this was just another autopsy so that was where he'd begin today.

At the very instant he deftly severed the main aorta, the 'dead man's' eyes flickered open.

It had taken much longer to get back than he had thought it would, but he had done it. He had lifted the curtain of death and looked beyond, he had seen what lay ahead and he had returned with that knowledge to share with all mankind.

The wonders he had witnessed. The incredible things he could relate to these doctors…

"I *TOLD* you I could do it!" he bellowed at the stunned circle of faces above him. But something seemed to be wrong. Very wrong. Why did they all look at him in that way? What had happened while he'd been away?

Professor Watson had already severed all major arteries to Charlie's heart before he realised that the man had 'returned' from the dead. He had even failed to notice that the once 'dead' organ had started to beat again at the very moment he had began the first incision and he now tried desperately to replace the throbbing heart back into the chest cavity, struggling with the haste of the hopeless… Already knowing that it was far too late to save his former friend.

Charlie Benton stared with pleading eyes into the face of his mentor.

"HELP ME PROFESSOR… *HELP ME!*"

He let out a soundless scream and his whole body shook and

trembled.

Charlie Benton returned to the other side. This time on a one way ticket.

TWO FOR DINNER

John Llewellyn Probert

"So are you a fan of Beethoven and all that sort of noisy bollocks then?"

Marcus Randall cut a thick strip from his exquisitely prepared steak and thrust the severed portion into his mouth. As he chewed he placed his elbows on the damask covering of the antique Georgian table and rested his chin on immaculately manicured hands, the light from the chandelier above glinting off both his gold wedding band and the heavy signet ring on his left little finger.

The much younger man at whom this comment had been addressed looked up at his dining companion with a slightly pained expression. Julian Partleton had been out of university for three years, but the company he had kept both there and since leaving was more inclined to discuss the finer points of classical music with *élan* rather than expletives. He had to cough to clear the nerves from his throat before he could reply.

"I think it's important to keep an open mind about all kinds of music," he said, still feeling too uncomfortable to eat much of the food that had been placed before him. Worried about incurring his host's displeasure he picked up his silver fork, only for it to slip from between fingers slick with anxious sweat. It fell to the floor, the thick pile of the Persian rug beneath their feet so thick and luxurious that the ornately engraved utensil barely made a sound as it landed.

"You've dropped your fork," said Randall, unnecessarily and with obvious pleasure.

"Yes... er... sorry," said Julian, bending down.

"Oh for God's sake don't pick it up," said his host, regarding his companion's bobbing shock of curly brown hair. "I'll get Hopkins to fetch you another."

The butler was summoned by a crimson silken pull cord to Randall's right, the like of which Julian had only seen in BBC

Two For Dinner

regency dramas. Tugging at the soft material produced a far-off clanging that signified the activation of some ancient but still functioning system of letting the servants know when they were wanted. For someone who looked nearly seventy Hopkins arrived remarkably quickly, left without saying a word, and returned almost as rapidly with a replacement utensil. Then he was gone again to leave the two men to discuss whatever it was Julian had been summoned to Randall's mansion to talk about.

They ate in silence for the next couple of minutes, Julian finding his steak easier to eat than he had been expecting, but then it had been prepared to standards better than he had ever enjoyed in a restaurant. Not that a music teacher's salary allowed him to take his wife out to anywhere even remotely expensive. And yet Jenny never complained, which was just one of many things that he often failed to appreciate about her.

"I make a point of employing a first class chef," said Randall, taking a swig from a large glass that was on its way to being emptied of a particularly fine Bordeaux for the second time that evening.

"Well if you can afford it why not?" said Julian, hoping he hadn't overstepped the mark.

"Exactly!" His host beamed in agreement. "Having spent so much time amassing a vast personal fortune it only makes sense that I should feel I deserve the best. The best food, the best wine, the best clothes (here he held up his arm to better display the elegantly cut black velvet dinner jacket he was wearing), and of course, the very best music teacher for Adrian."

Julian smiled at the compliment and inwardly breathed a sigh of relief. So *that* was why he was here. To discuss how Randall's seven-year-old was doing at his piano lessons. Thank God. But then what else, he reassured himself, could Randall have possibly wanted to talk about?

"He's a bright boy, Mr Randall, but I'm sure you know that already."

"Of course I do," said Randall, spearing the last roast potato on his plate and popping it whole into his mouth. "But then you're a very bright boy as well aren't you Mr Partleton? Music scholar at Canterbury wasn't it?"

"Organ scholar to be precise," said Julian.

Randall emptied his glass and poured another from the second bottle that had been opened.

"That's right. I do beg your pardon. One of those big church things I'll bet – the sort that keeps your hands and feet busy."

"It does take quiet a lot of skill to master it," said Julian. As he started to relax he suddenly realised how hungry he was. He began to tuck into the meal with relish. It was only when he was coming to the end that he realised Randall had been watching him eat without uttering another word.

"Did you enjoy that?" said the older man once he had swallowed the last mouthful.

"You know, I have to admit that I did," said Julian, wiping his mouth on a white napkin whose embroidered edge could have been gold lace for all he knew.

Randall fingered his glass.

"And you're feeling a little more relaxed now I sincerely hope?"

Julian nodded.

"Are we going to have dessert first or would you prefer to let the food go down and discuss Adrian's progress now?"

"Oh it's not Adrian I've brought you here to discuss," said Randall. "It's you. Or rather you and my wife."

Julian's stomach would have flipped over if it hadn't been quite so full. Oh God, he thought, Randall knew after all. He knew and Julian should never have come here. He should never have been so stupid as to accept a dinner invitation from this man. But he had so very few pupils at the moment and Randall paid so well that he hadn't wanted to risk upsetting him. And Jenny, lovely Jenny, his wife, to whom he had been married these past three years, had insisted he go.

But then she didn't know about his brief affair with Angela Randall.

Two For Dinner

Which Angela's husband obviously did. The man who was his employer, the man glaring at him from the other end of the table, the man he needed to get away from. Now.

Except that he couldn't.

For some reason his arms had been replaced by lead weights, and when he tried to move his legs it felt as if they had been glued to his chair. He tried to speak but this time only a slurred groan managed to escape his lips.

"I wondered when the drug in your drink would start to work," said Randall, getting to his feet and making his way slowly to the other end of the table. "You know that's one of the marvellous things about lack of breeding. You wouldn't know *this*," he picked up his nearly empty wine glass, "from the rather less than exclusive piss I've been letting you drink all evening. I see I was right in not wasting the good stuff on you. Christ all you have to do with some people is tell them they're drinking something posh and they believe you. No wonder so many restaurants these days turn a profit so easily if ignorant peasants like you patronise them. And there's no point trying to reply. Your vocal cords should be all but paralysed now. In a minute you'll be asleep." By now his face was inches from Julian's own. "And when you wake up, my friend, let me assure you that you will find yourself in rather less comfortable surroundings."

*

Julian came round to find himself in a large empty room lined with bare bricks. Bare that is, except for the broad wooden workbench at the far end, the one in front of which Randall was currently standing.

"Awake are you?" said his captor.

Julian tried to speak and was surprised to find he wasn't gagged. He took a deep breath and screamed.

"Good grief *that's* not going to do any good," said Randall. "Do you honestly think I would have left you with the capacity to speak if anyone might be able to hear you? *You* drove here in that clapped out little car of yours. *You* saw how isolated this place is. And don't think the servants will hear you – I've sent them all home and the nearest lives five miles away. So just to summarise, in case things aren't absolutely crystal clear – you and I are alone, miles from anywhere, in a position where we can now have a little chat man to man. Well, man to cheating philandering bastard. Who happens to be tied to a chair in front of me."

Julian had felt too fragile before but now he realised he could move neither his arms nor his legs. He looked down to see that he had been tied to the chair with what looked like wire.

"It's piano wire, actually," said Randall with a grin. "Cut from the very same Kemble grand at which you have sat so many times teaching my little Adrian that 'Middle C is on this Line' and all those other interminably dreary music exercises he has in that book of his. But you haven't actually been sitting at that piano quite as much as I had previously thought, have you? There have been times when Adrian has been left to practise while you have gone and done something else. And of course I'm not counting the times you must have come here with no intention of going near the piano at all. Possibly even running straight upstairs after letting yourself in?" Randall selected a Yale key from the bunch he had retrieved from Julian's jacket pocket. "I presume she gave it to you? It fits the back door perfectly."

"It's not what you think," Julian spluttered.

"Oh isn't it? You mean you haven't been seeing my wife on a regular basis with the intention of making her feel, shall we say, a little *happier?*"

"She was the one who suggested it," the music teacher spluttered as panic began to take hold.

"My dear fellow it matters not a jot to me who started it, but that you were instrumental in it happening at all. It does, after all, take two to tango. I do hope you appreciate the trouble I've gone to there to include a little musical pun. But enough of that – I am a very busy man, so I think it's time we started to take things a little more seriously."

Randall turned to pick something up from the bench. As he did so Julian strained to see the items on it. He caught sight of a number of tools, knives, and something in a tall glass jar which he could have sworn wriggled a little before Randall demanded his attention once again. The older man held up the pair of large pliers he had selected in one hand, and what Julian presumed was a chicken bone in the other.

"I don't do much DIY myself but it's useful to have a few tools around the house, don't you think?" Randall said as he placed the finger-sized bone between its jaws and showed just how little strength he needed to apply to crunch the grey-white ivory into a pinkish pulp. "Just in case you have any little jobs that need taking care of."

The older man shook the remains of the bone free from the pliers and allowed them to fall to the ground. He took a few steps towards Julian's quivering form.

"I was made to have piano lessons once, you know," he said. "Couldn't stand them. The teacher's name was Mrs Glossop and she looked exactly like her surname might imply – all rolls of fat and with tiny rimless spectacles hiding even tinier eyes." He held up his own right hand to regard it as he continued. "She had the most grotesque greasy, pudgy fingers that she would put over mine to try and improve my fingering. It was all I could do to stop myself vomiting all over the sleeves of one of the hideous hand-knitted cardigans she wore whatever the weather. And if that wasn't bad enough every time I knocked on her front door for the lesson that I was dreading anyway the two huge black dogs she owned would come galloping up and make such a noise behind the wood panelling that it was all I could do not to turn and run all the way home. Where of course my mother would have sent me straight back with a thick ear. So you could say I learned to dislike music teachers from an early age, and therefore I have had many,

Two For Dinner

many years to devise some very particular ways of making members of your particular profession suffer."

He was inches from Julian now.

"And do you know what I used to do when I got home from those dreadful music lessons?" he said, his voice quieter now he was nearer his subject, but all the more terrifying for it. "I used to read. And not just any stories – boys own stuff, Enid Blyton or any crap like that. I used to read horror stories. The more gruesome the better. There was one particular series from a British publisher that I used to love. In fact I have a full set of all thirty volumes upstairs, not that you're going to get to see them. They're far too fine a collector's item for the likes of you to be allowed to get their grubby little fingers on. Anyway, in one particular story someone ties up a horror writer and subjects him to all sorts of dreadful things – cuts his arms off, pops one of his eyes out, and tapes a commentary of what he's doing the entire time. Appalling stuff, and not terribly well written I realise now, but nevertheless it stayed with me."

Despite Julian's attempts to pull away, he was powerless to prevent Randall placing the jaws of the pliers either side of his little finger. The young man gasped as he felt the serrated edges grip his skin.

"I suppose losing any finger would be disastrous for someone like you," Randall said. "But if I'm going to spend some of my valuable time on you I suppose I ought to make it *really* count."

He relaxed the instrument, only to move it so that it now the fingernail and the soft pulp of Julian's right index finger was in its grasp.

"After all, an index finger is far more important to anyone," said Randall as he ever so slightly tightened his grip. "And when I think of where that finger might have been, well I'm sure you can understand why I might have something against it, other than the pliers I'm holding at the moment."

As Randall's pressure on the pliers' handles increased so did the biting pain in Julian's finger, building in intensity until he was sure the pulpy flesh of the tip would burst. Just as the music teacher braced himself for the inevitable crushing pain that was to come the grip relaxed.

"Yes I thought of crushing part of you," said Randall, backing away, "but then I remembered another more *horrible* way I could have revenge."

He straightened up and went back to the workbench. Julian looked down at his finger. He breathed a sigh of relief as he realised that, while it was reddened and bruised but there didn't seem to be any serious damage.

"Have you read any horror stories, Mr Partleton?" Randall still had his back to him.

Julian shook his head before realising his captor couldn't see him.

"No," he croaked.

"That's a pity," was the reply. "Because maybe if you had you would know what I intended to do with this, and that would make your terror all the greater."

Randall pulled on a pair of heavy gloves, picked up the glass jar and turned to face Julian once more.

Julian peered at what it contained. A slight, serpentine shape flicked from side to side as Randall brought it closer, so that now Julian could see that the shape possessed many pairs of legs, and two whip-like antennae.

And a pair of curved, clacking mandibles.

"There's another story in one of those books where a cuckolded man in Borneo takes revenge on his wife's lover by placing a large earwig into his ear. The creature then proceeds to eat through the poor chap's brain and lays clutches of eggs inside his head so the bastard has no hope of surviving." He held the glass jar close to Julian's face. "I couldn't get one of those earwigs, but I understand that the pain inflicted by the bite of this South American centipede is severe enough to make a man want to cut his own arm off rather than bear it. Of course it's not your arm I'm going to drop it onto. I think it would be more appropriately placed somewhere a little more relevant to the crime you have committed against me, don't you?"

He looked down at Julian's lap and began to unscrew the lid of the jar, shaking the container as he did so to further agitate the creature. As its head bumped against the side the creature tried to stab at the glass with needle-sharp mandibles, leaving streaks of dirty green fluid where it tried to bite at the walls of its prison. Randall reached in and picked the thing up by its tail, taking care to hold the squirming creature tightly. He walked up to Julian and held the centipede an inch from Julian's left eye.

"Losing an eye wouldn't be very nice either, would it?" he said. "Almost as bad as losing your fingers. Of course if this little fellow were to plunge those rather nasty looking pincers into your socket the poison would very quickly travel to your brain and you would be dead in moments. Whereas if we were to assist it in injecting the poison a little further away then you will have all the longer to regret your decision to show my wife the finer points of... fingering."

With his free hand Randall undid the belt of Julian's trousers and popped open the button.

"I've already told you there's no point in screaming," he said as he lowered the creature until its claws were beginning to brush against the thin material of Julian's boxer shorts, causing the young man to do just that. "And you have to admit that this way the punishment does indeed fit the crime."

Julian was about to pass out when Randall's gaze flicked back to the jar, and to the blackish fluid streaked down its inside.

"Oh, what a shame," he said, the creature still scrabbling to gain purchase on Julian's crotch as he turned to explain. "These little monsters only store up enough poison for one really good bite. We'll have to wait for another couple of hours before he's good to go again."

And with that Randall snatched the creature away, dropped it back into the jar and screwed the lid back on. He removed the gloves and stroked his chin in thought.

"What on earth am I to do with you now?" he said, turning back to the table. He picked up a rusty saw, twanged the blade, smiled and put it back down; a series of sharpened awls were tested on the pad of his left thumb before being found wanting; and a length of thick rubber tubing, a galvanised bucket and a large metal syringe were connected together before Randall snapped his fingers and left the room.

He returned a few moments later with an old fashioned alarm clock, a roll of copper wire, and a junction box. He proceeded to coil the wire around Julian's wrists and ankles, and then connected them via the alarm clock to the dusty black transformer which he then plugged into the mains electricity supply.

"There's a story about a man who is told that his rather dim-witted twelve-year-old son is in fact a genius, and so to test him he buries a treasure chest filled with chocolate and 'other sweetmeats', I believe the story says, in the garden and gives the boy clues. While the lad proves hopeless at thinking laterally he nevertheless *does* turn out to be something of a marvel at wiring his dad up to the mains and torturing him to find out where he's hidden the sweeties." Randall set the clock at five minutes to midnight. "Amazing what some kids will do for chocolate, isn't it? Although I've known some women to be willing to do so much more. Did you give Angela chocolates?" Julian shook his head. "No, I don't suppose you needed to. Giving her quite enough already I should imagine. Anyway it suddenly made me think of this, which should pass the time nicely, or rather the five minutes it will take for the clock to reach twelve, the connection to be made and the current to flow through the wires. I wonder if you'll die from the electrocution first or if there'll be enough time for you to see the wires slice off your hands and feet?"

He flicked the little metal switch across on the top of the device, and the clock began to tick.

"For God's sake, Marcus," said Julian, finally finding his

Two For Dinner

voice.

"For God's sake what exactly?" said Randall, his eyes on the clock face.

"You don't have to do this. It's not worth killing me over."

"Isn't it?" was the reply after Randall had waited for the minute hand to slide to three minutes to.

"No it's not! You're a successful man, far more successful than I'll ever be. More successful with money, more successful with women, more successful in life full stop. Kill me and you'll be throwing all of that away."

Two minutes to.

"You mean rather than mete out my revenge on you I should perhaps consider finding myself another wife?" said Randall, rubbing his chin as if in contemplation as another thirty seconds slid by. "Someone who might treat me better than Angela did?"

"Exactly," said Julian. "Let me go and I swear I won't say a word. And it won't be as if I can prove anything. Besides, I want to be with Jenny, I'm sure of that now, so in some ways you'd be the one left with power over me."

One minute to go.

"That's true I suppose," said Randall. "But are you really suggesting that I let you go to live happily ever after with your wife and be without one of my own?"

Thirty seconds.

"I mean let me go and let yourself go too – free yourself of her and put this entire incident behind you. No good can come of what you're doing here, but if you let me go then maybe you can leave this place with a clear conscience."

Fifteen seconds.

"A clear conscience, Marcus!"

Ten seconds.

"Not the conscience of a murderer!"

Five.

"A murderer Marcus, a cold-blooded murderer!"

Three.

204

Two For Dinner

"Marcus!"

Two.

"Jesus Christ, Marcus, *please!*"

One.

The minute hand slipped across and made the connection.

And nothing happened.

"I suppose you've got a point," said Randall, straightening up and going over to the junction box. He bent down and picked up the free end of wire that he had only pretended to attach to the one of the contacts. "Had you going though, didn't I?" he said with a grin.

Julian could only stare in dumb shock as Randall began to coil the wire up. "The question is," the older man said as he worked, "have I done enough for you to learn your lesson?"

Julian began to nod so fast he felt sick.

"Yes, yes, oh God yes."

"Well that's nice." Randall opened a large leather trunk, piled all the implements he had been using into, closed the lid, and locked it. "Time to put my things away then. Playtime's over."

He came over and began to untie Julian's ankles as the younger man stared at him in disbelief.

"You're letting me go?"

"Yes," said Randall. "I mean I don't think I'm going to see your face ever again. Am I?"

"God no, absolutely not," said Julian as his hands were freed and he was helped unsteadily to his feet. Once he had stopped shaking quite so much Randall released his grasp and pointed to the door.

"You are free to go," he said.

"Free to go?" Julian croaked. He took a tottering step towards the exit and then stopped. Surely it wasn't going to be that easy?

"What's the matter?" said Randall, washing his hands under the tap in the corner and drying them on a white cotton towel streaked with red stains.

Two For Dinner

"There's something waiting for me out there, isn't there?"

Randall put down the towel.

"I beg your pardon?"

Julian's voice was fast becoming little more that a series of choked, terrified sobs.

"Something waiting. Outside. You've got dogs. Or something. Worse."

Randall laid a hand on Julian's quivering shoulder.

"My dear fellow, allow me to give you my word that the only thing lying in wait for you outside this building is your car. To which this is the key."

He held up a shiny fob and pushed it into Julian's palm. Then he went over to the garage door, opened it, and stepped outside.

"You see?" came his voice. "No Rottweilers, no man-traps, no hidden shower of acid above the doorframe. It is a little chilly out here though – I would suggest you don't hang around getting to your car or you may catch a bit of a cold. Nothing to fear now. Naughty old Mr Randall's done everything he's intended to do."

Julian halted.

"You've cut the brake cables on my car."

Randall snorted.

"I have done nothing of the sort. Your car is as safe as it was when you drove it here. Anything that happens to you while you're in it is entirely your own responsibility. Go on."

Julian was almost through the door, but still something made him hesitate.

"Oh my dear chap for the last time I give you my word that nothing else of my doing will befall you this evening. It was merely my intention to scare you. I haven't harmed you, have I?" Julian shook his head. "Despite having ample opportunity, wouldn't you agree?" Julian nodded. "Well there you are then. Now hurry along. I want to lock up here so I can get to bed and read something to calm my nerves before turning in. Probably something by Charles Birkin or perhaps even a little Martin

Two For Dinner

Waddell – I feel in the mood for something a little mischievous."

Julian gritted his teeth and took one step forward.

Two steps.

Three.

And then he was outside. Outside in the dreary, damp, cold, *wonderful* night air. He took a deep breath and thanked God. His car was waiting only ten feet away. As he began to walk towards it he turned to see Randall watching him go. He was opening the door when a little of the cocky self-assuredness that had got him into trouble in the first place raised its head.

"You know I could always run off with Angela you know," he said.

Randall shook his head.

"I don't think so," was the reply.

"You think she'll stay with you, do you?" Now Julian was getting into the car. He put the keys in the ignition, started the engine and rolled down the window. "Well to be honest it'll be nice to get back to Jenny and some sense of normality," he called above the noise of the accelerator.

"Somehow I don't think that's going to happen either," said Randall, his voice colder.

"And why would that be?" said Julian, ready to drive away from this madman and into the arms of at least one woman this evening.

"Because, my dear chap," said Marcus Randall in the tone of a man who had never lost anything in his life, "Who on earth did you think we were eating for dinner?"

Dedicated to Herbert van Thal

www.ingramcontent.com/pod-product-compliance
Ingram Content Group UK Ltd.
Pitfield, Milton Keynes, MK11 3LW, UK
UKHW041410180426
11947UKWH00007B/47